Fall Too Well

By Erin Branscom

COZY CREEK/STANDALONES

Fall Too Well

Bagpipes & Buns

Just Another Summer Escape

WISTERIA COVE

The Pumpkin Spice Spell

Mistletoe & Magic

Hexes & Honeysuckle

BRIDGER FALLS

Forever to Me

Wild as Her

Always You

High Road

FREEDOM VALLEY

Falling Inn Love

Baked Inn Love

All Inn Thyme

Love Inn Books

Forever Inn Love

Snowed Inn

Fall Too Well

A COZY CREEK NOVEL

ERIN BRANSCOM

An Imprint of HarperCollins*Publishers*

HarperCollins books may be purchased for educational, business, or sales promotional use. For information, please email the Special Markets Department at SPsales@harpercollins.com.

hc.com

Originally published as *Fall Too Well* in the United States in 2024 by Erin Branscom.

Interior text design by Diahann Sturge-Campbell

Cowboy hat illustration © tribalium81/Stock.Adobe.com
Cup of tea illustration © cuttlefish84/Stock.Adobe.com

Library of Congress Cataloging-in-Publication Data has been applied for.

ISBN 978-0-06-346278-6

Printed in the United Kingdom

26 27 28 CPI 10 9 8 7 6 5 4 3 2

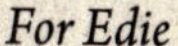

For Edie

CHAPTER 1

Everly

Until now, I couldn't picture myself getting arrested or into trouble with the law. I mean, I've done my fair share of stupid things, usually when I was a kid, alongside my best friend Hayley. But sitting on this front porch in the company of my best friend, taking in the setting sun and warm evening air, my mind drifts to all the possible ways I can get my ex-husband, Richie, to go far, far away and finally leave me alone. I picture him sailing away in a hot air balloon and never returning as I stand on the ground, happily waving goodbye forever. Then my thoughts go darker to him disappearing from the planet for good. And I could argue that I have just cause for these dark thoughts for all the hell he's put me through. My patience is running very low on having to deal with him constantly doing things to get under my skin and trying to get me to come back to him. It's never going to happen. Like signed, sealed, divorced never going to happen. My lawyer is baffled at how much he gets away with since the judge apparently had ties to his father. Lovely. A second chance with Richie has never been an option, yet he can't seem to get this through his dumb head.

Also, it's not wrong to feel like I deserve a little bit of revenge for the years of hell he put our daughter, Willow, and me through. It's like there's no way out from his relentless pestering. So, yes, I dream of him falling off a mountain or relocating for good—preferably to another planet. Sometimes I wish he was on that little submarine that went searching for the *Titanic*. I'm just so tired of dealing with him. Just leave a girl alone to live and enjoy her autumn. The fall season gives me life, and I don't need any nonsense right now.

When the thought of my daughter fills me with a warmth similar to a strong hug, I shield my hand over my eyes in a little salute. I squint at the sun beginning to set over the mountains draped in their fall golden hour glory and try to see her out in the field where Mack and one of his ranch hands are working on shoeing one of the horses. I heave a deep, satisfied sigh when I see Willow propped up on the fence near Mack, watching them intently work on the horse. She's clearly fascinated and in her element. Just like I was at her age at this very same ranch. They're too far away for me to hear what they're saying, but I know Willow's safe and having fun with Mack. The McCreedy ranch has been a very special place for me since I was growing up, and it makes me happy that Willow is here making her own memories. Mack is like a father figure to me, and he and Anna treat Willow as if she were their own granddaughter. In fact, we're lucky to have the McCreedy family, and I don't know what we'd do without them. We wouldn't be back here in Cozy Creek and safe without their support, that's for sure.

My eyes scan the familiar ranch that has always felt like a haven to me, the landscape awash with breathtaking burnt orange, bronze, and viridian. Autumn is showing off big today here at the ranch, and it's my favorite time of year. The mountains and all their stunning curves are full of the most vibrant autumn foliage I've ever seen.

The ranch is the most beautiful piece of land in Cozy Creek and has been in my best friend Hayley's mom's side of the family for three generations, Hayley being the fourth. Childhood memories fill me everywhere I look when I'm out here. The barn where Hayley broke her wrist when we took a donkey and a horse out for a ride without telling her parents, and the donkey had enough of our crap and bucked Hayley off. I had ridden back to get her brothers, Nash and Kincaid, to help us. The massive oak tree in the front yard that we took our prom pictures under and where I carved N + E up on one of the higher branches because I didn't think anyone would see it. Of course, Kincaid, Hayley's younger brother, found it and teased me relentlessly over it. *So* many memories here. And a few painful memories I don't want to remember. Mostly of the eldest McCreedy, Nash. Those memories I stuff deep down, bury them, lock them up, and have hidden the key where even I can't access them. Okay, well, I try not to access them, but it doesn't always work. Even the happy memories are marred by the way things ended between Nash and me when I left Cozy Creek.

It's basically a part-time job for me to avoid Nash in our small town. I hadn't come out to the ranch because I didn't want to run into him. I've turned down so many family dinners because I'm too big of a chicken to talk to him. I don't want to make it weird for him. It's his family after all. I'm just the add-on who he probably considers annoying as usual. I'm just the girl his sister is best friends with who had a childhood crush on him that he didn't reciprocate. He avoids me as well. It's an unspoken thing between us that we don't talk anymore. Hayley knows this, and while I know it bothers her, she's helped me steer clear of him. At first, this frustrated her, but now she just goes with it.

"You think he'll figure out it was us?" I ask as she looks over at me.

"Who, little Richie? Are you thinking about the shrimp again?" She crinkles her eyebrows at me as she chuckles, no doubt remembering what she did. "The smallest man who ever lived."

I bite my lip and nod, trying not to laugh at her song reference. And she's not wrong.

"That whole Taylor Swift album was like a dedication to your shitty marriage to little dick."

When Hayley came to pick up Willow and me that night we left Richie, she had been at a party. When I texted her that we needed help and it was an emergency, she left the party right away and snagged the shrimp platter on her way out. When she got to my house, she left shrimp tucked inside the metal curtain rods all over the house. She didn't tell me until a week later, and we both laughed until we thought we'd pee our pants. I'd asked her how and why she would think to do this. She simply shrugged and said, *I thought I'd eat the shrimp on the way to get you. Then I was too angry and upset to eat the shrimp, so I had some time to think about it on the way to your house, and that's what I decided to do.* Are we childish? Probably. Did Richie deserve it? Absolutely. Will he retaliate? I don't know. I don't want to think about Richie anymore.

"I just want him to leave me alone." I groan as I lean back in my chair.

"Yeah, he'll definitely know it was us." She snorts. "Who the hell else would stuff shrimp in his curtain rods to stink up his house?"

"You think we would look good in orange?" I raise my eyebrows, and she laughs.

"We *so* would. At least if we go to jail, we'll go together. Oh, and you can start a book club there," Hayley adds with a grin as she glances down at my oversized purse, which she no doubt knows holds my Kindle and at least one paperback. For backup of course. I can't help it. I love books so much. She calls it my "Rory Gilmore-ing" when I bring an extra book in my purse just in case I get bored wherever I go. I can't help it that fictional characters are often better than real people.

I snort and laugh. "It was still worth it."

"Yeah, it was." She sighs. "What brought this up?"

"I don't know. He's just been quiet lately, so I know he's got something planned. I can feel it. I know he's going to do something to screw up my life. And waiting for the other shoe to drop with him makes me anxious."

"Well, you have us now. You and Willow. You don't have to live like you're walking on eggshells. You feel worried or anxious? We're here for you. Always. You're back home where you belong, and we're living our best lives *as we should*," she emphasizes as she reaches over and gently squeezes my arm.

Being back here around people who love me and make me feel safe feels so good. I didn't have that for so long.

"You're right," I admit as I close my eyes and breathe in the fresh, crisp fall mountain air.

"Wouldn't it be great if we could just order you a good guy off DoorDash?" Hayley interrupts my thoughts by changing the subject. "He could just be dropped off hot and ready like a meal."

"What?" I look over at her and shake my head with a laugh. "No, thanks. And I don't even think DoorDash delivers this far out in the country."

"But seriously, there's just not a lot of options here in Cozy Creek. So I'll resort to finding you a good guy instead," she decrees as she sits opposite me on the oversized white rocking chairs on the porch of her parents' sprawling ranch home.

"Nope, there's no need. I'm good," I admit. Even though my divorce has been final for months, I'm in no position to start a relationship right now. I don't need to add to the chaos.

"Maybe we should just get away," she murmurs. "Go on a trip or something."

"You want to leave Cozy Creek?" Surprise fills me, and I realize that, for the first time, I don't want to leave. Willow and I have been back here in Cozy Creek for a little over six months now, and we're finally settling in and feeling at home. Plus, I can't imagine not being here during my favorite season. Autumn in Cozy Creek is the absolute best place to be on earth, hands down. The fall foliage is gorgeous, the weather is perfect, and I live for the cozy cardigan season. I have a countdown going throughout the rest of the year. And yes, summerween is a thing for me, too. Most of my thrifted and treasured home decor resembles an autumn theme. I'm not even sorry about it. It brings me joy and peace. And right now, I value peace more than anything.

"I don't know." She shakes a bottle of dark red nail polish and looks over at me. "Sometimes I just want to run away, wander, and travel. Be free."

I nod and sip one of the pumpkin spice lattes I brought to the ranch for us. It has long gone cold, but it still tastes so good.

"Now there's a cute guy," I mutter as I stare at the guy in the field with Mack. New fantasy unlocked. A hot ranch hand. Black chaps on his long legs as he leans over, a horse foot tucked between his muscular thighs as he works off in the distance. He has a black cowboy hat pulled low and a black button-down shirt stretched over his massive back and chest. Maybe I need to have a fling with a hot cowboy. Nothing serious, just a little fun. I tilt my head and think about the possibility. Yeah, I could have a little fun with a cowboy.

"What?" Hayley looks up and squints at her dad out in the field. Her eyes dart to the barn where a few trucks are parked, and she looks back at me and full-on belly laughs. She doesn't stop even after I playfully roll my eyes at her.

"What's *his* name?" I continue as I pretend to fan myself over the guy who is too far away to see his face. "Is *he* single? Be right back,

I'm buying a horse," I murmur as I watch him straighten, run his hand over the back of the horse, and start on a different foot. I used to know most of the ranch hands when I spent a lot of time growing up here, but since Willow and I have been back, I haven't come out to the ranch as often, so I'm not familiar with any of them anymore. But after watching this guy work on the horses, maybe I do need to come out here more and not just for the gorgeous mountain views. I have my reasons for staying away from the ranch. And those reasons are the ones locked up and buried. This guy gives off Rip Wheeler vibes from *Yellowstone,* and he is hot in his black shirt and black hat.

Hayley's still cracking up next to me in her chair and is now shaking her head at me with a big grin and a sparkle in her eyes. She looks like she's planning something.

"What?" I exclaim as I rock in my chair and stare at the man bent over, putting a shoe on one of the horses. "I can't even imagine myself dating after Richie burned me, but there's no harm in enjoying hot eye candy."

"Oh, nothing," she says with a devious grin. "Hot eye candy," she mutters with a chuckle.

She finishes painting her toes. "Richie didn't just burn you; he torched you," she adds with a look of disdain. "And that is why we don't feel bad about the shrimp."

This is what I love about Hayley. She's a girl's girl. She'll have your back and will only seek revenge if necessary. She loves everyone around her deeply and has a big, loyal McCreedy heart. She's my ride or die, and I love her so much.

I roll my eyes playfully and glance down at her nail polish, changing the subject. "What color is that? It's pretty."

"Vicious trollop," she says, keeping a straight face.

I snort-laugh. "Yeah, right." We've both watched *Gilmore Girls* a thousand times and repeatedly use phrases from the show. It's like a love language between us that makes us laugh.

I look up and straighten. Mack, the hot mystery man, and Willow are headed toward the barn. He looks slightly familiar, but he's still too far away. And with the black cowboy hat pulled low, it's hard to tell. Maybe it's Mack's friend Dane's son. I can't remember his name . . . But that doesn't seem right, either. Hmm.

Willow sees me watching and waves, and I wave back. She follows the two men into the barn with the horse.

Hayley tucks her nail polish in my purse next to the chair. "Here, you can go home and be a vicious trollop, too."

"Thanks," I say as I swallow the last of my drink. "Maybe you're right, and we do need to plan a trip together. Get away from here and have some fun. Maybe this spring."

I sense that Hayley needs to get away. She's been in Cozy Creek her whole life except when we were in college together for the first few years before I dropped out. I want her to be happy, so if taking a trip with her means that, I'll do it.

"We could always go visit my grandma Baa in Ireland. She's not getting any younger, and I'd like to go over and see her," she adds as she wiggles and examines her freshly painted toes.

"I don't know what I'd do with Willow," I admit. "But I've always wanted to visit Ireland."

"We can take her with us. Or does Richie ever pull his head out of his ass and keep her for like two weeks in the summer?"

"He's supposed to, but he doesn't like to take her for overnights. He makes up excuses like he doesn't want to make the drive. Says it's too far." I shrug as I shift in my chair and tuck my legs under me.

"It's not that far." She rolls her eyes. "Plus, I see him around town all the time. What's he doing here?"

"Tormenting me," I say with a deep sigh.

"Maybe she could stay with his parents," she suggests.

"Doubtful. They don't see her much, either. I could figure something out, though," I say as I reach to pet one of the cats who trails along my chair.

"We would have so much fun. And we could find cute Irish guys."

"Maybe you can introduce me to the cute ranch hand. He's got a great cowboy ass. And that cowboy hat," I mutter as I think about dating again. Navigating that with an eight-year-old will be tricky. But maybe I could do lunch and coffee dates on my breaks. I'm tired of being alone. I don't know what it would be like to get dressed up cute and go on dates and spend time getting to know someone. Sounds so foreign to me, but exciting. I want to be me again.

"Oh, I'll introduce you," she says with a smug grin as she shifts in her seat with anticipation. "In fact, here they come now."

Just the sight of this mystery man has my palms clamming up and my stomach knotting in anticipation. Whereas my mind and imagination are very much in working order, it's been so long since I've felt an inkling of desire or stir of interest that my poor body is in revolt.

CHAPTER 2

Everly

As they get closer, it dawns on me why the man looks so familiar. He removes his cowboy hat and runs his hand through his wavy dark hair that matches his sister's. I close my eyes and shake my head in horror and embarrassment. He's the very last man on the planet that I should be thinking about. He's off-limits.

Nash.

No, no, no.

I gasp. "No." I shake my head at Hayley, who finds this even more hilarious and laughs even harder in her chair. "Not a word. I swear I will kill you if you tell him I said any of that. Dead and buried, Hayley. I mean it. *Oh my God.*"

I thought the ranch hand was hot, and it was Nash. Freaking Nash. The boy I've had a crush on since I was seven years old. He held my hand at my mom's funeral but then kept me at arm's length all through school even though he knew I liked him. He treated me, at best, like a pesky friend to his little sister who was off-limits and broke my heart on a regular basis. Most of the time, he didn't even know he was doing it. He'd do it by dating and screwing any girl in town and ignoring me. After high school, I bravely confided in him right before I left for college that I loved him, and he told me that I was too young even though he's only two years older than Hayley and me. Looking back, he was wild then. There's no way we'd have made anything serious work. Nash seemed like he couldn't be tamed. He was more into partying and getting into trouble. I didn't want that with Nash. I didn't want to be just another girl to him. I wanted to be *the* girl.

A few years later, when I unexpectedly found out I was pregnant with Willow and told him, he begged me not to marry Richie. But it was too late. He could have had me, but he didn't want me. I didn't want him to take pity on me. I wanted him to truly want me. I figured there was no way that would happen, when I was barely twenty and having a baby. I felt like I had no choice but to marry the father of my baby and do what I thought was right. At that point, my dad had already left Cozy Creek and moved away to start over with his new family, so I felt like I had no one. I couldn't tell Hayley I was in love with her brother and he'd rejected me. I had already made things weird with Nash; I couldn't make them weird with Hayley. Now that I look back, Richie was my biggest mistake. I should have stayed in Cozy Creek and figured it out as a single mom. I would have been so much better off, and so would Willow. But hindsight is twenty-twenty, right? Instead, I gave some of my precious younger years to dickhead Richie, who did nothing but treat me like crap.

And here is Nash now, heading our way. He's walking next to my daughter like it's no big deal. I stiffen and straighten in my chair. Things didn't end well between us after that night he begged me not to marry Richie when I told him I was pregnant. I haven't been around him since we returned to town, and nobody talks about what happened with Nash. As I said, it's been a part-time job of mine to avoid him at all costs.

"Hey, sweetheart, are you and my girl here staying for dinner? Last I heard, Nana Anna has on a big pot of hearty chili and honey cornbread," Mack cheerfully calls with a faint hint of his Irish accent.

He smiles at me as he stands before us on the porch, plopping his worn and wrinkled hand playfully on Willow's head. She grins up at Mack with her missing front teeth. My heart swells watching them together, an ache lingering in my chest seeing her so happy with the people who gave me unconditional love as a child when I desperately needed it. She's never had a grandfather figure treat her like this. Both sets of her biological grandparents are emotionally and physically unavailable. My dad lives in Florida and hasn't even met Willow. And Richie's side of the family is cold and detached. We see them rarely and only on formal occasions. This is why the McCreedys mean so much to us. Except Nash. He's made it clear that he wants nothing to do with me. I've been back in Cozy Creek for a while now, and he's made zero effort to even be a friend.

"Willow's been a big helper with the horses. We have a future rancher on our hands. She has it in her bones; I can tell." Mack beams proudly at all of us, and I can't help but smile, disarming the awkwardness a little in Nash's presence. I know how happy this makes Willow. All she's talked about are horses, and horse shows are all she wants to watch on streaming apps. She's a goner for ranching and horse life.

I've known Mack all my life. My mother was best friends with his wife, Anna, until she died. The McCreedys took losing my mother as hard as my father and I did. My father did his best to raise me after her death, but he was a long-haul truck driver who was gone for long periods of time. When he was gone, I stayed out here at the ranch. I had chores just like the rest of the kids, and they always included me in all their family traditions and activities.

"We actually have to get going," I say softly, feeling nervous and trying not to look at Nash. He's standing next to his father and staring at Hayley and me, probably trying to figure out why she's been manically laughing, and I look horrified and embarrassed.

As I should. *Freaking Nash.* I should have known. I've always been drawn to him. No matter what I do to convince myself that he's not the one, my heart tells me I'm lying. He's always been the one. No other person on the planet has ever had this effect on me, and I really wish he wouldn't, but apparently, my heart will do whatever the hell it wants to. Even fall for someone who doesn't love me back. The world is a cruel place.

I feel like the air has left my chest. He's staring right at me with an unreadable expression. Gone is the boy I once knew, and in his place is the man I always thought he'd become. And he looks good. Better than good. Freaking fine as hell. He's got massive shoulders now, making me wonder what it would feel like to wrap my arms around them and hold him tight. The black button-up shirt he's wearing stretches tight across his broad, muscled chest. His black cowboy hat is pulled low again. His wide, square jaw is covered in scruff, but it's neatly trimmed, making him look even darker and more mysterious. His expression is still unreadable. Nash has always felt mysterious, but I prided myself on being able to read him and his expressions. In fact, when we were younger, we could have entire conversations with just our eyes. He was the best hide-and-seek partner. No one could ever find us out here on the ranch. But now, I realize I don't know this Nash. His dark brown eyes are hard to see, but I know he's looking at me. I feel like I'm on a stage, and a giant spotlight is on me. It's hot, making my cardigan on this cool evening feel like a heated blanket wrapped around me. Everything feels way too hot.

"Oh, bummer. Will we see you on Sunday for dinner?" Mack asks, still looking hopeful.

"I'll check my calendar," I promise hesitantly, looking at Nash and back at Hayley, trying to focus anywhere but Nash. It's so obvious to everyone, and while Hayley finds it funny, I can feel the disappointment radiating off Mack. I know he just wants us to all be together again.

Mack says softly, "Well, then . . ."

Hayley says nothing but watches this little reunion with highly amused fascination. I will get to her later. She knows this and says nothing when my eyes dart to hers. The looks I've been sneaking at her could incinerate her if I had those powers.

I clear my throat. "We'd better get going. I have supper going in the slow cooker at home, and Willow has school tomorrow. Thanks for letting her hang out with the horses." I stand and grab for my purse, almost losing my balance with nervousness.

"I'll walk you to your car." Hayley smirks at her brother, and his eyes narrow on her briefly. He's well aware something is going on between us, yet thankfully, he has the decency to say nothing and look away, not making eye contact or fully acknowledging me.

"Please tell Anna we said goodbye," I say softly to Mack as I kiss his cheek. It's awkward that I don't address Nash and give him a wide berth, but I don't know what else to do. He's a stranger to me now. We're not friends; we're barely acquaintances. Something I never imagined we'd ever be, but here we are. In the past eight years, we've had one other interaction—that night I left Richie when they all came to get Willow and me. I've caught glimpses of him around town, but I've avoided him. I've been known to dart into local businesses if I see him out and about, and I've avoided Bookers Pub at all costs. Hayley has begged me to come and help her bake in the pub kitchen, but I won't step foot into Bookers. He lives above it, and it's too risky. I'm afraid I'll run into him. I don't even know what I'd say if I did talk to him. But it's not like he goes out of his way to talk to me either.

"You bring our little girl out here anytime," Mack says. "We need to get her on a horse and get her comfortable riding. The sooner, the better."

I smile and nod, knowing she would love that. "Thanks, Mack."

The night I left Richie, I made one phone call to Hayley, telling her that Willow and I needed out immediately. The McCreedy family and their three trucks pulled up in front of our house no less than forty-five minutes later. Nash, Mack, Hayley, Anna, and Kincaid silently packed our belongings, loaded the boxes in their trucks, and drove us back to Cozy Creek. No questions were asked; they just showed up for us. I thanked them profusely. I'm lucky these people love us the way that they do. Well, all of them but Nash. He looks at me like I'm nothing to him.

Mack had a few things to say that night, and Hayley definitely had more than a few things to say about the situation, but in the end, they just wanted us safe. And that's how we ended up back in Cozy Creek. And let me tell you, coming back to your hometown after you got pregnant and married the town jerk has not been an experience I'd wish on anyone. I've had to endure a lot of gossip and people who have opinions about all my life choices. One could say it's none of their business, but you know how it goes in a small town. It took me a long time to get people to let me back in and trust me. My part-time job at the library has definitely helped.

"Bye," I call as Willow reluctantly slides her hand in mine and looks back at them.

Willow slips out of my hand and runs back to give Mack and Nash a hug, and I can see how much being here means to her as well. She really appreciated them letting her help with the horses.

I take in Nash's surprise at Willow's gesture, his big hand hesitating as it comes down to rest on Willow's head, a much softer look in his eyes there and then gone as Willow returns to my side.

It's hard for me to process the kindness he shows Willow, yet not me. At least if Nash and I can't even be friends, I can be grateful for how kind he is to my little girl.

"Bye, sweetheart," Mack calls, and Nash lifts a hand and waves to Willow as he leans back against the porch railing. I briefly look back but feel like I need to focus on every step in front of me, or I will trip from nervousness.

The air almost completely leaves my chest when Nash's eyes follow me to the car.

"You're dead," I whisper to Hayley after I get Willow in the back seat. But she's not. I'll always forgive her. She's my best friend, and she knows it.

She throws her head back and laughs so hard. "Your hot cowboy," she mocks as she pretends to throw up.

I shake my head with mock betrayal as I give her a dry look. "I bet you're pretty proud of yourself, aren't you?"

"That was great. And we'll discuss it *later*," she says with a huge grin as she motions to Willow.

"I'll call you after I get Willow to bed."

"I'm looking forward to it," she calls as she waves. "See you later, vicious trollop."

"Did you have fun today, baby?" I ask Willow as I slide into my seat, trying to calm down so I can drive and focus on her.

"Mom, I love it here *so* much. When can we come back?" Willow asks from the back seat.

"I'm glad you do. We'll be back soon," I promise, and we head back to town.

Just not when Nash is here.

"Okay," she happily agrees. "Mack says they can teach me how to ride. Can we come back this weekend?"

"We'll see, honey. I'm glad you're having fun with the horses."

We may both be healing from the hell that Richie put us through, but at least we're doing alright. I let out my breath, knowing we're going to be okay. Things are getting better being back in Cozy Creek.

Finally.

I may not have been around Nash for the past eight years, but he has always been with me. My heart has always belonged to him. A man who never wanted my heart in the first place. As much as I try to deny this, it's there and always has been. He's like the forbidden fruit. And I need to continue avoiding him, not lusting after him like a vicious little trollop.

CHAPTER 3

Everly

Okay, spill, what's up with you and my brother?" Hayley demands in a playful but serious tone through the phone as I close Willow's bedroom door with a loud creak, reminding myself to oil that so it's quieter.

"You could barely look at him. At first, I went along with your ridiculous game to avoid each other. But now it's time to move past this. You both need to get it together," she scolds like she's tired of us.

I settle in on my cozy couch and tuck my feet under me, stretching a soft orange-and-brown flannel blanket over my legs, and say with defeat, "I know. I don't even know where to begin with everything, Hayles."

"Explain it to me then, because we miss you at Sunday dinners at the ranch. Nash tiptoes around you, but I think he misses you, too."

He misses me.

I wonder if he's said anything to her. He sure hasn't said anything to me. Not a single word. He looks at me like I'm the biggest disappointment. At least, it feels that way to me. I'm proud of myself and all that I've worked hard for, but proving myself to this town that still sees me as the motherless and now fatherless single mom who married the richest, slimiest guy in town and then divorced him has not been an easy image to live up to. It's embarrassing, and I feel ashamed. Like I can't get anything right.

"I don't miss Nash," I lie. "And I'm sorry. I don't mean to make things weird for your family. I just don't know how to fix things with Nash. Things just are the way they are, I guess."

"Well, first off, it's *our* family. You're included in that. And you're not weird. Okay, maybe a little weird," she teases. "But seriously, why are you guys like this? You used to be so close. We all were. Now, we can't even have Sunday dinners," she complains.

I sigh and sink further into the couch in defeat. I knew we'd eventually circle back to this conversation, and I couldn't put it off forever.

It's harder to hide the fact that I don't talk to Nash from Hayley because they both work at the pub together, and he's always there, which means I can't see her at work because Nash is there. See? Complicated.

Hayley and Nash co-own the pub in town called Bookers, a popular hangout for locals and tourists. Hayley works there in the early mornings to late afternoons and runs a micro bakery out of the kitchen. Nash runs everything on the evening shift. They took the old dusty pub and made it an extremely popular tourist and local hangout with a restaurant and great food. Since I don't step foot in there, I only know this from the takeout Hayley has brought me. They're also known for having the best sandwiches on delicious homemade sourdough bread. People come from all over to eat there and purchase Hayley's fresh-baked bread daily. She's an incredible baker and businesswoman. Hayley and Nash's Grandma Baa owns a very successful bakery in Ireland, and Hayley learned a lot from her. I'm proud of them both for what they've accomplished.

"Nash and I haven't talked since I got pregnant with Willow and moved away with Richie. I hurt him," I whisper.

I'll never forget the night it all went downhill. It was pouring rain that night. I stood there in front of him outside the barn, telling him that I was pregnant. Devastation poured over his face as he listened to me. He'd asked me whose baby it was. When I said it was Richie's, he had shaken his head.

"Anyone but his," he'd pleaded, not accepting my answer.

Shame filled me that night. "I'm sorry," I'd whispered.

Nash looked desperate and had begged me, "Don't go with him. Stay here with me. I'll help you. He's not a good guy, Everly."

"You didn't want me when I left for college. Why would you want me now that I'm pregnant with another guy's baby? A guy you hate."

"I was waiting for you!" he'd shouted, making me jump. I'd never seen him look this anguished and upset.

"No, you weren't, Nash. You were busy being the town fuck boy. You were not waiting for me," I'd said angrily. And the look on his face when I'd said that to him still haunts me today.

Richie and I got married and moved to the next town over. And I've regretted it every day since. Hurting Nash like that and disappointing the McCreedys by moving away and cutting off everyone I loved has left me with deep regret. I've loved Nash for so long that I don't remember a time when I did not love him. It started as a childhood crush, and by the time I got to high school, I thought he was the love of my life. And it hurt like hell when I realized that he didn't love me back, or at least made me feel that he never loved me the same way. But then that night in the rain, he'd asked me to stay. He'd begged. And I never understood why he did that. His words, telling me that he was waiting for me, slashed into me like a thousand tiny knives, shredding my heart because his words never matched his actions. Not when he didn't give me the time of day. There hadn't been any waiting around at all. I lashed out at him because I wanted him to bleed the way he made me bleed. But still, the guilt is crippling, even now.

I couldn't have stayed. Because the truth is that Richie had threatened that if I went anywhere near Nash or the McCreedys, he'd take my baby from me. And I knew he would. He ended up making my life miserable anyway. I should've just stayed in Cozy Creek. Richie has the resources to fight me with his family's money. That's why I didn't try to leave for so long, even when we were living with him, and I had no support system. I stayed away because I couldn't risk losing Willow. Hayley and I kept in touch but had to be secretive about it. Looking back, I can't believe I let Richie isolate me and take everything from me. Never again will I let that happen to me.

"It's been a long time. Nash doesn't seem hurt. He seems like he wants you to come around more. And he really likes Willow," Hayley says softly, her voice not accepting the excuses I'm rolling out one by one.

I reach for my acorn-shaped steaming mug of tea and cup it in my hands, the warmth comforting me. "Does he talk about me?" I ask tentatively but also curious.

Hayley scoffs and then jokes, "No, he would never talk about his feelings, especially not to me, his sister. You know Nash."

No, I really don't know Nash. Not anymore. And that makes me feel sad. As kids, all of us were inseparable. Even in high school, when Nash had a reputation for being the bad boy and getting into trouble, and Hayley and I were getting good grades and joining as many clubs and after-school activities as we could squeeze in to get into good colleges, we still knew we could call Nash, and he'd be there for us. He treated me like a pesky little annoying sister back then, but he'd give us rides if we went to parties. He always looked out for us, sometimes even when we didn't know it at the time. That was just how he was. He was an asshole, but he was *our* asshole. No one messed with Nash or his family. And the McCreedys are one of the most respected families in Cozy Creek. Few people have anything bad to say about any of them. They'll be the first people to help anyone who needs it. Meanwhile, my family was more like the family on *Shameless*. Frank Gallagher was like my father, Brian, and unfortunately, I didn't have a Fiona to raise me. But I did have the McCreedys. And for the most part, I think I turned out okay. I'm still working on it, though. I'm currently working a part-time job at the Cozy Creek Public Library but hope to have a full-time position there when my mentor retires. Willow and I are getting by, but it hasn't been easy. I haven't been able to give Willow a lot of things, but I can give her a safe and happy place to live in our cozy little house in town that was once my childhood home.

Even though Nash would get into trouble in high school, most people overlooked it because of his family and chalked it up to teenage rebellion. And most of Nash's trouble was harmless. He was the kid who only fought because someone was getting bullied. But he did like to get into shenanigans with his buddies. Let's just say every cop in town knows Nash on a first-name basis and has given him rides home on more than one occasion.

"Are you still there?" she asks, shaking me out of my thoughts as I trace the plaid lines on the blanket in my lap.

"Yeah," I say, bringing my thoughts back to the conversation. "Do you think Richie will ever leave us alone?" I change the subject.

I don't like to think about the night we left, but it was up there on the list as one of the worst nights of my life. Richie had been binge drinking for days leading up to that night. He was screaming at Willow and me and breaking things around the house. He never put his hands on Willow or me, but he scared us. And things were getting worse. I felt like that was going to be the next step for him, so I had to get us out. When I went to check on Willow during his rage that night and found her shaking and hiding under her bed, I was done. Nash said nothing to me that night. He just loaded up our stuff while Richie remained passed out on the couch in our living room, a bottle lying next to him leaking into the couch that was no longer my problem. They got us out of there quickly. I'm relieved that I've never had to go back there. And I hope the shrimp still smells terrible.

"Hayley," I whisper.

"What?"

"I love you. Thanks for always having my back."

"Right back at you."

"I'll try to make it normal with Nash," I promise.

"You two need to get it together," she says with a deep sigh.

AFTER I DO a quick tidy of my house and blow out my pumpkin-scented candle, I check my phone as I go to put it on the charger next to my bed. I scan the notifications and see a text from Richie. I close my eyes and groan. The devil himself.

Richie: I took the car back.

The blood rushes to my ears, drowning out the sound of everything else as I rush to the front window and peer out the curtains. Anger pulses through me in frustration that leaves me bone-deep weary. This man will not stop until he takes everything from me.

Nope. I'm not giving in to whatever game he's trying to play now. I think about the many responses on the tip of my tongue, but I say nothing. I take deep breaths and contemplate how I'll budget a vehicle into our already stretched-to-the-max budget on my part-time librarian salary.

Richie: Come home and you can have it back.

I take a deep breath and look up at the ceiling, trying to find some patience and not respond. But right now, I'm fresh out of patience.

Me: I would rather work 7 days a week, 18 hours a day to pay for a new car than live in the same zip code as you ever again.

Richie: Have fun walking.

Anger sears through me when I think about the games he plays with me and how it affects Willow. He never even bothers to ask about her. I would block his number, but he'll just find other ways to come around. If he texts me, at least I can save the texts for my lawyer. And he would take away our only form of transportation as a form of manipulation. Well, the joke's on him because we live in the middle of town. We can walk to her school, which is just a few blocks away. The library is just a few blocks in the opposite direction, so I can walk there, too. And the general store is on Main Street as well, so we can get groceries on foot. I'll just make frequent trips. I don't need that car. It'll be an inconvenience for a while, but I'll figure it out. *Enjoy your shrimp, buddy.*

Now that I'm too worked up to go to bed, I go to the kitchen and pick up the broom and sweep, then head outside to empty the trash. Shaking my head angrily at Richie's bullshit, I hurry over to the trash barrel. At twenty-eight years old, I shouldn't be afraid of the dark, but it is what it is. It's not so much the thought of the dark as it is the thought of who could be hiding in the shadows. The feeling that Richie would stop at nothing to intimidate and try to scare me. I worry he could still be loitering nearby. Running up the stairs, one of them snaps under me, and I fall back and land hard on my butt on the pavement. I groan as I lie there and curse the universe. I wiggle my fingers and toes and cautiously sit up. Nothing feels broken. Relief fills me as I stand, careful to sidestep the broken stair.

I stalk to the bar in the kitchen where my laptop is closed and flip it open. I will be emailing my property manager. I shake my head, anger pulsing through me. What if that had been Willow who fell? Or if I'd broken my leg? I don't even have a car anymore. How the heck can I walk everywhere on a broken leg?

I open my email and type up a strongly worded message about the back stairs and how I fell, and one is now broken and needs to be repaired. I probably was too harsh and mostly still mad about Richie, but it's too late. I've already hit send. Hopefully, they'll get it fixed soon. I'm more mad at Richie right now, but I'm sore from falling, and that's not helping things either.

I trudge to bed, turning off the lamp on my bedside table. The moonlight shines in my room, and I sigh. I've screwed everything up with Nash. I wonder if we could ever get back to being friends like we were. Hayley is right. It's time to work it out so I can come back around. Willow needs the ranch and the McCreedys as much as I do. I can't mess things up with them. We need them.

CHAPTER 4

Nash

Hey, Pumpkin Jack, why don't you come help me with this," Hayley calls as she hefts the liquor order on top of the bar and begins to unload it.

I grumble as I make my way around the bar to help her get the rest. I hate it when our delivery guy just drops it off in the back and doesn't tell me. "Hey, yourself," I grump at her for calling me Pumpkin Jack. She knows I hate fall, so she teases me about it every chance she gets. Hayley and I get along well, and we have fun working together. Sure, we have our typical sibling squabbles, but co-owning the pub has been good for us. I couldn't have afforded the pub on my own without her help. When we each turned twenty-five, we got an inheritance from our maternal grandparents. The local run-down pub was circling the drain, so Hayley and I put our money together to buy and fix it up to what it is today. And I'm proud as hell of what we've built. I also invested money in a few properties around town and set up a property management company. I've kept it private for a reason. This town made its mind up about me years ago, so there is no need to try to change it. Now, I live a simple life above the pub and invest as much as I can back into my business. I value my solitude more than anything. I work several days a week as the local horse farrier and at the pub in the evenings. I own three busy businesses and don't have much of a social life, so it's good that I get to do what I love every day. Plus, staying busy keeps my mind off Everly being back in town. But if I'm honest with myself, Everly rarely leaves my thoughts.

Working with the horses is my greatest passion. The pub is fine, but taking care of horses is where I come alive. I'm a rancher in my blood through and through. I've built a great list of regular clients who trust me with their horses. I've even had some younger locals express interest in apprenticing with me, which I'm considering.

"You mad at me?" Hayley grins and cocks her head. She knows what she did. Bringing Everly out to the ranch when she knew I'd be there. It's unspoken that I don't go out there while she's there. I've seen Everly duck into the coffee shop if she sees me coming, and she hasn't stepped foot in Bookers despite Hayley co-owning it with me. Those two are thick as thieves, and it's not lost on me that she has not come in here. They always meet at the library, which I also don't get to go into anymore since she's back and apparently working there. That's been an issue because I miss Anne Marie, the librarian who has been running that joint since I was a little kid. Anne Marie has been my go-between, holding papers for tenants to sign so I could keep the anonymity of my property management business, but now I have had to get creative. It irritates the hell out of me that Everly and I don't talk, and she evades me. And it hurts. Because it's a reminder that no matter how much I love her, she avoids me.

"You know it's about time you both grow up and bury the hatchet? Also, you should know she was checking you out when you were with Dad and Willow. She called you a hot cowboy and said she was going to buy a horse because of you." She cracks up with laughter at her own statement and waggles her eyebrows at me.

"Jesus, what are you talking about?" I mutter. But that got my attention. *What?* Why would she be checking me out? What's up with that? She acts like I don't exist and she wants nothing to do with me. I shot my shot all those years ago, and she walked away, turning me down. She went with *him*. The town douchebag. And now that I know how he treated them all those years, it makes me livid with pure undiluted rage when I think about what it must have been like for them. I should have had my shit together back then, and maybe she would have chosen and trusted me. Instead, I was a piece of shit she couldn't trust, and I can't blame her. Every decision since that night has been to make me a better man who can be depended on.

"She didn't even know that you're a horse farrier. It seems that the two of you have a lot of catching up to do." She gives me a dubious look, then she turns serious. "She's been back for months now, and Mom and Dad want everyone to be able to come to Sunday dinners. She's been lonely, Nash. Please work it out with her. We finally got them back."

I'll admit that dug at me when she said that. *We finally got them back.* They got them back, not me, not yet. I don't want Everly to be lonely. Far from it. I've been giving her the space she seems to need so I don't make her feel awkward. Because every time she's seen me or been around me, she seems to want to go the other way. It also physically hurts me to see her and not have her in my life. But I'll take that pain if it means she's safe now and happy back home in Cozy Creek.

And the fact that I love Everly so much, and then she has this cute miniature version of herself who runs around, hanging on every word when I teach her about horses. She has the same eyes as the ones I fell in love with all those years ago. How can I not want them both to be happy and have everything they deserve?

"Fine, she can go, and I won't." I shrug nonchalantly as I unpack the liquor order and turn to stock the shelves, hoping she'll leave it at that. But I know that I'll probably still show up. For some reason, I'm finding it harder and harder to stay away from Everly and her ridiculously cute kid. She's like a magnet that pulls at my heartstrings every single time I see her or feel her near me.

"Come on, don't be like that," she says, looking disappointed. "I just wish things could go back to the way they were when we were all friends."

"That's up to Everly." I turn and break down a box and stack it next to the bar.

She furrows her brow. "What's that supposed to mean?"

"If she wants me around, fine. If not, it's not a big deal," I murmur as I continue to unpack boxes, breaking them down and stacking them in a neat pile.

She stares at me for a beat and nods, grinning like she's got something sneaky planned up her sleeve. Leave it to Hayley to get involved when it comes to Everly and me. Luckily, she changes the subject, but I know she's up to something.

"What do you think about us hosting a local speed dating event here at the pub? I think it'll be fun," she adds.

"Knock yourself out. It can't hurt to bring more people in," I agree. But I'm still thinking about what she said about Everly. I've looked out for her since she's been home. Then it dawns on me that she might participate in the speed dating if Hayley is, and I realize I don't like that either. But that isn't very likely since she doesn't come into the pub.

"Are you and Everly doing the speed dating?" I turn to ask her just in case, suddenly not liking this speed dating idea after all. I don't need some losers around my sister and her best friend. And especially Everly. I realize I just gave her a reason to ask me more questions.

"Um, yeah, probably." She carries boxes to the back and asks, "Why?"

"Absolutely not," I say as I follow her with the rest of the boxes.

"What do you mean? It'll be fun. You should do it too."

I glare at her like she's nuts. "No."

"We'll see, you big grump," she calls to my back as I head out and ignore her ridiculous idea. I won't be doing any speed dating. And like hell Everly will either. I've seen these tourist assholes in the pub, and I don't want any of them around her.

I don't like the thought of Everly dating anyone. I don't want another Richie for her. Watching her live through that the first time was awful enough. I fucking hate that guy.

I get to my office above the pub and open my laptop to scan through emails. I'm deleting the junk when I land on one from Everly. My heart clenches for a moment. She has no idea I'm her property manager, and I have to keep it that way. A few years ago, when Everly's dad put his very old and run-down house up for sale to move to Florida to start a new life with his new family, not bothering to stay in contact with Everly (freaking prick), I privately purchased the property and repaired and updated it. I worked hard to renovate it, but then it sat empty for over a year. I never felt right renting it to anyone. I had been debating on what to do with it. I almost moved into it myself, but when Everly moved back, I knew it was meant to be for her. Then I really wondered if the universe was fucking with me when she reached out to my property management company via email inquiring about renting her old home, having no idea that it was me. And I rented it to her for about a third of what I could have rented it for because I knew she had a part-time job at the library and was in the middle of a divorce. I set up a two-year lease to make damn sure she wasn't going anywhere and would have a safe home for her and her daughter in her newly remodeled childhood home.

I open the email, then freeze at what I read and scrub a hand over my face.

Oh shit.

> To Whom It May Concern:
>
> Can someone please fix our back stairs? I fell down when one of the treads broke, and it's not safe. I have a little girl who could have fallen. If I'd have broken my leg, I couldn't walk to work. Please fix the stairs as soon as possible.
>
> Your 2906 tenant,
> Everly Sparks

I close my eyes and rub the bridge of my nose. I have so many questions. Is she okay? Why the hell didn't she call me? Then I remembered of course she wouldn't call me. She hates me. I resist the urge to call her and make sure she's alright right here and now. I look at the clock and realize she's probably going to lunch soon. I can look down Main Street from my office, and I'll be able to see her when she walks to the coffee shop across the street. I don't always catch her, but I've noticed that she does this regularly at the same time if I just so happen to be working at my desk around lunchtime. I read the email two more times and feel reassured she has no idea it's me. And why is she walking to work? What happened to her car? I make a mental note to check into that. Secretly, of course.

I know she loved the home that she grew up in. She used to say it was the only piece of her mother she had left. When I cleaned and renovated it, I found things I couldn't throw away, which I have saved for her in a box. Behind the old fridge was a handwritten grocery list that looked like something her mother had written. It was old and worn, with what looked like doodling from a child on it. It didn't look like Brian wrote it. Brian didn't strike me as the type of dad who wrote out grocery lists. I don't even think he kept many groceries in the house, considering he was often on the road as a truck driver or had his ass parked at the pub when he was home, leaving Everly to stay at our house most of the time. When her mother died, dinner and grocery lists died with her. Stuck down in the trim of the house in the primary bedroom, I'd found a laminated bookmark that Everly had made her mom for Mother's Day in preschool with a picture of them together before Natalie got sick. Things that her dad probably wouldn't have saved for her. Brian wasn't a bad guy, but he wasn't a great dad either. When his wife died, he didn't seem to know what to do with that grief or the seven-year-old he was left to raise alone. Since Natalie was good friends with my mom, Everly was out at the ranch when Brian was gone for long stretches of time. When Natalie was diagnosed with cancer, she only had a few months left and was sick a lot. My mom helped her out and kept Everly since Brian was gone. He didn't seem to care much about being there for his wife during her last months of life. On more than one occasion, my dad had to go get him from the pub and take him home when he drank too much. When my dad realized Everly was left home alone often, he made sure she came out to the ranch more and put bunk beds in Hayley's room for them. My parents unofficially adopted Everly, and that was that.

We were raised together, but I never saw Everly as a sister. I always had a deep connection with her. There's no denying that. But she was also my little sister's best friend. Even though she had a big crush on me, I knew she was going to college, and I was the town fuckup at the time. I didn't want to get in the way and keep her from going to school and following her dreams.

I email her back and hope that she responds and lets me know that she's okay. I'm playing with fire here.

> Ms. Sparks,
>
> I'm sorry about the stairs. They will be repaired as soon as possible. Are you okay? Please don't ever hesitate to reach out if you need anything further, and I'll repair the stairs quickly.
>
> Management

I sift through paperwork and hope that message is enough to reassure her and not give anything away. I made a mental note to run to the hardware store tonight before work and get what I need to rebuild the back stairs. I won't risk her or Willow being unsafe. I'll get to it when I know she's at work so she won't catch me repairing it.

It's a small town, and my pub is the heart of our town. I can see everyone coming and going out the big bay windows of my office and the pub below. Everly is a creature of habit and takes Willow to school at the same time and then heads to the library. She takes her lunch break and walks in front of the pub nearly every day, so I know that, too. It's not like I go out of my way to watch her. And this is why it's impossible to rid myself of thoughts of Everly. She's everywhere, yet still so far out of my reach.

I glance over at my laptop and back again quickly when I see that another email has come through from her while I was working. I quickly click on it, my heart racing fast.

To the person I was rude to,

Thank you. I'm so sorry that I was rude. I'm just having a really bad week and falling down the stairs was not on my bingo card for life right now. Thank you for fixing the stairs. I feel bad now for being so harsh. I'm sure you're just doing your job.

Your very sorry and rude 2906 tenant,
Everly Sparks

I want to know what is causing her to have a bad week. I wish we weren't in the place where I can't call her or text her and ask. I've been looking after her for months without her knowing it, and it bothers me that I don't know. So I email her back, and despite telling myself I'm nuts for this, I hit the send button anyway.

Ms. Sparks,

I'm sorry again about the stairs. They will be fixed this week. In the meantime, is there anything else I can help with? You mentioned you were having a bad week. I hope it gets better.

A new friend, a.k.a. management

Too much? Probably. I don't care. It's been hard not being able to talk to her since she's been back for several months. She spends most of her time with Hayley, but our unspoken avoidance, which is that we don't talk and steer clear of each other, is stupid. I've never liked any of this. I want to be in her life again. I want her to let me in.

I look down through my large glass windows and see her coming out of the library and down Main Street. It's hard to miss her. She's the most beautiful woman I've ever seen, and she turns heads everywhere she goes. Her long, wavy dark blond hair is pulled up today on top of her head in a messy bun, her bright blue eyes light up a room when she smiles, and she has on her usual red lipstick that does things to me every time I see her wearing it. Her purse is slung across her chest, and she has on a light brown sweater, jeans, and brown boots. She smiles and waves to people she knows. And I swear my heart squeezes every time I see her, wishing she'd smile at me like that. She has one of the most captivating smiles, lighting up every room she enters and stopping me in my tracks. She always has.

I watch as she stops to talk to Ruth, the local eccentric inn owner who knows everyone. I see her hug her and continue as she calls back something to her. Everly tips her head back and laughs. Watching Everly come out of her shell since she's been back has been amazing, like a butterfly coming out of her cocoon. She was hesitant and insecure at first, but slowly but surely, she won everyone in town over with her kindness and smile. She stops to peer in the window of one of the shops and then continues, disappearing into the coffee shop across the street where she'll no doubt exit with two coffees to go or a tray sometimes if she's bringing Hayley one, too.

Now that she's passed by and I know it's clear, I lean back, nab my keys, and make my way down to my truck. I drive past her house and notice her car isn't there. I didn't recall seeing it at the library earlier either. Interesting. I hurry and purchase all the lumber and hardware that I'll need to reinforce the stairs before the hardware store closes and tuck it all in my truck bed, then slide the cover over it to hide it. I don't need Hayley asking me what the lumber is for and then hearing Everly mention she needs her stairs repaired and doing the math. I have a good reason for people not to know my business. Mainly the people who are dicks, like the Sullivans. Richie Sullivan's father is the town manager, and he's been known to make the lives of people he doesn't like a living hell, and businesses aren't off-limits. He especially likes to sabotage businesses if it's in his best interest or if anyone crosses him the wrong way. The bullying this man has gotten away with astounds me. I don't need him to have any information about me or my business to use as ammo. The amount of hate I have for the Sullivans is in abundance. I won't let them hurt the people I love ever again.

CHAPTER 5

Nash

When I finally make it back to my office, I check my email and am disappointed when I don't find any new emails from Everly. Heat fills me as I realize I'm being ridiculous. What am I even doing? I need to just stop. I head downstairs and get ready to work my shift at the pub. *Stop thinking about her.* She's not mine and not any of my business. I've already gone too far by being a dirtbag and not telling her that I'm her landlord.

Luckily, it's a busy night for the pub. Our regulars are in their usual spots around the bar, and the tables are full of people having happy hour drinks and appetizers. We have bruschetta with fresh tomatoes from the farmers' market on Hayley's toasted baguette bread tonight. It's always a hit, and we've been popping up on tourists' social media and travel blogs, so business has never been better. We need to consider hiring another bartender and someone to help Hayley out in the kitchen. She started baking to supplement Bookers, but it has become a local little best-kept secret to get the finest baked goods around. It's not something we planned on, but Hayley enjoys it, and the baked goods are a big draw for people who want to eat at the pub.

When the pub went up for sale a few years ago, I had already worked here, starting out as a barback and then a part-time bartender for seven years. I knew the ins and outs of Bookers and what I would do to make it even better. I saw an opportunity and seized it. I dragged Hayley into it with me because she's got a head for business like no one else. Plus, she was able to put the restaurant part of it together better than I ever could. She and I created a business plan and ran with it while she finished her MBA. Owning a pub wasn't her dream, but owning a business is something she's fantastic at, so we looked at it as an investment for her. And it's been a hit. We both agreed that if either of us didn't want it anymore, we'd buy each other out, but to start, we needed each other. And it's proven to be a great investment. Hayley is an early bird, and I'm a night owl, so it works out. We've run it smoothly for the most part at separate times, and most importantly, we've had fun with it together.

I lift my chin in hello to a few of the regulars at the pub and get to work. Work is what keeps me busy and sane at this point. I try to work away the feelings for the woman I can't have. In some ways, I had always dreamed that maybe she'd return to Cozy Creek and see what I'd done with my life. Perhaps she'd be proud of me in some stupid way. I can't remember a time when I didn't love Everly. Every little memory of her was like a million paper cuts to my soul. Everly is love. She's the person who will always make me feel like she's connected to me in every way. She's like a piece of my soul, and I feel whole when she's near me. I can't remember a point in my childhood when she wasn't a part of the memories. After high school, I was busy getting into trouble, into fights, then later working at the pub, then straightening up and going to horse farrier training, doing my apprenticeship, and figuring out my shit. By the time I pulled my head out, I'd lost Everly, and it was my fault. I fucked it all up, and there's no way to unfuck it up now. Everly got pregnant in college and married the town asshat and son of an even bigger asshat, Richard Sullivan. Hayley so eloquently calls them a bag of dicks, and she's not wrong. They're some of the worst people I've ever met. My life is busy and empty at the same time. Most days, the silence is so fucking loud and lonely.

One of the best things about owning and operating the local town watering hole is that we hear everything. Whether we want to or not, we hear all the gossip, drama, and everything happening. Cozy Creek is a small town, and like most small towns, people love to sit around and gossip. For example, who is having an affair with whom in town. Which town administrative people are doing dirty things. And Richard Sullivan is a dirty town manager. I have enough dirt on him to bury him if his son doesn't stop messing with Everly.

I do a final sweep of the pub and look around. All the chairs are up, and everything is wiped down and ready for the morning. I glance down at my watch. Hayley will be here to start baking in a few hours. That gives me a few hours to measure the stairs and cut all the wood to finish it when I know Everly will be at work later today.

Grabbing my grandpa's old dented green metal toolbox, I throw it in my truck, back it up to the small garage behind the pub, and get to work.

Richie Sullivan played professional hockey for a few years but wasn't very good. His attitude and ego were even worse, so no one was surprised when he was cut loose early from his team and lost his contract. Nobody likes Richie Sullivan as much as Richie does. He still thinks he's a hockey legend even though that's far from the truth, and everyone knows it but him. He took his hockey money and opened a car dealership. I personally would never buy a vehicle from him, but apparently, people do.

I walk down the street to check the measurements. Scanning the street, I look for Everly's car, but I'm still not seeing it.

Hmm.

The cottage has a few faint lights glowing inside, but it's late, so everyone is likely asleep. I turn on my flashlight and quietly make my way around back to measure the stairs, making a note on my phone. I see the broken tread and grimace. I should have just replaced these stairs before she moved in. I didn't know they'd give out. After getting my measurements, I quietly head back to the pub to measure and cut the wood.

I've always preferred to work while everyone else sleeps, so I'm up at night for the most part. Less interaction with people. People in this town made up their minds about me a long time ago. I used to think I could be successful and prove that I wasn't the shithead kid they all thought I was. Now, I don't care what anyone thinks. Well, maybe what the horses think. My clients can't talk, and that's nice, too.

Anyone but Everly, that is. I used to think she'd come back and see who I'd become and be proud of me. So far, she doesn't seem to see me at all.

CHAPTER 6

Everly

I glance away from my computer to make sure Anne Marie isn't nearby and sit back in my chair for a minute. Luckily, she's pretending to be busy helping a patron at the checkout counter while catching up on some local Cozy Creek gossip. Our Cozy Creek library is small but a surprisingly busy place for our cozy little town. Hence the name. It's our hidden gem that the rest of the world has begun to discover, and we seem to be growing. Anne Marie, our town librarian, has made this library what it is. The programs she's set up for the past few decades are impressive and invaluable to our community. I'm proud to work here, and truth be told, it's one of my favorite places on earth. I have so many memories here. The smell of books, orange furniture polish, and coffee makes me smile. All is right with the world when I come through these doors—as it should be. And I also want that for anyone else who passes through the doors. We're doing important work here, and it matters.

I'm thinking about the emails I received from the property management company. I feel terrible for the first rude email that I sent. And then the person who responded was so nice. I decided to write back and can't keep the smile off my face. Maybe I'll make a new friend here. God knows I could use more friends here in Cozy Creek. It's been hard making friends as a grown-up.

To the kind person who puts up with a rude tenant:

Thank you for your kind response even though I don't deserve it. I'm just struggling right now. I moved back to Cozy Creek last spring, and it's been a tough adjustment. I don't know whether I need a hug, an extra-large coffee, two months of sleep, a shot of tequila, or eight hundred and twenty-seven chicken nuggets. I'm working and struggling with everything, and life is just hard right now. But it'll be fine. Thank you for your kindness. I'm sure you didn't want to hear all of this. Please let me know if you hear of any part-time jobs in Cozy Creek. I'm looking for a part-time job to make more money. But don't worry, I will always pay my rent on time, and I appreciate you renting this home to me. This house is very special, and you have no idea how grateful I am. I try to take good care of it.

Signed,
Your 2906 tenant who pays rent on time first and foremost.

I need fresh air. Standing, I stretch and grab my purse. "Anne Marie, I'm going to grab a coffee. You want one?"

Her head pops back into the office. "Yes, please. It's also pumpkin bread day. Can you see if Hayley has any left? I have cash in my top drawer."

I wave my hand at her, smiling. "I'll get it. Be right back."

I love working at the library with her. She's always been a wild card. She's not your typical seventy-five-year-old librarian. No, she's a spitfire. She's usually adorned in animal prints and bold patterns. Her signature large multicolored glasses are always fun, and she changes them up daily, depending on her outfit. Today, they're bright orange on a string hanging from her neck, and she's adorned in cheetah-print pants and a black shirt. I can't help but smile when I'm around Anne Marie. She's mentored me into who I am today. One of the things that I love about her is that she has always worn bright red lipstick for as long as I've known her. And call me crazy, but it works for her.

When I was seventeen and sitting in the library talking books and drinking coffee with her and Hayley, I asked her why she always wore her signature bright red lipstick. She had explained to me that when she was younger, she had been married, and her husband had cut her down, belittled her, and kept her from working outside the home and using her library science degree. He also hated it if she wore any kind of makeup even though she'd liked it. She said it made her feel pretty. He'd wanted a very traditional wife who didn't work, stayed home, and took care of a house full of kids. And she explained that while there was nothing wrong with that, it just wasn't what she wanted. She wanted to be free to be herself without having to answer to anyone who didn't support her ambitions.

She explained to us that during that time, she did what nobody else was doing. She paved a different path for herself. When they'd ended up getting a divorce, she started wearing bright red lipstick every day as her act of rebellion. It made her feel confident and beautiful. She told us to find our favorite signature lipstick color, wear it proudly, and always do whatever makes us happy. And wouldn't you know, she had two tubes of lipstick sitting on the counter for us when we walked in a week later. I've used up all that lipstick, but the empty tube is still in the zipper part of my purse today as a reminder to be happy even over a decade later. Anne Marie and Anna McCreedy are the closest I'll ever get to a grandmother and mother.

What she said to me that day didn't register at the time, but later, when I felt broken down while living with Richie, I thought about Anne Marie a lot and how she was brave and decided to choose a different path for herself. So one day, I bought bright red lipstick and began to wear it. Call me crazy, but it gave me more confidence and the courage to advocate for myself. Who knew red lipstick could do that? I sure didn't understand it until I did. And Richie hated it. All of it. The lipstick, the confidence, the advocation. All the red flags added up, and eventually, there were so many it felt like the carnival was in town. So I left. And I've worn red lipstick ever since. Because it makes me feel good. Only now, I wear a lip stain, so it doesn't come off and lasts all day. Anne Marie was tickled when I bought her a tube, and now that's all she wears, too. Anne Marie will never know how much she's done for me and how much she means to me. Who knew good friendship and red lipstick could change a woman's life?

Anne Marie talks about retiring next year, and when I was hired as a part-time librarian, we talked about me taking her position when that day came. I would love that, but I also don't want her to retire. But when she does, I know we'll still be close. Even though I was gone for several years, Anne Marie welcomed me back into Cozy Creek and the library like I'd never been gone, and she loves Willow just like a granddaughter. She's like the town grandmother to many. I try to learn everything I possibly can from her so that when I take over for her, I can carry on her legacy here in Cozy Creek. Those are big shoes to fill, but I'll do whatever it takes. No one loves this library more than me and Anne Marie.

I send Hayley a text to meet me in the center of town and bring me bread if she has any, and she replies she's on her way to our meeting spot.

Sometimes I wonder what it's like to go into Bookers and eat dinner with Willow or have a drink with Hayley. To not have to worry about what Nash would think or say if he saw me. He probably doesn't even want me there.

I avoid Nash because I don't know how to interact with him now, and I'm so nervous that he wants nothing to do with me. He will break my heart again, and I don't think I can bear that. But the problem is, I still want everything to do with him.

CHAPTER 7

Everly

"I need you to do speed dating with me," Hayley announces as she plops down next to me. She hands me a brown-handled bag with pumpkins and leaves printed on it, and I smile because I know she's brought me yummy bread. But then I side-eye her at her random dating statement as I hand her a pumpkin spice latte, which neither of us can seem to get enough of this time of year.

"I do not need to speed date or whatever you call it, but thanks for the bread." I grin as I pull my cardigan tight around me in the brisk fall mountain air as I get comfy on our favorite bench outside of the library, crossing my legs. It is gorgeous outside today but a little chilly. "I *so* need this weather." I look down the street at all the pumpkins on display, brightly colored orange, purple, and yellow mums, and light posts decorated for fall with cornstalks and leaves sprinkling the sidewalks. *It's perfect here,* I think as I take a sip of my coffee. Mmm.

"I'm talking about just casual, fun dating." She holds up her hand. "And before you say anything, you know Mom or Anne Marie would watch Willow for you anytime. She's always welcome at the ranch, and she loves it there. If we'd let her, she'd probably sleep in the barn with the horses. And we could even do a sleepover in case you want to have some sexy overnight time." She wiggles her eyebrows.

I stare at her with a dry look. "Why the sudden interest in my dating life? I just got out of the worst marriage ever. I don't need to date. In fact, I'm in my old-lady era now. I work at a library. I bake, read books, and drink tea. I'm in bed by nine o'clock reading. This is my life now. I won't find an eligible man who would want that under eighty years old."

"Hey now, you can always rock an older guy." She shrugs, then grins after she pauses to take a sip of her coffee. "Mr. Fitzsimmons is a widower now. He might be interested."

"Stop it." I playfully laugh. "Anyway, what are you up to with all this dating nonsense?"

"I'm so glad you asked. I'm putting together a speed dating event at the pub, and I need you to help," she says full of excitement.

"We can put up a sign at the library," I offer, silently praying that is all the help she needs.

"No, I need your actual help with the event and to be my wing lady. We can do it together."

"At the pub?" I stare at her like she's crazy. She knows the pub is off-limits for a million Nash reasons, no matter how often she sneakily brings it up.

"Yes," she says, sipping her coffee while trying to look serious.

"Absolutely not." I shake my head. "Not setting foot in the pub."

"Come on, I *really* need your help. It'll be on a Saturday night, and Mom would have no problem keeping Willow." She throws that in with the hope she's covering every obstacle so I won't say no. I know her MO.

Saturday night. When Nash works. Not that I know his schedule or anything.

"No," I plead.

"Why?" she asks over her coffee cup before she takes a sip.

"I'm not coming to the pub when Nash works, and I'm not doing speed dating," I say, looking at her like she's nuts.

It was hard for me when I first came back to Cozy Creek. I'm the daughter of a single father who drank too much and had his own seat at the local pub. He preferred a different pub, not Bookers, but I still don't need history repeating itself. I've always felt like I'm the girl from the wrong side of the tracks, and Richie did a great job of reminding me of this. Going to the pub feels like what my dad did to me. He was always at the pub. Now that I'm back as a single mom, I've worked hard for people to take me seriously. I'm not doing speed dating and looking like I'm desperate and on the hunt for a new man. I'm good. I don't need to give the town any more fodder to judge me on. I was joking about the hot cowboy at the ranch who turned out to be Nash. I'm in the look-but-don't-touch era. No shade on pubs, but I just can't do that to Willow. I know it's totally classy and modern and more like a restaurant now, but still. Bad memories of my dad taking up residence there instead of spending time with me have left me happy in my old-lady-bookish era.

"Anne Marie could watch her?" she suggests. "Willow's always begging to stay at Anne Marie's. Plus, if I promise her bread for life, she'd do anything, I know it."

"She'd do it anyway. It's not only Willow, but you also know why I can't go. Nash." I add the last part softly.

"It's a big pub, and there'll be a lot going on. You probably won't even see him," she says as she shakes her head. "I can probably convince him to just take the night off. He needs it," she adds as she rolls her eyes.

I wonder what that means, but I don't want to seem curious, so I don't ask, and I continue to argue.

"Look, I know you've done a good job respecting that I don't want to talk about him up until recently. But we have to keep doing that. It's the only way."

"The only way for what?" she asks.

"For me to get over him," I finally whisper, looking down at my lap.

"Everly. You still love him?" she asks softly.

"I don't know that I ever stopped." I sigh and lean back against the bench. "Soulmates come in the form of friends, too. Sometimes it's not about romance. It's someone who makes you feel whole and who understands you the most when the rest of the world doesn't seem to understand you at all. And for me, that's what hurt the most. Losing Nash. I felt like he was my best friend soulmate. Other than you of course, but with Nash, it was just like there was something I can't quite articulate."

I don't look at Hayley because I'm afraid of what my face will reveal. She's quiet but reaches over and squeezes my hand. "Keep telling yourself that, friend. We all know that you've always had a deep connection with Nash. You two are like magnets. You always fought and made your way back to each other."

Until now.

Almost a decade has gone by, and I feel like I've lived so much life without Nash. And it feels wrong. I've missed him. But I don't know how we can go back to the way we were. I've messed it up.

Then I remember what she just said and turn to her. "Keep telling myself what?"

"He's never been *just* your friend. Look, I saw firsthand the freaky bond you both have. It was unique. I mean, we're *best* friends. But you know deep down Nash was always more than that to you. I saw it, and I know you felt it. Sometimes you can't fight it. Fate will win."

I nod and look down, kicking a pebble with my shoe. "I don't know."

My heart still feels bruised from losing him even though it's been years.

We sit and drink our coffee in quiet for a moment, and I think about what she's saying. It's hard to mend a fence you thought could never be mended. I look over at our beautiful library standing so tall in the distance with the mountains in the background full of all the gorgeous fall foliage popping all around us. Sometimes I think fixing things with Nash feels about as daunting as climbing the towering mountains in the distance. It's just too hard.

"Maybe you could start by coming by the pub. You could come and eat dinner and say hello to Nash. Start slow."

I just look over at her when she says his name. Just hearing his name makes me have goose bumps on my forearms.

"You've avoided each other for long enough. Time to rip off the bandage and get on with life. Whether together or not, you can't avoid each other forever."

She's right, and I know it. But I don't want to admit it. I take another sip of my coffee. I won't tell you how many I've drunk already today. Don't judge me; I'm having a mini breakdown.

"Why are you so down?" she asks as if she can read my thoughts.

I guess I'd better just tell her and get it over with.

"Richie took my car," I admit. "It was in his name, and he had let me use it through the dealership, but we had nothing in writing on it, so legally, he can do it. It was my fault for trusting him. But it was a shitty thing to do."

"He what? When did he do that?" she asks with a disgusted look. "He has a whole dealership full of cars."

"He just took it last night and texted me that I could move back home if I wanted it back."

"And what did you say to that rat bastard?" she asks, looking heated.

"That we'll be just fine walking." I take a sip of my coffee and raise my chin defiantly. We don't need him. Plus, I heard Jimmy Huber just set up a Huber ride-share business, so I can just take a Huber if I need to. I mentally remind myself to plug his number into my phone later.

"Little dick owns a freaking car dealership. He doesn't *need* that car. He's a manipulative bastard who would leave his child without transportation just to be a controlling psycho."

"I know." I shrug. "But there's nothing I can do."

"Unbelievable. You can drive Bobby. I'll talk to Mom and Dad."

"I don't need Bobby, but thanks," I say, thinking of the old ranch truck that we've all borrowed a time or two. It's basically more rust than truck at this point, but it gets from point a to point b. We all learned to drive using Bobby and made more donuts in the fields than we'll ever admit to our parents. "We can walk until it gets too cold, then I'll figure something out." I watch as the leaves trickle down from the trees in the distance.

"I hope the shrimp is smelling even worse now." She twists up her lip as she shakes her head.

I bite back my laughter and nod. "Me, too. I wish I could tell him how stupid he is. I'm just so tired of fighting with him."

"So what will you say to Richie next time he comes around? Because you know he'll keep playing games." She shakes her head, looking angry on my behalf.

I look over at Hayley, who is always so good at articulating things. "How do you tell someone that they're stupid in a professional manner?" I ask, trying to lighten the mood and make her laugh.

She bites her lip for a moment, then smiles. "Knowledge has always been chasing you, but you've always been faster."

I laugh. "Richie would probably take that as a compliment and not get the insult."

"He definitely underestimated you. He never thought you'd leave him. Always needs his ego stroked. And when was the last time he even saw Willow?"

I think about when he saw her last. "It's been a while. He says he can't have her right now because he's too busy. And honestly, I'm okay with that. I don't like the idea of her being with him when she's not comfortable with him. They never had much of a relationship when we lived together. It felt strained and forced. She would cry when he drove away with her for a visit, and he would get upset that it took her the entire drive back to his house to calm down and stop crying, yet she never stopped asking to call me. Sometimes he wouldn't even make it to his house before he brought her back to me and said he couldn't stand her acting like that."

Hayley looks beside herself with anger as she listens to me. "Acting like what? Having actual human feelings?"

"Right. I would bring her home and tuck her in next to me, holding her while she slept from exhaustion from crying. And I hate it. She doesn't feel comfortable with him."

"I don't blame her. I'm not even comfortable with Richie. What was he like with her when you all lived together?" Her brows knit together as she shakes her head.

I bite my lip as I think and then admit, "He was gone most of the time. Went on a lot of business trips for work. Really, that was just a way for him not to deal with us. When he was around, he was manipulating and controlling, and we were miserable. We were happiest when he was gone. We were practically strangers living alongside each other for years, but I couldn't leave because he threatened to take her. Now, I know that makes no sense because he doesn't even want her. He played us for years and used her to keep me there."

"You did the right thing by getting out. I know it hasn't been easy." She flips her phone over to check the time.

I couldn't stay with Richie a minute longer. When I saw how Willow was when he was around, I knew it was time to go. He wouldn't make it easy on me, but I knew I had to get out.

Going to college had been my only hobby and escape for the entire marriage. I took as many online classes as I could and stayed busy while Richie was gone. I quietly finished my online degrees without fanfare, and when I received my diplomas in the mail, I promptly tucked them away out of sight. Richie never cared about me taking classes, and he even joked that it was my "little hobby." I don't think he ever realized that I earned a master's degree on the down low. That shows how uninvolved he was in our lives. It was Richie's world, and we were just living in it. It was time for me to start living too. And in order to do that, I had to leave.

"What does your lawyer say about the car?" she asks as she turns to face me.

"I haven't contacted her about it yet. But there's probably nothing we can do." I shake my head in defeat.

"We're going to figure this out, Ev."

"I need another part-time job. The library isn't enough." I sigh.

"I could always use your help baking at the pub. My baking orders have taken off, and I sell out every week. It's an easy part-time job, and you're good at cooking and baking. You can even bring Willow with you."

I think about her offer. I would like to bake. But not at the pub. Nash would practically be my boss since he co-owns it. This would mean I would interact with and see him regularly. And I will admit that part thrills me and makes my heart clench at the same time. I can't handle him not wanting to see me. That hurts worse than avoiding him.

"What are you thinking?" she says as she watches me.

I stare at her but can't help but smile. "You're incorrigible." I know what she's doing. She's trying to get me to come in when Nash works because she wants us to figure out our stuff.

I playfully roll my eyes. I know she's trying to help, but this is against everything I've done to keep roadblocks up around Nash. "I don't know. I'll think about it."

"I promise it would be okay. He won't give you a hard time."

"He looks at me like he hates me," I say quietly.

"He doesn't hate you," Hayley promises. "We all want you at Sunday dinners."

"Does *he* want me at Sunday dinners?" I ask dubiously.

She shrugs. "*Our* family misses you and wants you there. Plus, you know Mom's dinners are the best."

I do know this. Anna pours her soul into these dinners, making delicious meals you'll never forget. She does themes like Italian, Mexican, Midwest comfort, Asian, and more. She goes all out with her decorations, special dishes, and even makes mouthwatering desserts. Growing up, I've had the best food I'll ever have at Anna's table. Nobody turns down a dinner invitation from Anna.

"Family is important, Ev. And you're our family. We need you, too."

I close my eyes. She's wearing me down, and she knows it. I know she's right, and adding Willow into that reminds me that she does need this, probably as much as I do. I will make a point to ease back into things with Nash and stop being a baby.

One thing I've learned is that family isn't always the one you come from. It's the one that you make.

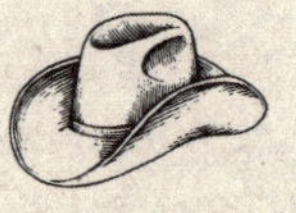

CHAPTER 8

Nash

"Guess what it smells like outside?" Hayley asks with a grin as she appears next to me at the empty and closed pub where I was catching up on paperwork in peace and quiet before she appeared like a little leprechaun.

My eyes dart to hers, but I don't turn my head. She slides a coffee cup across the bar top toward me that looks like fall threw up all over it with leaves and pumpkins. She thinks I hate fall. And Christmas, too. All the seasons. I have my reasons for this, and they're valid.

"Do tell," I say hesitantly, taking the warm cup and placing it in front of me as if it were a bug. But it smells really good. It's probably some ridiculous fall drink that she knows I'll pretend not to like and then drink every drop later when she's not watching. But I won't be caught ordering that for myself or showing her that I like it or anything else about fall.

"Fall," she says blissfully with eyes that are lit up. "The leaves smell crisp, the air is brisk, and the food and drinks are ten out of ten right now. It's amazing," she says as she sinks onto the barstool beside me.

"I'm going to need you to pump the brakes there, pumpkin spice," I say dryly as I sift through my paperwork.

"Why are you such a Scrooge about fall, anyway? It never used to bother you when we were kids. You participated in everything. You loved the haunted houses, fall festivals, and all of it just as much as I did."

"I don't hate fall." I give her an incredulous look. I reach for more papers and stack them neatly and lay them flat again. "I've grown up, unlike some people. I like grown-up things."

"Could have fooled me. You're a grump about all things fall. Come to think of it really any of the seasons."

I stopped liking fall when Everly left. It was her favorite season, and we did a lot of fall stuff together—haunted houses, fall festivals, and pumpkin carving. And it all reminds me of her, so I stayed away from all of that. Ultimately, it's just better for me not to do the things that remind me of her. I've worked hard to avoid the memories.

"Are you doing horse work today?" She nods to the stack of papers in front of me.

"Just finishing up some paperwork, then I'll head out to see a client and be back to work the pub tonight." I left out that I'm also going to Everly's to replace her stairs. I have the stair treads cut and hardware ready so I can do it quickly before she realizes someone is there. I have checked my email repeatedly, and there hasn't been a response. I shouldn't have sent the last one. I can't help it; I want to know how she's doing. I never ask Hayley any questions about Everly, but I never stop her when she mentions Everly and Willow. And since they're friends, Hayley does mention her a lot. I secretly love it.

I change the subject and glance at the time on my phone. "What are you baking today?"

"Pumpkin bread. I'll have them packaged up and ready to go for tonight. Eighteen are spoken for and pre-paid, so they're just for pickup."

"You're killing it, Hayles. Proud of you." I squeeze her shoulder as I stand and shove my paperwork into my bag. "Save one for me."

"Are you finally ready to admit that you like fall treats?" she teases, then turns serious. "Thanks. Don't get sappy on me, big bro."

I can tell my words hit her where they needed, and she continues, "Speaking of . . . I need to run something by you."

"What's that?"

"Everly might be baking for us. She's been looking for another part-time job, and I can double my baking orders and sell more bread if I have her help," she says cautiously, watching my reaction.

I swallow, hoping I'm playing it cool. I clear my throat and shrug. "Yeah, that's fine. Whatever you need."

"Really?" She eyes me skeptically.

"Yeah, whatever." I am playing it cool, but inside, I'm anything but cool.

"Okay," she says slowly as she watches me like she's waiting for me to react differently.

"I'm going to head out now that you're here to take over. Gotta get to it," I say casually even though a million thoughts run through my head.

Why does she want to work here at the pub? Doesn't she know I'm here, and she won't be able to avoid me? I need to process this. I have to get out of here.

"Later, Nash," she says as she ties on her apron and pulls her hair into a knot on top of her head. That means she's going into baking mode, and we're done.

When I get upstairs, I flip open my computer to check and see if I have any emails, and I quickly sit and scoot my chair up when I see one from Everly. I read it twice and smile. Then respond.

Ms. Sparks,

I have spoken with the owner, and your rent will be forgiven for the next three months due to the fall on the stairs. We would like to sincerely express our heartfelt apologies for your inconvenience. We hope this makes things a little easier for you for the next few months. If I hear of any part-time positions, I will be sure to forward them your way. Also, feel free to text me at the number on your rental agreement if you need anything. Looking forward to helping in any way that makes things easier for you.

Management

I have a separate phone that I rarely use, but I keep it for my property management. I have gotten away with keeping everything under the radar, but there's one small issue. I used Anne Marie at the library for my person to leave paperwork and keys with, and when Everly came back, I talked with her and asked her to please keep my business confidential. She had given me a hug and reassured me that she would. I just hope that agreement holds up. She's the only person in town who knows I own property, and I need to keep it that way. She's trustworthy, and I hope that still rings true even though she works with Everly. I hadn't anticipated Everly working at the library when she returned. I run my fingers through my messy hair and head out to take care of a few horses. I've been trying to work on as many of my horses as possible before the weather turns, and it gets colder, and the snow comes. We have a big ski season here, and the pub is always busy during the fall and winter. Spring through fall is my time to take care of my client's horses, and I want to make sure they're all taken care of and maintained going into winter.

I LEAN DOWN and trim one of Soupy's hooves and hear Mrs. Caraway calling her chickens off in the distance. She's always been one of my favorite clients. Eccentric woman who loves all her animals. Her horse that she named Soupy is not a fan of anyone but me, and she loves to remind me of that. But she also regularly sends me home with fresh eggs and homemade treats in Tupperware and still calls me her honey boy. Like I'm five years old and not thirty and a grown man. I shake my head and chuckle. I set Soupy's hoof down and lean over to scratch his forehead and pull him toward me and kiss his forehead. "Love you, too, Soupy."

"See, I told you he only loves you," she says from the doorway, and I look over to see Mrs. Caraway standing there watching me and smiling. "My Soupy knows good people."

"Well, Soupy *is* a good boy, aren't you?" I say as I pat his back and scratch his face before I lean down to pick up my tools. "He should be good to go until our next appointment, but you can call me if anything comes up. Still no idea how he got that shoe off?"

"No, no clue." She shrugs. "I look forward to your visits, honey boy. Now, take this. I made fresh apple cider donuts, your favorite."

I know that Soupy is rough on his hooves, but I suspect Mrs. Caraway is lonely, and she doesn't mind when I have to come out extra to fix Soupy's shoes when he has mishaps. But they seem to be happening more and more often. I play along with it and always come and spend a little extra time chatting with her. I know she's older and lonely since her husband passed away.

"Thanks, Mrs. Caraway. I appreciate your treats. Keep Soupy here from knocking his shoes off," I say as I load my toolbox into the back of my truck and shut the gate.

"Drive carefully, honey boy. See you next time!" she happily sings with a wave as she stands next to Soupy, her horse with wild and crazy red hair.

They are by far my favorite clients, and her treats really are the best. I eat all of them on the way back to town. I won't tell Hayles this, but fall really is my favorite too.

CHAPTER 9

Nash

I barely had a spare minute tonight before I realized it was after midnight and time to close. I love it when work flies by, and I stay busy until the end. I finished closing and hit the light before heading up the back stairs and stopping at my computer to check if she emailed me back. She did, and I sat to read, plopping down and placing my hand under my jaw, exhausted but curious to see what she had to say.

> Dear CC Management,
>
> Oh my goodness, you did NOT have to do that! I will admit that it will help me out to catch up a little bit, and I appreciate it so much. Seriously, I'm blown away by your generosity. Thank you. I will admit I'm curious as to who you are. Are you a Cozy Creek local? Is it okay if I ask your name and how old you are? I could always use a friend. Maybe you could, too?
>
> Signed,
> Your thankful and new friend 2906 tenant
>
> P.S. Please call me Everly.

I chuckled at her email and sent a quick response. I'm glad I could help her with the rent. Another reason I want this to be anonymous is that I know that I'm toeing the line with these emails. I should shut my computer and stop emailing. But I can't.

Everly,

It's not a problem at all. Sorry that your stairs were a mess. I hope they look okay. I knocked them out today. My name is Reed, and I'm thirty. Tell me a little about yourself. And I can always use a friend, as well.

Reed

Guilt pricks at me for lying to her, but I can't tell her who I am. Part of it is true. Reed is part of my last name, and I really am thirty. *Not technically lying*, I tell myself. Maybe she'll never know, and we can just be emailing friends.

I shower to wash the day off me, having it out with my dick. I spend more time with my hand than a woman because I can't do casual sex with random women anymore. And if dirty thoughts of Everly send me over the finish line, I try not to dwell on it too much. I lean my head against the cold tile of my shower and sigh. I didn't realize I'd be this lonely when I pictured my life after doing everything I set out to do. Working at the pub and managing my farrier clients and then my properties leaves me exhausted. Sometimes I wish I could control-alt-delete these feelings because I'm tired of feeling like all I do is work and sleep and have no life. I have tried to move on and find someone to settle down with. Believe me, I've tried. I can't settle down with anyone because they aren't Everly. No one will ever be like her or mean as much as she means to me.

For the first time in a long time, I fall asleep relaxed and at peace. I have a small piece of her back. It might not be like it was, but it's better than having nothing at all.

I WAKE UP to a soft noise clamoring below me in the pub kitchen. Soft music plays, and there is the occasional clank of a pan in the sink, oven door shutting, and typical kitchen sounds. I close my eyes and remember that it's Saturday, and Hayley is baking before we open. Which means she probably has coffee ready. I brush my teeth quickly, pulling on a T-shirt before heading down the back stairs. But when I get to the bottom of the stairs, my breath hitches, and I halt when I see Everly and no Hayley in sight.

She leans against the counter, with a coffee mug in her hands as she stares off like she's deep in thought. I take in the soft smile on her face as she hums to the music. Her eyes are a little tired but still the same stunning blue, and her curves are accentuated by the apron that cinches at her waist. She's so beautiful, taking my breath away in this quiet moment. When my feet hit the bottom of the stairs, her eyes slide to me and grow wide. She freezes with the mug to her lips.

"Good morning," I say quietly as I stand there and stuff my hands in the pockets of my joggers. I don't want to make her feel uncomfortable, and I seem to do that just by existing in her presence.

She stares at me, and I don't miss the way her eyes scan me and land on my face as she stands straighter, quickly looking away. "Good morning. Er, um, Hayley isn't feeling well and asked me to cover for her this morning."

I blink and try to hold back a grin. No way Hayley is sick. I don't think her body even knows how to get sick. She is orchestrating something here, that's for sure. Everly might have fallen for it, but I see through my sister's bullshit. She was fine yesterday and loves her quiet Saturday mornings for baking. She plays music and gets all her stuff done with no one around to bother her. No way she's sick.

"Thanks for helping. We could use your help around here. It's nice of you to offer," I say softly.

Hearing this, she seems surprised and softens, and says shyly, "Would you like some coffee? I made plenty."

I take in the kitchen, tidy but functional and industrial, something we splurged on when we updated the pub. She has all the ovens full and going. Everly seems at home here already, and it smells fantastic. I didn't even know she could bake like this.

"I'd take a cup to go if you've got extra," I say, trying to be casual.

She turns and grabs a cup and begins to fill it, her hand shaking slightly.

She looks beautiful with her face flushed from the kitchen, her black apron over her snug white T-shirt, and jeans that hug her ass just right. Her hair is pulled up in a messy bun, and a few of the tendrils escape, and her bright lipstick does things for me. I haven't seen her around without it since she's been back. It makes me imagine her lips and what I'd like to do with them. Run my finger over the plump bottom and kiss her while biting it.

I shouldn't think about her like this. But what was all that talk about her telling Hayley she was checking me out? Maybe she doesn't dislike me as much as I thought.

Since she's been back, she doesn't make small talk with me. This is the most she's interacted with me. Maybe we're getting somewhere. Jesus, about damn time. I've waited for her to come around for months. When we brought her back to Cozy Creek, she was so broken and sad. I hated it, but I knew she needed a soft place to fall and make her feel safe. And as much as I wanted it to be, I knew that wouldn't be me. She let me know that she didn't feel the same way all those years ago. I often think about that night and what I should have said to convince her to stay. I still second-guess everything about that night she told me she was pregnant.

She turns and reaches for the fridge handle and almost crashes into me. I reach out to steady her, my eyes going to hers, my hands bracing her biceps as I hold her to me, not pushing her away, feeling her heat against mine. I hold her firmly but gently, not wanting to hurt her in any way. I notice her breath catch and those red lips parting softly. The feel of her smooth skin at the point where the material of her T-shirt sleeve ends. My thumbs absentmindedly sweep back and forth, savoring the feel of her, intoxicating and heady. But the look in her eyes is the thing that fells me. She's affected by our proximity. She . . . likes it.

"I'm . . . sorry," she stammers, her face flushing as she looks up at me, her lips quirking.

"It's okay," I murmur, wondering what it would be like to hold her like this more often. I like it.

She looks to the side of us nervously like she wants to flee, so I scoot back a little and keep my hands on her to steady her.

She stills. "What are you doing?"

"Keeping you from falling," I say as I release her arms and take the cup she has set on the counter for me.

"No, I mean talking to me. I thought you didn't want to talk to me," she says, but all I can focus on is her lips, plump and red, and her bright white teeth. I wonder if my lips would be stained red for the rest of the day if I kissed her lips.

"Who said I don't want to talk to you?" I scan her face as my lips curl into a smile even though I'm trying to play it cool.

"You just . . . don't," she huffs, but her eyes dart back to mine. Then they travel down my face and over my chest, and she looks to the side again quickly.

Yep. Getting somewhere.

"Maybe we should change that," I offer as I lean back against the counter and reach to take a sip of my coffee, remaining in her space as I try not to stare at her.

"Did you mix up our coffees?" I ask as I set it back down.

She frowns, looking confused. "No. You always used to drink pumpkin-flavored drinks when we were friends."

When we were friends.

Fuck.

I say nothing and stare at her, my smile gone and feeling deflated. She stares back defiantly. And as defiant as she tries to be, I know the truth, the real Everly. She misses me.

I smirk and grin at her, taking another sip as I raise my eyebrows. She thinks she's pushing me away. Her attitude makes me want to be around her even more. I'm done with these games we've been playing. And she needs to be done too. I gave her time. Now I'm going to see if she's done with me. If she is, it's going to hurt like hell. But fuck, I miss her, I realize as an ache fills my chest.

"So it's gonna be like that," I mutter over my mug.

"Gonna be like what?" she challenges.

"We have things to work out, Ev." I reach out and tuck a lock of blond hair behind her ear that has escaped from her messy bun. My fingers run along her cheekbone, making her close her eyes, and she leans into me slightly and stills.

"Like what?" she repeats nervously, still not moving away from my touch.

"Like why you think we're no longer friends," I say as I reach over for her cup and hand it to her.

"Well, we're not. I don't know what we are, but we're not friends," she says evenly as she sets her cup down and walks over to check the oven. Using the dish towel tucked into her apron, she slides out pans of sourdough bread, slides in more, and sets the timer, then turns to look at me.

I can't take my eyes off her.

I look at her and smile. "We'll see about that," I call as I turn and head out the back door, closing it softly behind me.

A good start.

I make my way out as I take a big swig of my coffee. It tastes like memories of Everly. Memories I'm going to do my best to fix.

Yeah. Today's gonna be a good fuckin' day.

I take my usual run and add a few extra miles to burn off some excess energy. Everly is long gone when I get back, but an email awaits me in my inbox.

> Reed,
>
> Thank you so much for fixing my stairs. They look beautiful and are super sturdy now. Willow (my daughter) and I appreciate it very much. I was hoping to thank you in person and meet you. I will admit, it is kind of fun communicating through emails. Maybe we can try text, but if email is what you're more comfortable with, that's fine, too.
>
> You asked about me, so I'll tell you, and hopefully not bore you to death.
>
> I'm twenty-eight and a single mom of a horse-loving eight-year-old. She's a good kid, in the third grade, and pesters me daily for horseback riding lessons, which I'm hoping to make happen for her soon.

I love to read, and I especially love everything about fall. If that doesn't scare you off as far as being my friend, then please text or keep emailing. My friend jokes that I'm basically a seventy-year-old in a twenty-eight-year-old's body. I love to decorate and work hard to make our home cozy. I love thrifting and DIY home projects. I'm a foodie through and through and love to cook and bake. I've been making a different fall soup and bread for us nearly every day and love trying out new recipes. How about you? Tag, you're it.

Everly

I chuckle at this and decide to be as close to honest as I can. I'm insanely curious about all of this. I want to know what soups she's making and what projects she's working on. I've missed her. Everly has always been the right woman, wrong time. And while she's back, I risk her not feeling the same as I feel for her and especially worry about what will happen when she realizes I'm her landlord. I'm playing with fire here, risking messing things up again. But I can't bring myself to stop emailing. I miss her so damn much.

Everly,

Not scared so far. I'm thirty, single, never married, and I work a lot. I manage properties and pretty much just stay busy with work. I love horses too and hope to have some of my own someday. I have a property outside of Cozy Creek that I plan to build a home on someday when I have my own family. That's what I've been working hard toward.

What are your favorite things about fall? What soup did you make today? I'm not going to lie, you have me curious about these soups and breads. I can cook but not very well. But I love to eat.

Reed

I'm surprised when a response comes back quickly as if she's waiting.

Reed,

Today's soup of the day is Italian meatball with a loaf of crusty homemade sourdough bread. Your dream of building a home outside of Cozy Creek sounds divine. There's nowhere as beautiful as Cozy Creek. My friends own a big ranch outside of town. I practically grew up there, and it's the most special place in the world to me. You won't find a more spectacular view, especially in the fall. And in the winter? The snowcapped mountains are so beautiful they'll practically make you cry. What do you think your house will be like when you build it? Do you have a dream for it?

Everly

Her writing about the ranch being home fills me with hope. Maybe I will have a chance with her. I'm not sure what that would look like, and I will admit, it scares me. Am I good enough for her? Everly deserves the world, and I want to be the one to give it to her.

I want to be the one to make her smile and feel safe. Nothing about her body language this morning said rejection. It was an invitation. It was confusing. Like she wanted me too.

We've been emailing back and forth, and I have lost track of time. I love this and need this. I think she does, too. And hell yeah, I have a dream for that home. With her in it.

CHAPTER 10

Everly

I slide a pan of pumpkin bread into the oven and turn on my favorite show to binge-watch, *Gilmore Girls*. I light the new apple cider and nutmeg candle that I saved from my birthday, glancing over when I hear a soft knock on the front door. I see Hayley bending down to pick something up from my front porch.

"Hey, how are you feeling?" I ask as I open and hold the door for her. She comes in carrying a bottle of tequila, a takeout box of something, and an envelope.

"Oh, much better." She waves it off as if it was nothing that she called me in a pinch, begging me to fill in for her baking when she had a touch of the flu. *The made-up flu,* I think to myself.

"Thanks for filling in for me. I had to stop by to see what the soup of the day is and see if you have any extra." She grins as she sets the items on my kitchen table.

"Of course, I always make extra. What's all this?" I ask as I open the box and find it full of warm chicken nuggets.

"I don't know. It was all on your porch," she says as she kicks off her boots. "I thought you ordered something."

I open the envelope and find a gift card to Cozy Creek Coffee House for an amount that makes my eyes widen as I mentally calculate all of the coffee I can buy with it. A note is included.

Everly,

I can't provide all 827 chicken nuggets, a hug, or a nap. But here's the rest. Enjoy!

Reed

I tuck the note in my back pocket before Hayley sees it. I'm not ready to answer questions about Reed quite yet. I haven't figured out our friendship, but he is becoming a close friend, and I like chatting with him. I'm touched that he took the time to deliver these gifts. He paid attention to me and made me feel listened to and taken care of, two things I lack in life.

"It's a gift card for coffee, a large box of chicken nuggets, and a bottle of tequila." I pick up the bottle and turn it to show her. I haven't drunk tequila in years. I'm mostly a coffee and tea type of girl. But it excites me to have a secret friend to talk to and share day-to-day things.

"That's top shelf. Good stuff," Hayley muses. "Who gave you all this?"

I shrug, trying to play it off.

"It's so random," she says, turning on the kettle to make herself tea.

I've been enjoying our secret friendship. I kind of don't want to ruin what we have going on. It's been fun, and I look forward to our emails. I found myself sad a few times when there wasn't a return email.

"A very random assortment of gifts," she says as she reaches into the box and takes a bite of a chicken nugget, covering her mouth as she chews. "They're still warm, and they're good."

I reach in for one and take a bite. "These *are* good."

"I'm not sure how you get signed up for random gift delivery, but

I'd like to be added to the list for that service," Hayley teases as she pulls out a chair and sits.

"It is nice," I agree. "And today I have beef and barley soup. I have Italian meatball left, too," I offer, trying to change the subject.

"I'll take whatever. It all sounds so delicious. So I talked to Nash and got the green light on speed dating. I have it set up for Saturdays when we do karaoke. It's going to be fun."

"It'll be good for the pub, but I wouldn't call that fun," I decree as I stir the soup.

"You're coming, right?" she asks as she cuts off the end of a loaf of bread, spreads butter on it, and looks up at me.

"Um, no, that sounds terrible, Hayley. I thought you were joking about me participating." I wrinkle my nose and look at her like she's nuts.

She pleads with me with her puppy eyes. "Noooooo, you need this as much as I do. I told you we're not going to find nice guys delivered by DoorDash," she reminds me, her voice laced with humor. "But apparently, you're getting all kinds of random things delivered, so I mean, who knows at this point? Maybe as a society, we're evolving to that level."

"I definitely do not need to find a guy. I'm all set. Been there, done that, got the T-shirt," I say as I pull down three bowls. "And that T-shirt can go in the trash," I mutter.

"Hey, Willow tree, can I have a hug?" Hayley leans over and calls down the hall. "Also, your mom has chicken nuggets!"

"Hi," Willow calls as she emerges carrying a toy horse whose mane she's been trying to braid. I melt when I see she's made homemade paper horseshoes and taped them to the horse's feet. She wraps her arms around Hayley, laying her head on her chest.

"I love your kid," Hayley mouths to me as she squeezes Willow back.

And my heart melts seeing them together. A pang also hits my heart, as we lost so many years of being away and not having Hayley and her parents in our lives when we lived in the city. And Nash. But I'm not going there right now. I'm still confused about our interaction the other day. It left me feeling like I'm second-guessing everything as far as Nash is concerned.

"I like your horse. You still going to do lessons out at the ranch with Pops?" Hayley asks her.

"Yes!" Willow exclaims as she looks over at me to confirm.

I smile and nod. "We need to talk to him and set it up."

"Nash is also good with lessons too, you know. And look, you can do horseshoes, too? No way! Nash would love this." She smiles as she pulls out her phone, snaps a picture of her toy, and sends it to him.

I try not to feel jealous that she gets to casually text Nash whenever she wants. I wonder what he'd even say if I texted him. I don't even have his number anymore. I picture Nash giving Willow lessons, and my heart can't even take the vision of those two together. I wonder what he thinks of her paper horseshoes.

Willow grabs a chicken nugget and heads back to her room, happy to hear that the horse lessons are still a thing, regardless of who is giving them. I smile because I love seeing her happy and relaxed here. I look around at our home, and I'm proud of the life we've created. It's peaceful, cozy, and it's ours.

Hayley leans back in her chair and pleads, "Please do the speed dating with me. It'll be fun."

"It does *not* sound fun." I pull out a chair and sit across from her, putting my chin on my hands as I stare at her.

"Okay, then at least consider doing it once with me and give me feedback on the experience to improve it for the next round."

I guess that wouldn't hurt. It does mean going there when Nash is possibly around. After that moment in the kitchen the other day, I was a mess. I mixed up the wrong batter for pumpkin bread, and I couldn't get my head on straight after he touched me. I loved it when he held my arms. I've thought about it ever since. I rub my arms absentmindedly, where his touch felt like a surge through me that left me feeling short-circuited. But no way am I telling her this about her brother.

"I guess I could help you once. I'll have to check with Anne Marie about watching Willow."

"Mom would do it, too. She'd love having Willow out for a sleepover," Hayley said, taking another chicken nugget.

"I don't have a vehicle anymore," I reminded her. "Anne Marie is just around the block."

Hayley takes a deep breath and lets it out. "Asshole," she mouths, referring to Richie taking the car back.

"So what's the plan?" I give her a reluctant side-eye. She knows I'm going to support her, but I'm not excited about it.

"I'm so glad you asked," she says, swinging her legs in and leaning toward me excitedly.

"This Saturday, along with the speed dating, we're having a 2000s throwback theme night. We'll have great music, good appetizers, dancing, and of course, karaoke. It's going to be so much fun."

I smile because she's so enthusiastic, and I will admit that it maybe sounds just a little bit fun. I haven't had a girls' night out in years. That is sad to say, but it's true. I guess one night out at Bookers couldn't hurt. Hayley and I love karaoke and sang a ton for fun in high school and college.

"Let's see what you have to wear," Hayley says as she stands and heads toward my room.

"A sweater and jeans will be fine, I'm sure," I call back to her. I don't have the money for new clothes.

"What are you wearing?" I ask as I follow her into my room, and she opens my closet.

Hayley looks at the contents of my closet incredulously. "I'm getting a new outfit. I'm trying to figure out what you have that doesn't scream old lady librarian."

I groan. It's like she can read my mind. I'm content to become an old lady librarian at this point. I'm already on my way to making that happen. I already have the job, cozy cottage, and tea brewing.

"But I *am* an old lady librarian," I protest as she moves hangers to the left and frowns even more.

"No, you're not. We're dressing beautiful and sexy. I want you to feel confident."

"I *do* feel confident in my sweaters and leggings," I mutter.

"You have nothing. We're going shopping," she announces as she pulls out her phone and types something into it.

"I don't have that in my budget right now," I point out as I sit on my bed and look up at the ceiling in protest.

She looks up from her phone. "Mom's finishing shopping at the general store and coming to watch Willow. We're going out to get new outfits. And probably makeup. It's on me." She holds up her hand. "I don't want to hear it. Consider it a baking bonus. You have helped me so much, and it's time for me to help you. Plus, you're doing me a favor by helping with the speed dating. I owe you."

"You do help me . . ." I say before she ignores me and heads back down the hall.

I shake my head and smile as I follow her, knowing I won't win this one. I peek into Willow's room, where she's coloring. "Hey, Willow, let's eat."

We're having soup, chicken nuggets, and some of my homemade sourdough bread when Anna comes in my back door and waves as she sets down a few bags of what looks like baked goods and a few containers of food. I love Anna. She is what I imagine my own mom would be like if she were still alive. I don't have a lot of memories of her, but Anna tells me stories. She even keeps a notebook, and when she has a memory of my mom, she writes it down for me. I've read it a few times since I've been home, and I cherish every memory she saves for me.

"Hi, Anna, thanks for coming. You didn't have to do this," I say as I take her coat and give her a quick hug. Hayley rolls her eyes at me and smiles, mouthing at her mom, "Yes, you did."

"I wanted to spend some time with this kiddo," she says, plopping a kiss on Willow's head as she slides into a chair next to her at the table.

"I have some soup on if you're hungry."

She smiles and nods. "It smells good in here. I think I will have some in a little bit. Glad you two girls are going out. What do you have planned?"

"Shopping for an outfit for speed dating, apparently," I say dryly.

"Speed dating? Now that sounds like fun for you two." She rubs her hands together with a grin.

"If you say so," I say as I rinse the bowls and set them in the dishwasher. I turn, and Anna's already chatting with Willow. Seeing them together makes me wonder what my mom would have been like with Willow. I look around my kitchen and feel her here. Even though I have very few memories of her, I miss her and wonder what she would have been like.

Hayley leans in and hugs her mom. "Thanks, Mom. We'll be back late; we're going to the city to shop."

"The city?" I protest.

She waves her hand. "You know we won't find what we need here. We're on a mission. I have just the idea of what we need."

Oh boy.

"Go, go, go," Anna says as she pulls my plaid jacket and purse off the hook by the door and hands them to me, urging me along.

"Okay, thank you, I'll check in . . ."

"Bye," Hayley calls and waves, trying to get me to the door.

"Bye, sweetie," I say, giving Willow a hug. "I won't be long," I call as Hayley steers me out the door before I can come up with another excuse.

After three hours of what Hayley calls power shopping and a few new outfits later, complete with shoes, makeup, and hair products despite my protesting, I will admit that I do feel pretty. And I haven't felt this way in a long time. For the past several years, I've poured all my energy into school and taking care of Willow and Richie. I really put myself last. Survival mode was not fun and not a place that I want to live in again. Finding my way back to myself here in Cozy Creek has been liberating. I've been working hard to set up our home, which has been nice. I guess it's my turn now. And Hayley and I have had the best time. This really was my Julia Roberts from *Pretty Woman* moment when I got to cut loose, and I felt like . . . well, me again. Everly. Not a mom, but me. I needed this. I had my makeup done and have a bag of new makeup in Hayley's trunk. I paid close attention when she explained the makeup to me, and I can't remember the last time I've curled my hair and not just thrown it up in a messy bun or ponytail, always trimming the ends and my bangs myself.

On the way back to Cozy Creek, I turn the radio down in the car. "Thanks, Hayles. I needed this."

"I know you did. That was so much fun." She gives me a wicked grin. "Hey, want to go steal your old car back?"

"No. Richie would probably call the cops on me, and I'll go to jail." I snort. "And he'd enjoy that too much."

"What a dick."

"If the name fits," I mutter as my phone vibrates in my lap. I look at it and cringe. "Speak of the devil."

"Answer it. Let's hear what little dickie poo has to say." She smirks with an evil playful look on her face.

Feeling a little snarky, I slide the answer button and put him on speaker. "Yes," I say in my steady and what I like to call my professional librarian voice that I've perfected. Richie hates it when I don't give in and argue back with him. Boundaries are his worst nightmare.

"'Bout time you answer. I've been calling and texting," Richie huffs, and I hear commotion in the background around him like he's out somewhere.

"What do you need, Richie?" I ask, remaining calm.

"You coming back?" he demands.

"Nope," I say with a pop of the *p* at the end, hoping he gets my emphasis on the word.

"What are you going to do?" he berates in a condescending voice. "You can't afford a vehicle on your measly little librarian paycheck. You're barely making ends meet. I'm not even sure how you're even making it. Unless you have some part-time escort job I'm not aware of. Where are you getting your money?"

I take a deep breath before I answer and remember to keep it professional. "My household budget is none of your concern. Is there anything else you need to talk to me about concerning our child?"

Hayley flips on her turn signal and stops at a light. Looking over at me, she shakes her head with disgust at the way Richie speaks to me.

"Give up, Everly. Come home where you belong. It stinks, and I need you to take care of whatever it is. I'm too busy to deal with this." His voice is full of frustration.

Hayley and I lock our eyes, and I cover my mouth. Hayley can barely contain her laughter. Our eyes are wide, and we're breathing heavily, trying not to laugh.

"Maybe you could hire a housekeeper to maintain your home," I say nonchalantly.

"I hired someone. And they say they won't come back until I figure out the odor," he bites out. "This is your job, Everly. You need to come home."

"I don't know what to tell you. Maintaining a house that size is a lot of work, but you'll need to figure it out. We're divorced now," I remind him evenly, proud of myself for keeping my cool.

"I know we're divorced, Everly. You should never have left me. And you know it's wrong. You need to be here where you belong. Come fix this."

"I'm going to have to let you go, Richie. I hope you can resolve your odor issue," I say, barely keeping it under control. "Bye now."

I disconnect, and Hayley and I are hysterical with laughter. "Your odor issue," she repeats and dissolves in another fit of laughter.

"Well deserved. When he finds out what it is, we're screwed," I say but still cackle.

"He can't prove it was us."

I sigh, and my shoulders sag. "When is he going to stop making Willow's and my lives miserable?"

"He needs to back off and leave you alone. I should have Nash talk to him."

"No, don't do that," I say quickly, but she's already parking and getting out.

"Meanwhile, you'll be a hot lady for speed dating, so whatever." She grabs bags from the back, and we head up the stairs, still on our fun shopping high despite Richie trying to kill the mood.

She stops and looks down at the steps. "Are these new?"

"Yeah, my old ones broke, and the property manager replaced them," I say as I notice a metal box that looks like a toolbox tucked behind the stairs, and I remind myself to check it in the morning. The landlord probably left it here, and it'll give me another reason to email and talk to Reed.

"They look nice. Good thing you have a good landlord. You really lucked out getting this place again. I wish you could have just bought it."

"I'm just grateful we get to live here." I have very few memories of my mom, but this was the house I lived in from birth up until I went to college. It's the only place I can still feel and remember her. I can still picture her standing in front of the stove making dinner and coloring with me at the kitchen table just like I do with Willow now. My dad sold it and moved to Florida with his new wife and stepdaughters. I hear from him usually around Christmas when he sends a family Christmas card with their family smiling in the photo. And every time he does that, it practically guts me. He rarely calls and doesn't ask about Willow, and he hasn't been a participant in our lives. It was a painful time when he was moving and asked me to come and look at some of my mom's old things before he donated them. He'd looked at me and said, "I have a chance to start over and have a real family. You get that, right? I need this, kiddo." He'd thought I would be happy for him when he told me this, and that's when I realized I wasn't included in the equation at all.

And those words devastated me. Because I needed a family, too. I needed him, and he was never there for me. When I was growing up and he was home, he chose to spend that time at the pub and not with me. And now seeing him being a sober father to his new kids makes me feel like something was wrong with me. Why didn't he want me? And he could include me with his new family, but he doesn't. I don't know if that is his new wife's doing or his, but it has been that way ever since. And that is that. I had the McCreedys. Until I didn't. And now I have them back again. I'd do anything for any of them, apparently even speed dating.

I CHECK MY email even though it's late. I should be going to sleep because my alarm will wake me up early. I have no new emails from him, but I decide to write to him anyway.

> Reed,
>
> Thank you for the gift card, tequila, and chicken nuggets. That was a nice surprise, and you didn't have to do that. And a funny one. I will admit, I'm intrigued about you. Where could I find you if I wanted to repay the favor and drop off soup or bread since you've asked about them? If you're not

dating someone, I mean. I don't want to bother you. I'm sorry if that's too forward.

Thank you again,
Everly

Too much? Probably, but he sounds like a nice guy, and I like chatting with him. It's easy and fun. Maybe speed dating would be like this, and I should put myself out there after all.

I drift off to sleep, and Nash fills my dreams as he often does.

CHAPTER 11

Everly

It's speed dating night, and I'm nervous. *Really nervous.* I'm not even worried about speed dating. I'm nervous about seeing Nash after the moment we had in the kitchen the other day and what he'll say to me. Will he even talk to me? I've always felt like he was way out of my league, but now I'm figuring out who I am. I'm a different person now, and it's clear he is, too. We don't know each other anymore. Every time I'm out at the ranch, I learn something else that I missed out on when I was gone.

With Willow safely dropped off at Anne Marie's for the night, I quickly walk back to my house and get ready for the night out with Hayley. I love my new clothes, and I am ready to feel sexy and beautiful for the first time since becoming a mom and now newly single. Nothing wrong with a little flirting and a few cocktails, I suppose. I'm stepping out of my comfort zone. Who knows, maybe Reed will even show up.

Standing in my bathroom in my new black lace panties and black lace halter bra while I curl and tame my long hair, I remember to check for an email back from Reed. I grab my phone from the charger on my bedside table and see an unread email from him waiting for me. My heart flutters as I open it and read it.

Everly,

I thought you might need some things from your list. What're your plans for the weekend? Anything fun going on in Cozy Creek? I am single. How about you?

Hope you are having a good weekend,
Reed

What do I even say to that? I'm single, but I've been in love with my best friend's older brother since I was a little kid, and I'm tortured by his existence daily. Then, a few days ago, we had a moment, and now I'm confused as hell? I don't even know what to write. While I like talking to Reed, I wish it was Nash talking to me like this. I want Nash to care about my weekend plans and if I'm seeing someone.

I secretly hope Nash will be there to participate in the speed dating, especially when I'm dressed up. God, I feel like a high schooler again with a crush.

I bite my lip and debate on whether I should respond. What the hell, I shrug, as I type out my response. *Can't leave the guy hanging,* I tell myself.

Reed,

I'm also single and busy with life. I don't have much time for anything other than emailing and texting. Haha. Although I'm going way out of my comfort zone this weekend and attending a speed dating event at Bookers mostly to support my best friend Hayley, one of the owners. I'm not usually into that type of stuff because the pub scene isn't really my place. I'm more of a quiet date night kind of person. What about you? What's your ideal date if you were to go on one?

Everly

Nerves fill me as I hit the send button. Can't take back that email now. I put on my high-waisted black slacks, which look amazing, and my open-toed black heels. I put on the black halter top with sparkles that Hayley chose for me. My hair is down and loose in waves with the top pulled back in a knot with tendrils around my face. Hayley was right; this is the perfect throwback outfit. I feel a little bit like my old self before Richie sucked all my self-esteem out of me. While I apply the final coat of my signature red lipstick, which is nonnegotiable, I feel like a different person. My makeup is the best I've ever done, and my eyeliner took too long to perfect, making my blue eyes pop. I turn in the mirror and say, "Not bad."

Another email comes through, and I'm giddy as I check it.

Everly,

Good to know. Not everyone is into the whole pub scene, and that's okay. It's nice that you're supporting your friend with her event. My ideal date would be to take someone out to my property and go on a horseback ride and have a picnic. I'm a simple guy. Anything outdoors is fun for me. What about you? What's your idea of a fun date?

Reed

I look around my cozy house and have second thoughts about speed dating. I just want to stay home and email Reed. I'm pathetic.

Maybe I could feign a migraine. Surely, Hayley would understand. In under ten minutes, I could take my makeup off and park myself in front of the TV in my pajamas with my popcorn and hot chocolate. It feels good to flirt and talk with someone even though I secretly wish it was Nash. I bite my lip and debate this for a moment as a text goes across my phone.

> **Hayley:** Where are you? I need help. I'm freaking out. A ton of tourists posted about this event on social media, and we are JAM-PACKED!! Please get down here! And don't even think about bailing on me! I need you, Ev!

I sigh and reach for my purse. I agreed to help her, so I can't let her down. Ready or not, here I come. I throw on my black coat, which is a little dressier, then slide on my black flats. I carry my heels for the quick walk down to the pub. I spray one more coat of hairspray on my hair, hoping it holds up.

Looking back at my computer, I quickly send a response, not even able to help myself.

> Reed,
>
> My ideal date would depend on the time of the year. Right now, fall is my ultimate favorite season. Every year I make an entire bucket list I could make date nights out of. Haha. So far, my daughter and I have been working through the list.
>
> Some of my favorites would be going to a fall festival like the Oktoberfest, a drive-in movie, a fall hike, popcorn and spooky movies, an outdoor picnic, coffee at a bookshop,

just to name a few. Okay, I'm off to speed dating now. Wish me luck. Honestly, I'd rather just stay home and keep emailing you.

Hope you're having a good weekend as well,
Everly

I think about what Richie would have done if I'd worn an outfit like this and gone out with a friend. It would never have happened, not just because it's speed dating, which I wouldn't have gone to while I was married, but Richie didn't encourage the idea of me having friends or any sort of life outside of being at home and taking care of Willow. I had a few mom friends when Willow was little and had a few playdates with them and the kids, but he didn't want people at our house, and he would throw fits when I went anywhere, so I just stopped and stayed home and focused on Willow and my classes. I poured myself into my classes. Looking back, I now know that Richie never loved me, and I should have left sooner. He wanted me to be his household manager and handle things for him. I lived in *his* house, and he loved to remind me of that. I glance back at my little house and feel my heart warm with pride. This is *my* house, and it is full of peace and love. I mean, it's not technically mine because we're renting, but it's our home. And I'm so proud of it and grateful to have it.

When I get to the corner, I quickly slide on my heels and tuck my flats into my bag. I glance at my reflection in the side window and fluff my hair. Well, here goes nothing.

I open the door to Bookers. The atmosphere is lively, and the music is loud. Someone is setting up karaoke on the stage, and people are already milling around, laughing and talking. I look around and realize how beautiful it is here and feel a pang of regret that I haven't been here before. It has rich dark walnut wooden booths and dark green academia vibes throughout the space—very masculine, warm, and welcoming. Old pictures of our town and people grace the walls in various vintage frames with other town memorabilia, and it makes me want to take the time out to come back and explore it one day when it's not so dark, busy, and loud. The lighting is dim, dark, romantic, and fun. The tables are set up for speed dating, and the stools are filled along the bar, where people order drinks.

Hayley looks up from the bar as she pours a drink and waves. She has a young male bartender beside her that I don't know and another young girl beside him. Nash isn't in sight as I quickly scan the bar. Regret fills me when I don't see him. I'm surprised he's not there as busy as it is. A few barbacks bring glasses and drinks back and forth from the kitchen.

"Everly, you look hot!" Hayley calls over to me. She rounds the bar and looks me up and down. "Smoking hot."

"I look *nothing* like me," I admit, suddenly feeling self-conscious and smoothing down my shirt.

"I know, that's the point." She grins. "Tonight, we're going to let our hair down, act like the young, single women we are, and have fun."

"You look so beautiful, Hayles. Seriously." I smile as I slide up onto a stool and rest my forearms on the counter.

She's in a sequined top that shows her ample cleavage, dark denim jeans that are tight, pointy black sparkling heels, and her makeup is done to the nines like mine. She splurged on makeup and clothes with me. Her dark hair, the same color as Nash's, cascades in long curls down her back. Her sea-green eyes shine and pop with her dark red lipstick. She's a bombshell. How she's still single, I'll never understand. With Hayley, it's always felt like she's had one foot propped outside the door, as if she doesn't really want to be here in Cozy Creek. Our small town is not overflowing with eligible bachelors, but we get our fair share of tourists. Most of them are annoying, but I suppose it's good for the pub. And I've noticed that Hayley has had some things going on for the past few months. I can't put my finger on it, but it's almost like she's unhappy about something. Restless. I make a mental note to talk to her about it soon. Just not tonight. Tonight is about her and her event. I look around and notice the place is packed, and I am ready to help in any way that I can.

"Everly, have you met Marcus and Courtney?" Hayley calls over her shoulder.

I smile and wave over the loud bar noise. Marcus lifts a tray of beers and grins as he saunters off. "Stay dangerous, ladies."

I laugh at his teasing and look around curiously. I wonder if Reed ever comes in here and what he looks like. I suddenly feel nervous. I could run into him, and I wouldn't even know who he was. And Nash. *Where is Nash?*

"Hey, do you know a local guy named Reed?" I ask lamely, taking a sip of my drink and trying to play it cool. Hayley knows all the townie people, so if he's been in here, she'd know.

She tilts her head as if she's thinking, *Doesn't ring a bell. Why?*

"Oh, never mind," I say as Hayley slides a few drinks over to a server and mops down the bar top and shoots me a curious look.

It's possible Reed isn't a pub person, either.

Hayley was right. Tonight is the night we have fun. We dressed up and get to feel pretty and be young and carefree and not have any worries. I could use a few hours without worrying about motherhood, bills, a crazy ex, and what everyone else thinks I should be doing. I'm doing this for me. I need this.

"Come on," she says, hooking an arm around my shoulders as

she pulls me over to where long tables have been set up for the speed dating event.

Oh boy.

SPEED DATING WAS interesting and not at all what I expected. There was a line on each side, and we had two minutes with each person. When it was done, if we clicked with anyone, we could get a drink and talk more or dance. It was simple, casual, and not a big deal. I'm glad I helped Hayley. She and I both laughed a lot and had fun. Hayley should put it on again because it seems to be a hit with most people. A lot of people have gotten together and are talking and dancing now that the ice has been broken, so to speak. It just wasn't for me. I basically went through each guy, hoping one of them might be Reed. Sadly, none of them were. I'm still curious about who he is and what he looks like. When I wasn't vetting guys and trying to figure out who they were, I scanned the bar for Nash, but he never showed up. Karaoke is going full swing, and that's been fun to watch, too. Hayley and I both signed up to sing a few songs. We've always loved karaoke, and it's our jam. We used to put on performances for the animals from our little karaoke machine out in her barn. I keep my eye on the bar, and when Nash doesn't make an appearance, I want to ask Hayley where he is, but I don't want to admit that I'm looking for him. I assume that he just has the night off like she said he might. Maybe he's on a date. Thinking of that makes my heart sink. What does Nash do in his spare time? Does he have a girlfriend?

Hayley and I aren't too bad at singing. I mean, I'm not going to win an *American Idol* or *The Voice* competition anytime soon, but I can hold my own, and she can too. I sing "All Too Well," Taylor's Version, of course. Hayley sings along with me, and then she sings "Timeless," which got couples dancing, and I could tell it made her happy. I didn't find anyone I wanted to connect with more. Probably because I kept looking around for Nash. I even snuck to the back of the kitchen earlier and hung my purse up where the aprons are stored on hooks, hoping to catch even a tiny glimpse of Nash hiding out, but he wasn't there either. There was no sign of him anywhere.

Hayley and I commandeer the end of the bar, where it's a little quieter and darker. She makes drinks on the other side to help the bartender, who has been busy nonstop. I'd offer to help, but I'm terrible at bartending. I barely know what drinks are what, so I am of no help. Finally, I cannot take it anymore, so I ask, "Where's Nash?"

The corners of her mouth smirk while she pours a few more beers and slides them down to Marcus and Courtney. "Been waiting for you to ask me that all night. I've seen you looking for him."

"I have not—" I start to protest, but we both know it's true. I can't fool Hayley. She knows me too well.

She cuts me off and points at the glass windows above the bar. "He's working up in his office."

I sit back on my stool. He's been upstairs the whole time and hasn't even come down. Confusion fills me. "Why isn't he working? It's so busy in here."

She shrugs. "He didn't want to make it weird for you. I told him you needed this."

I bite my lip, trying not to show my disappointment. He didn't want to see me. I shake my head because this isn't right. It's his pub. He can do whatever he wants. All I can say to her is, "Oh." But I'm not fooling her. She can see the disappointment on my face.

"But you can run this up to him if you want to help." She smiles and raises her eyebrows as she hands me a beer she just topped off and grabs a plate of bacon cheddar cheese fries from the kitchen window. "Another loaded cheese fries," she calls back and turns to me with a grin.

I start to object, and she says, "Hurry before they get cold. Nobody likes cold fries." She winks as she pulls two more glasses out and fills them, turning to help another customer.

"I guess I can do this." I swallow nervously as I slide off my stool, trying to play it cool.

Hayley gives me another wicked grin as she continues making drinks. I anxiously make my way up the back stairs, hoping I don't spill anything or freak out with nerves. I'll just hand it to him and leave. Yeah, I can do this. Get in and get out. Plus, I want to see his office. From down below, it looks like it could be Batman's lair up there, so I'm kind of curious.

I stand nervously in front of the door with a sign on it that says management. Suddenly, I'm more nervous than I was for speed dating. My two cocktails have long worn off, not giving me the liquid courage I need right now.

Hopefully, he just takes the food, and it's not super awkward.

CHAPTER 12

Nash

"This is *my* fucking pub," I grumble in my office as I shred a piece of junk mail into a pile on my desk and glare at the fun happening down below. Why do I have to be banished to my office by my sister when I can see Everly through the one-way window down there having fun in *my* pub? She looks beautiful and sexy as hell. I watched as she did the ridiculous speed dating while smiling and being nice to all these stupid assholes who were staring at her tits and ass. I hate every fucking minute of this. She's by far the most beautiful person in the entire bar, and every single one of those assholes knows it. She's way too good for any of them. I want to toss every one of them out and tell them never to return. I close my eyes and realize this is why Hayley made me stay up here. I watch Everly flip her curly hair over her shoulder and wonder what it would feel like to wrap my fist around it. I'd pull her against me to kiss those deep red lips and find out what she tastes like. I close my eyes, picturing it and wanting what I can't have. This is why I'm brooding and nursing a glass of whiskey. I startle when there's a knock on my office door.

"What?" I clip as I spin in my chair, expecting Hayley or Marcus to come in with a question.

"Hi," Everly says softly, standing in the doorway in her fuck-me heels that make my cock instantly go hard. She has bright red polish on her toes that peek through. I'm speechless. But besides her looking fucking amazing, she's Everly. The woman who will always claim my heart regardless of anything she can possibly throw my way. Have a kid with another man? Still mine. Move away and not talk to me anymore? Still would show up at any time and do anything for her. Nothing can change the way I feel about her. It's like a prison sentence I can't escape. I will always want what I can't have—the person who doesn't want me back.

But what the hell is she doing up here? She looks scared and nervous, so I lean back and uncross my arms, trying to relax, reminding myself to breathe around her.

She clears her throat like she's finding courage and makes her way toward me, and I freeze as she gets closer and sets a plate and a beer down on my desk. I try to nonchalantly close my laptop and stand and lean against the desk, folding my arms across my chest, unsure of what to make of her coming up here. "What are you doing, Everly?" I ask her quietly. When she leans down, her hair smells like vanilla and coconut, and I like it. My whole body likes it.

"I was just bringing you the food you ordered from Hayley." She nods to the desk like it's obvious. Her eyes land on the junk mail I've shredded angrily into a pile.

"What are you doing *here*?" I repeat more tersely and abruptly than I mean to be because I'm hanging by a thread with her standing in front of me smelling so good and looking so damn beautiful.

I notice her eyes shutter, losing the warmth they held mere seconds ago, her gaze falling to some spot over my shoulder as she bites her lip, and I notice her lipstick doesn't budge. The bright red stays in place, and it makes me want to pull her into me and kiss her until she moans against my mouth and messes up that lipstick. Her posture loses some of the confidence she had walking in, and I can't tell what she's thinking, but it feels like she questions whether I want her here or not.

"I'll just be going. Um . . . enjoy your food," she murmurs and turns to leave, trying to look anywhere in the room but at me.

Before she can make it to the door in those fuck-me shoes, I've moved in front of her. She plows into me, her hands coming up to rest on my chest. Her hands stay square on my chest, my heart beating even faster and her eyes gazing into mine. I wonder if she can feel my heart racing through my rib cage at her tentative touch. If she's aware of how she affects me. Her wide eyes are focused on me, but not how I thought she'd be looking at me. She's staring back at me the same way I am looking at her—full of desire, want, and heat.

She's had two cocktails and three waters. I haven't missed much down there. Then she came up here to see me. We have servers on the floor who could have brought me food. Food that I didn't ask for, I should mention. Hayley had a hand in this, but I'm not mad about it.

Her eyes look just as hungry as mine probably look. She swallows and bites her lip nervously, eyes still locked on mine until they unlock and travel down to my mouth and back to my eyes.

"Nash," she whispers, and it hasn't gone unnoticed that she still hasn't taken her hands off my chest. Where she's touching me, my body burns with heat. Jesus, my body reacts to her so much.

"One more time, beautiful. What are you doing here?" I murmur. Her eyes widen, and her lips slightly part, making me twitch.

"I just came to help Hayley," she says, eyes finally darting to the sides, showing me that's not true at all.

"You sure? Who did you wear this outfit for?" I ask softly, my fingers tracing the halter of her top at her neck.

"Me," she says defiantly, tipping her chin up.

A smile spreads across my face. "There she is."

"What?" she asks. Her eyes narrow, confirming the sass that's back in Everly. When she came back to Cozy Creek, it was as if the spark was out of her eyes. Watching her find herself again when she moved back here has been a relief. A lot of us worried about her when she first came back after what that prick put her through. He tore her down and destroyed her. I think about how I wish I could destroy Richie for what he's done to Everly and Willow.

"I knew you were in there somewhere. Been waiting for your sass to come back."

Her head tilts, and she says dryly, "Really, Nash?"

Before I can stop myself, my thumb goes to her lip, and I drag the pad of it over her plump bottom lip and watch as her lipstick doesn't smear. Fascinated, I watch her mouth. She leans closer, eyes closing.

"The real question here, Nash, is what are *you* doing?" she says quietly, her voice cracking as she continues to lean into me.

"Trying to figure you out," I murmur as her eyes are back on mine. Her hands remain on me, and I'm pleased she hasn't let go.

"What's there to figure out?" she says, her eyes landing on my mouth and then lingering.

I dip my head to hers and whisper in her ear, "I'm going to kiss you, Everly. Say no if you don't want that to happen." My eyes scan her face. She blinks, and her chin tips up slightly, giving me all the permission I need. I start at her lips, kiss along her chin, then return to her lips. I give her the kiss I've been building up on all fucking night while watching her down there. A kiss almost ten years in the making. Something I've wanted since she was twenty years old, and I was just figuring out *who* I wanted from life, not *what.*

I murmur against her lips, "So fucking beautiful, Everly. Brave, strong, stubborn woman." I trail my mouth along the edge of her jaw, punctuating each of my words with a soft kiss, basking in the flutter of Everly's lashes as she fights to keep her gaze on mine. "But why are you here in my office?" I murmur as my lips kiss her ear and nip at her earlobe. Her breath hitches, and she leans into me, not answering. "Don't make me ask again."

"Maybe I was here to see you," she admits, but she no longer looks at me because her body is so close to mine that I can't see her eyes.

My mouth crashes into hers again, pulling her to me. Her arms wrap around my neck, pulling me in closer, deeper. I kiss her hungrily, slipping my tongue around hers to taste her and feeling like she's my kryptonite. Always the one I couldn't have and shouldn't have, yet all I want at the same time. I'm taking what I want tonight, and she wants it too. Kissing her is a risk. And I might be either fucking everything up between us or fixing something that should have been fixed a long time ago. I'm betting on the latter.

I reach down, shove the beer and plate of fries over, and wrap my hands around her ass. I pull her up to me and set her on the desk. Her legs wrap around my waist, clamping around my hips, those shoes making me desire her so badly. I kiss her neck as she leans back, the dip of her sparkly top offering me the soft swell of her breasts when she arches her back, almost offering me a taste as I grip her bottom.

I claim her mouth, pulling her to me as her arms pull me closer, deeper, wanting me just as hungrily as I want her. God, I've missed her for almost a decade now. And she's been off-limits. Tonight changes everything. I didn't expect this, but I'm taking it.

"Hey, we got an issue down here and need . . . Oh shit, sorry, man," Marcus says from behind us as he steps back out of my office and closes the door quickly.

I glance at the door, then lean over the window to see what's going on down in the bar. I scan and find the issue where a small crowd has gathered. Richie motherfucking Sullivan. *Fuckin' great.* He ruins everything good for her. I should have known. She can't even have a night out with her friend without that dickweed popping up.

"What's wrong?" she asks as she leans over to look. Her body tenses, and she steps back when she sees Richie. "Can they see up here?"

"No. It's a one-way window, tinted to make it look like part of the wall. So I can keep an eye on things down in the pub when I work up here." For reasons like Richie Sullivan.

She grimaces as she watches Richie exchanging words with someone I don't recognize, but I can see the tension building down there. People don't look happy that he's here and don't like whatever he's saying to the other patron.

"Maybe we can just ignore him," she murmurs angrily as her hand goes to her mouth where I've kissed her, almost like she is trying to figure out if that kiss just happened.

"Any idea why your douchebag ex is in my pub?" I grumble as I watch him.

"I don't know. I try not to ever talk to him," she says defiantly, crossing her arms.

Hearing that fills me with relief. I don't want him anywhere near her.

"Listen, I need you to stay up here. Don't come down until he's gone. Let me take care of this for you."

"Oh, hell no," she says, climbing off the desk and straightening her shirt and hair.

Her hair is messy like she has sex hair, and we didn't even make it to second base. Jesus. This isn't going to go well at all.

I'm just gazing at her, looking like she does, and knowing I'm responsible. The elation and pride that swells in me when I realize it won't go well if Richie sees her this way. I just want her to be okay, and I don't give two shits what that dickhead Richie thinks. The last thing I want to do is complicate Everly's life.

"What?" she asks, her hand coming to her lips.

"Why have you been avoiding me?" I ask. My hand goes to her chin, and I cup it and stroke the sides of her jaw.

She leans into me, her eyes on mine. "The same reason you've been avoiding *me*."

I just stare at her, trying to figure out what to say, when I hear Marcus call up again, "Bossman!"

"Coming!" I look at her again and warn, "We're not finished with this conversation."

"Oh, is that what we're calling this?" she says with a smile that's cute as hell.

"We can call it whatever you want, but we'll be continuing this," I say before I reluctantly head downstairs to take out the trash, a.k.a. Richie Sullivan.

I pass through the kitchen and into the pub and see Richie with a blond woman named Meghan, a regular at the pub. She leaves with a lot of the other regulars. Some married, some not. She takes what she wants and doesn't care who her actions affect. I can't put it all on her since the patrons she leaves with go willingly. But I can't say she is a person I'd hold in high regard. Marcus and I refer to her as the black widow. She's come on to me for months to hook up, and I've always politely declined and redirected her. I'm not a hookup kind of guy anymore, especially with one who does it in my pub regularly with so many others. My town fuck boy reputation isn't as valid as Everly once thought it was. The truth is, I haven't dated or been with a woman in months. Since before Everly came back.

I watch quietly from the back to assess what's going on, and I see Richie has acquired a small audience around him. Mainly because his ego is too big, and he's just not a good person. His golden boy years are over, and everyone knows it but Richie.

Richie's in the middle of loudly telling a sexist joke, and I notice a few people around him have the decency to look away awkwardly. He looks at his audience for approval, and his eyes narrow when they land on me. He doesn't look surprised, so I'm guessing he's being obnoxious and disorderly to summon me to start something. We've never gotten along, and we never will.

I lean back, cross my arms, and observe him without giving a reaction. I'm glad the people around him refuse to help him feel comfortable with his inappropriate joke. Everyone should react to this dickhead like that.

Taking a swig of his beer, Richie narrows his eyes and says across the bar, "I heard my wife was in here. Where is she?"

His wife. Laughable. She's not his wife anymore. I knew when their divorce was final because Hayley had a little celebration for her. I stayed away from it, but trust me, I was celebrating too. The whole town was.

I cock my head and stare at him, trying to come across as confused and bored, not saying anything as a few people around him chuckle and murmur and move away.

"She's probably back washing dishes because she can't pay her tab." He laughs, looking around. At least he looks perturbed when no one laughs with him at Everly's insult. What Richie forgets is that we all love Everly around here, and we don't think his jokes are funny, especially at her expense. Shithead.

Before I can address that shitty comment, he glares at me, but I realize he's not staring at me. He's scowling behind me, and I look back as Everly walks up and stands next to me, glowering at him.

I give no reaction and continue to stare at Richie.

We're side by side touching, and her warmth makes me feel even more protective of her.

"Oh, so it's like that. I should have known you were fucking by now," Richie clips bitterly. "Probably for free drinks since she can't afford them."

My eyebrows raise, and I look at Everly. I know how this is going to go, but it's not going to go how Richie thinks it will go. And by that, I mean not well for him.

Richie stalks over to us and angrily hisses at Everly, "Why are you dressed like a fucking slut?"

"Watch it." I growl the words out as I put my hand square to his chest. He halts and glares over at me.

"Don't touch me unless you want me to lay your ass out, McCreedy," he slurs, swaying at the touch of my hand that's still holding him back.

I say nothing and continue to stare at him. He can't read my expression, and it's confusing him. Just as I suspected, I can tell wherever he came from, he's already been drinking, and he's already had too many.

"Answer me, bitch," he grunts as he raises his voice at Everly. She flinches, looking at him like she doesn't know whether to run or cry. She stands frozen next to me. The fact that he called her that and is humiliating her in front of everyone makes my blood boil, but I remain calm. The old me would have punched him, and that's what he's expecting, but I have the upper hand here. This is my pub, and I have Everly on my arm. He's out of control, and he's going to lose it. Plus, after whatever happened up in that office, I don't want to scare her off and for her to think I'm that same reckless bad boy from high school. I've changed, and I need her to see that. I'm going to prove it to her.

"Who do you think you're talking to?" I ask in a voice meant to be calm, but it comes out eerily scary, even to me.

"I'm talking to my wife," Richie sputters.

"I'm pretty sure she's *not* your wife. And you need to leave my pub. Now."

"How long have you been fucking her?" he spits out, reaching out to push off me. "You've always wanted my seconds."

Before he can say another word, I have him spun around, his arm behind his back, and he's out of the pub and out onto the sidewalk, a maneuver I've mastered in the years of owning this pub and long before when I worked here as a barback. Sometimes people get rowdy, and the trick is to remove people before they get ugly. Everly is still inside, and Richie is confused at this sudden movement landing him outside on the sidewalk.

I'm still somehow maintaining control, but it's hanging on by a thread. I get my shot in, though, by saying quietly, "Nah, Rich. You can't claim something you never really had. You know she's always been mine."

I'm baiting him, and he's taking it. He rears back and hits me square on the cheek, and I stand there and let him land that hit. I barely flinch because I knew it was coming and anticipated this before we ever even made it out onto the sidewalk. What Richie didn't see was the Cozy Creek's police cruiser parked across the street with an officer sitting in it. He's watching this whole thing go down and is now quickly heading our way. Perfect timing. I couldn't have orchestrated this outcome better.

My hands remain at my sides, and I look at Richie and smile. He tips his head, confused at my response.

Now I can press charges. Tarnish his little reputation and protect Everly and keep him from coming into my pub.

Richie is pulled back and placed in handcuffs, and I realize that our audience has grown considerably, but I remain calm. Everly watches, full of concern, her cheeks still flushed and her eyes shiny with unspilled tears from behind me, and turns to leave with Hayley as Richie is still yelling at her and threatening to take Willow away from her, his words now slurring even more with anger and embarrassment. He looks panicked as he glances at the officer and then back at me, suddenly realizing that no one is taking his side.

"He started it!" he yells to the crowd. "You all saw it."

People in the crowd cross their arms and shake their heads in dismay, looking at Richie as if he's crazy, which makes Richie fight this even more.

"No trespassing," I tell him and the officer. "You are never allowed in Bookers ever again. And I will be pressing charges for assault."

Richie sputters and then glares at me, his eyes narrowing to slits. "You'll pay for this."

"And we can document these threats too," I say calmly as I nod to the officer and head back inside, tucking my hands in my pockets like this is no big deal. Because it isn't. Part of owning a pub means sometimes I have to take out the trash, and I was happy to take out this particular trash.

And I want so badly to find Everly, but she's gone, and we're closing.

What the hell happened tonight?

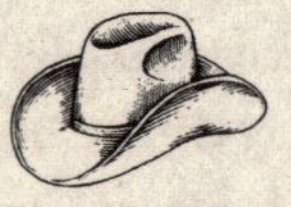

CHAPTER 13

Nash

Ice to my face, I check my email. It's late, and the bar is long closed when it finally comes through.

> Reed,
>
> I hope you had a good night. I went out with my best friend Hayley. She co-owns Bookers with her brother. I don't know if you've been there or not. It's a nice place. I have started to help her bake for the restaurant part of the pub. If you ever want to meet up, I'd love to say hi.
>
> Sorry to bother you. It's just been a weird night.
>
> Have a good one,
> Everly
>
> P.S. If you ever want to text me, you can.

I do want to text her, but not as Reed. I want to text her and find out if she's okay. She left after I threw Richie out, and I want to know how she's doing. But I also don't want to freak her out.

I've wanted to nail his ass to the wall for years. But Richie is going to sink himself with how he acts. It's just a matter of time.

I reach for my extra phone that I use for property management. I power it on and make sure it still has battery. I type in Everly's number.

Me: Hi. It's Reed.

I blow out a puff of air and look up at the ceiling. I hate lying to her.

Everly: Hi, I just emailed. Assuming you got it? Thought it would be easier to text and take it out of the 90s. Although *You've Got Mail* is one of my all-time favorite movies.

Me: Never seen it.

Everly: Really? You should watch it. It's a classic.

Me: I've heard of it. Why was your night weird? You okay?

Everly: It was confusing. I'm divorced, and I ran into my ex. He said some nasty things to me in front of everyone at the pub. It was embarrassing. I was just trying to have a good night, and he ruined it.

Me: Want me to beat him up? Haha jk

Everly: Lol, no. Thanks, though. It was like a *Jerry Springer* episode. He punched a guy and ended up getting arrested.

He punched a guy? I'm "a guy"? Remembering to stay in character, I continue.

Me: That sounds upsetting. Who did he punch?

Everly: He punched my best friend's brother. And before that happened, her brother and I had an . . . unexpected moment.

Me: What was unexpected? Do you like the brother?

Everly: Honestly? I've always loved him. But he doesn't feel the same for me. Or at least I thought he didn't. Until tonight, that is.

It's not lost on me that she said loved. She didn't say like. Relief fills my chest, and I roll my fist over my chest as it squeezes. I needed to know she felt the same, and she does. I continue the conversation, feeling like a jerk, but I can't help it.

Me: And what happened to your ex and this guy?

Everly: I'm not sure. I didn't stick around. After getting into trouble, I was so embarrassed about what he said to me and what was happening that I left. I shouldn't have been there. I should have been at home with my daughter. The pub is not where I want to be a regular unless I'm baking in the back. That I can handle.

Me: Why do you think you shouldn't have been there? You have a right to go out with your friends and have fun, don't you?

Everly: I need to just settle for being single forever. I'm not cut out for dating.

Me: What do you mean by that?

Everly: I don't know how to do this whole dating thing. I'm not girlfriend material.

Me: ?

Everly: I don't know how to be a girlfriend. I'm a wife. I want to see him every day and cook dinner together. I want to be in love and take care of him. Spend every day and make memories together. But dating is like, yeah, see you at 8 on Saturday. See how that sucks?

Me: Damn. That sounds incredible. Whoever gets that with you is a lucky guy.

Everly: Haha. I'm not lucky. I'm a mess. I feel terrible bothering you with this. I can't talk to my friend about him since it's her brother. Too weird.

Me: Sounds like he likes you back. Maybe you should talk to him.

Everly: What if he doesn't, and it makes things even more strained between us? We used to be close. Now we haven't talked in years.

Me: You never know until you try. Call him.

Everly: Okay, I will before I lose my nerve. Thank you, Reed.

Me: No problem. Let me know how it goes.

My personal phone rings in my pocket, so I pull it out and see her name light up the screen. I close my eyes and swallow.

"Everly," I say softly.

"Hi," she murmurs. "I'm sorry to call you so late. Did I wake you?"

"I own a pub, beautiful. I keep late hours. Just winding down."

She sighs. "I'm really sorry about tonight, Nash. I shouldn't have—"

"Shouldn't have what?" I interrupt before she can tell me she shouldn't have kissed me because I don't think I can take it if she does.

When I touched her and kissed her at the pub, I didn't miss the way our skin zinged when we touched. The way she had goose bumps when I had her in my arms. There's no denying we still have insane chemistry together. And if she tries to tell me anything different, I don't think I can handle hearing it after all this.

"I should have just stayed home. I knew Richie would probably start something if he knew I was out tonight."

Annoyance fills me, hearing that she can't have fun with her friend without Richie making her life miserable.

"Ev, you are not responsible for his behavior. You're allowed to have a life and shouldn't have to put up with him crossing the line like this."

It's quiet for a minute, and she says softly, "What was that kiss about?"

"That kiss? That was you and me finally realizing what is meant to be." I take my shot, not even holding back.

"You like me?" she asks, and I hear the confusion in her voice.

Like her? She has no clue. No clue about the pain and turmoil I've dealt with by not having her in my life. I can't even take it anymore, and I have to tell her the truth. I'm not sure what's compelling me to lay it all out there for her, but I can't hold back anymore. We have to hash this out. I can't keep going on like this with her.

So I lay down every single card I have and hope to fucking God she gets it and understands why I did what I did.

"It's always been true. I wasn't good enough for you. You deserved someone who could take care of you and support you. Everly, back then, I could barely support myself. I couldn't give you what you needed. I had to push you away so you'd go live your life, go to college, and achieve all your goals and dreams. With me, you wouldn't have done any of that. I was going to hold you back."

"No, Nash. You were good enough."

"I wasn't. I was a screwup back then, and we both know it," I level with her.

She sighs, and I continue, "Beautiful, I love you. Always have, always will. And that might be a lot to hit you with right now. But you need to know. It's true, and it's always been true. This isn't some random I love you bullshit. You know you've always meant more to me than anyone."

She's so quiet that you could hear a pin drop.

"Everly?" Closing my eyes, I'm wondering if I've gone too far.

"I'm still here," she says. "Why do you call me beautiful?"

"Because you hate the nickname Babe. You told me in high school that a few boys called you Babe and made fun of you because it's a pig. I beat them up. Do you remember that?"

"Yes," she breathes softly.

"But you should know that I intend on ending this silence between us. I want you to know my feelings and what I want to do about them."

"And that is?" she asks.

"I'm claiming what's mine."

Her breath hitches. "Nash . . ."

CHAPTER 14

Everly

He loves me. And he's always loved me.

I take this in as I stare out the window at the library while I wait for closing time the day after the speed dating. I've always known something was special about Nash. I just didn't think he felt the same way I did. And here he was, laying it all out after all this time, not even hesitating. He didn't waver; he just said what he felt. And he's felt this way all along. It's like time was robbed from us. He's always held something back when it comes to me. A block has been between us that I could never break through. Now that I'm back and starting to figure out my stuff, he's letting me know his intentions. It scares me and excites me at the same time. Part of me wants to run and the other part of me wants to jump in. Nash is the person who was always there when we were growing up. A friend and an ally. As time passed, I fell hard for him, and then I realized somewhere along the way that I couldn't imagine living my life without him in it in some way. That's why it was so painful when I didn't have him or his family in my life. It didn't go the way I thought it was supposed to go. Deep down, he was always the love of my life. And I thought I'd blown it. But now? Now, everything has changed.

It was a busy day for the library, so I didn't have much time to process everything, but my mind has been spinning since Nash kissed me and told me he loved me. And I kissed him back, and I loved every minute of it. It was so hot and sexy. If Marcus hadn't interrupted us, I think we would have had the hottest make-out session ever. I wanted him, and holy shit, he wanted me. And I blame this interruption on Richie, fucking Richie. He always has to show up and mess up everything good in my life. He tries to take away everything that I love that matters to me. I don't understand why he can't comprehend that we are done. He has no ties to me.

Oh my God. I still can't get over what Nash said.

This is not what I expected. Ever since that night when I came back, he's barely looked at me, and I had no idea how he felt. We talked for a while, and I didn't want to hang up, but I could tell he was exhausted. My mind pans back to what he'd said.

"Let me show you, Ev."

"Show me what?" I stupidly asked.

"How much you mean to me," he'd said.

I close my eyes. I had no idea he's loved me all this time. Finding this out has rocked my world. I'm confused and angry that I loved him for years and didn't feel like he loved me back. And now he just drops this bomb on me. A shot from that bottle of tequila at home that Reed left on my porch sounds pretty good right about now.

Reed. I need to check in with him and see how he's doing. I check my email, and there's nothing there and no texts. Damn.

It's fifteen minutes till closing time. Dusk is setting in, and the sunset from the library windows is showing off big time. This is my favorite part of closing. The view.

I lean over the counter to check as a text flashes across the screen.

Anne Marie: Honey, I'm keeping Willow tonight. We've got big plans to watch *Halloweentown* and eat popcorn. Go and have some fun!

I smile because I love how Anne Marie enjoys spending time with Willow. She's become even more special to us since we've been back in Cozy Creek. I'm glad Willow has all these people who love her like they loved me. For the longest time, it was just Willow and me and the occasional appearance of Richie.

I quickly send a response, thanking her and letting her know I'll pick up Willow later. I power down my computer and gather my lunch bag, water bottle, and purse. I slide into my coat and tie my scarf around my neck since it's gotten much cooler at night now. I need to figure out our vehicle situation soon. Maybe I can shop for a used car next weekend. Not paying rent for a few months will certainly help with the cost of a new vehicle.

Richie has been eerily quiet since last night at the bar. I figured he'd blow up my phone by calling, texting, or even possibly showing up at the library today. Nothing. I'm relieved, but at the same time, I'm wondering what he's planning. Whatever it is won't be good. There's no way he's just going to let this go. I'm expecting an all-out war.

Shivering at the thought of Richie, I head out and lock the doors. When I feel someone nearby, I whirl around nervously, already on edge from thoughts of Richie.

Nash.

He stands in a tan Carhartt jacket, hands in his pockets, and a black cowboy hat tipped low. His mouth is turned up slightly, his jaw dark and scruffy.

"Nash. What are you doing here?" I stand nervously, seeing him for the first time since our phone call when everything changed. For me at least.

"Just making sure you're okay," he says with his smooth-as-whiskey voice.

I close my eyes for a second. "I'm okay." It's been a long time since I had someone check on me. In fact, I haven't had that other than Hayley in the past few years.

"Where's your car?" he asks as he faces me.

"I don't have it anymore. I'm getting a new one," I admit.

"He took it, didn't he?" His eyes seem to darken.

I nod, unsure what to say. I don't want to make more issues with Nash where Richie is concerned.

Nash turns and says, "Your ex and his family resemble cactuses. Full of pricks."

I throw my head back and laugh. "You aren't wrong."

This whole town has issues with the Sullivans. They are notorious for doing whatever they want, and it doesn't matter who they run over to do it.

He shuffles his feet, looking perplexed and then straightens and blows out a breath. "Can I take you and Willow out to dinner?"

He wants to take me *and* Willow to dinner. The way he includes her makes my heart squeeze.

I clear my throat. "I actually have dinner in the slow cooker at home. I had planned on feeding Willow, but she's staying at Anne Marie's for the evening to watch a movie. We could go to my house," I suggest softly, suddenly feeling nervous about him being in my space for some reason.

Something in his face twitches, and his mouth turns up slightly.

Also, I'm not sure my nerves can handle being alone with him and out at a restaurant or having the town see us and add to the already long list of gossip I have going about Richie, Nash, and me.

I'm frozen in front of the library, taking him in as he stands tall before me with his hat pulled low. He's looking at me like he's trying to figure me out.

"I'm down for soup," he finally says, reaching for my hand. He guides me onto the sidewalk, tucking me next to him effortlessly. This is probably good because I've already forgotten how my feet work. My hand tingles in his; it's big, warm, and rough against my smooth and smaller hand.

"Who said it was soup?" I question, and I look at him.

"I've heard about your soup of the day and bread you've been baking with Hayley," he offers as a reason.

We're quiet on the way to my house. We don't talk, but it's not awkward. It's as easy as it used to be with Nash. Luckily, it's dark, but we pass a few people out and about who give us surprised and then curious looks. Most people know we ran around together as kids but then haven't been seen together until last night. Last night changed everything. I think about that kiss he gave me and shiver, goose bumps going up my arm. I look up at him, walking next to me. He glances down at me and grins.

"What kind of soup did you make?" he asks, trying to make conversation.

I'm trying to pull it together. His fingers intertwined with mine feel so nice.

"Cheesy chicken potato."

He squeezes my hand and grins in response.

We pass Bookers, and he says to hold on a minute. He goes in the back kitchen door and then comes out with a loaf of sourdough that Hayley made.

"Soup *and* fresh bread," he says as he holds up the bread, then slides his hand back into mine. We make it the rest of the way to my house without me tripping or saying something dumb.

"How did you know I didn't make bread at home already?"

"Because you worked all day, beautiful," he says.

I'm so nervous I can barely see straight, and my hand shakes as I try to open my door. I finally get it unlocked and hold it for Nash.

He seems huge and out of place in my entryway, which is right in the living room. He looks around and takes it in.

"I lucked out being able to rent my old place." I nervously pick up a blanket and fold it over the side of the couch. I had no idea he'd be coming by, or I'd have picked up more. I run my hand through my hair, nervous I'm going to mess this up with him and say something wrong or just fall on my face.

Nash watches me and closes the distance between us. He pulls me into his arms, and I rest my head on his shoulder as he says, "I like it. It looks so warm and welcoming in here."

He smells so good—minty and a mixture of pine and clean. I love being near him.

I take in my small sectional and old stone fireplace with a television mounted above it that Mack had hung for me. I have warm blankets stacked on an old rustic ladder, fall-scented candles sprinkled throughout the house, and a homemade braided rug that took me months to make under the couch. Three large wooden bookshelves are on one wall and filled with books that Willow and I both read. Plants of various varieties and colors are displayed throughout the house, adding a pop of green with the thrifted terracotta pots, colorful tapestries, and throw pillows. It's home for us, and I love it here. I'm grateful every single day for this place. Our sanctuary.

"I love all your books," he says. "There are so many."

"I am a librarian after all." I smile.

"You've always loved books. The plant obsession? That must be new because you and Hayley killed any plant we had growing up," he says as he gazes around the room thoughtfully.

"It is a new hobby and something I've gotten better at, thank you very much," I say casually as I watch him walk around and take in our space. He seems to like it.

"Place looks good." He takes his coat off and hangs it on the hook by the door, looking like he belongs here. My breath hitches as I watch him in his hunter-green-and-black flannel shirt stretched across his chest.

"Thanks. The property was renovated, and they did a great job. It's beautiful. I'm so thankful Willow and I can rent it."

He doesn't say anything but continues to look around, running his hand over the railing that has been sanded and stained dark.

"Smells good in here." His lip twitches as he walks into the dining room and kitchen.

"Let me get you some dinner," I say quickly as I hang my coat next to his and motion for him to have a seat at the bar in front of the stove.

I stir the slow cooker contents, then reach for the bread and set it on the cutting board. I think of what to say and finally just say it. "Thank you for sticking up for me last night. I'm sorry he showed up and caused a scene."

"Nothing for you to be sorry about. You didn't do anything wrong. Richie has to take responsibility for his own actions, not you," he says as he picks up Willow's and my fall bucket list on the table and scans it. In bright autumn colors, we've made a list of all the things we want to do together this fall season. A few have check marks next to them, but not for everything. Willow loves it, and we've been making new memories and traditions.

"That's our fall bucket list," I say as I ladle soup into two of our rustic soup bowls that I got from a local pottery shop and set out a few small matching plates. I quickly slice the bread and set out the butter.

"It looks fun," he says as he reads, and his eyebrows rise. "We used to do many of these same things when we were kids."

"We did," I say softly. "I'm trying to keep the magic going for Willow."

"You're a good mom," he says gently as his tongue wets his lower lip, and my thighs squeeze as I watch him.

I smile and bite my lip. "I try."

He tilts his head, thinking before he says, "I'm going to lay it out, Everly. I don't want to go another day without you in my life. I don't know what that means for you, but for me, I want to find out."

Oh my God. And this is so like him. He's not one to beat around the bush. He has always loved with his whole heart and has done anything he wanted, fully committed.

"Why now?" I ask. "I didn't think you felt this way."

"Well, now you know. What are you thinking? Where do you stand?" he asks as he watches me walk over to the counter and set the soup bowls down.

"I want to find out, too. But I'm scared," I admit.

"What are you scared of?" Standing, he closes the distance between us, pulling me to him.

"I'm scared that things won't work out, and then I'll be even more divided with you and your family, Nash. Hayley, Kincaid, and your mom and dad are all the family I have besides Anne Marie. If we don't work out, I have a lot to lose. So does Willow," I admit as I stare up at him, his eyes completely drawing me in.

I close my eyes. *Focus, Everly,* I remind myself.

"You think I don't have a lot to lose? I already lost you once, Ev. I'm not going to let anything mess this up, especially since Willow is involved," he says as his brown eyes seem to darken with intensity.

I look down and lay out two napkins and spoons, trying to keep my hands busy and not show how nervous I am. "I don't want this to be a temporary thing. I can't take that."

"Beautiful, you're nothing casual. You're forever."

My heart clenches, and I close my eyes. "I wish I had gone with you."

He tilts his head slightly. "That was then, this is now, and we have the chance to start fresh."

"It's different now. I have Willow. I'm different. I suspect you are, too. We don't really know each other as the people we are now. It's been . . . a long time."

"I know you have a kid. I like her a lot. And I suspect we're not all *that* different. I want to get to know you and be in your life again. Do you want that, too?" he asks me as if it's just that simple of a question. Like checking a box for yes or no.

Nothing is simple when it comes to my feelings about Nash. My feelings are so freaking big that I would never call them simple.

I bite my lip and nod. "It comes with a crazy ex for me, though. He won't like it that you're in our lives, and he'll do his worst to make sure we feel that."

He shrugs. "Okay. He can do his worst. It won't keep me away. Not this time."

God, this is why I have always loved this man. He isn't bothered and is confident in what he wants. And he wants *me*. What the heck is my life right now?

He leans up against my counter, making me feel warmer and safer somehow. My cozy little home has always been where I felt relaxed and comfortable, especially since making it my own. But having him here in this space makes it somehow feel right. Like all is well with the world, and he was supposed to be here with us all along.

He leans over and pulls me to him, kissing the top of my head.

My arms circle him, and I lay my head on his chest. I look up at him. "Are you hungry?"

"Starving," he says as he looks at me, and I wonder if he means for the soup or for me.

Ohhhhh.

CHAPTER 15

Everly

When I hug him, he has more muscles than I remember him having, and his body is hard and solid. A body that does more hard laborious work instead of a body that was made in the gym.

We sit at the kitchen bar together to eat soup and bread and catch up. Thankfully, I start to feel less nervous and more at home with Nash. I sneak glances at him every so often, wondering if he's really here, in front of me and in the flesh.

"So tell me about your farrier business?" I ask him as I finish my soup and push my bowl forward.

He smiles and lights up when he says, "I started apprenticing not long after you left, and I love it. I love working with the horses, and it's been a good, solid business."

"I always figured you'd work on the ranch and do something with horses. The pub was a surprise, though," I add as I sneak a look at him, trying to pinch myself that he's really here in my kitchen.

Sliding out his phone, he pulls up a picture and shows it to me. It's a selfie of him and a wild red-haired horse. I reach out and take it, looking at the picture and smiling. "That's Soupy," he says as he flips through even more selfies with different horses.

I laugh. "Okay, these are adorable. You really love the horses, don't you?"

"I do," he admits with a grin.

"Who is your favorite?" I ask, looking at the selfies with a smile.

"Soupy," he says without hesitating.

"I love this, and I love that you are happy with this. But why the pub, too?" I'm confused because, looking at the pictures, it's obvious he's happiest with the horses.

He looks over at me. "I think everyone in this town thought I'd end up in jail or on a wanted poster. I liked surprising them by being successful and having my own businesses."

"I never doubted you, Nash. You were always going to be something special. You just had to figure out what that was. But there's still time for that if you want to choose jail," I tease.

He laughs. "No jail for me. I love the horses, and I like the pub with Hayley."

"You're doing great. I'm proud of you," I say softly, laying my hand over his arm. But it doesn't pass by what he said about loving the horses and liking the pub.

"Do you like working at the library?" He takes a bite of his bread.

I nod. "I love working at the library. I want to help people and provide as many resources to our community as I can. Do what Anne Marie has done for all of us and keep her legacy going even after she retires."

He nods. "You seem happy. And she does a lot for this community."

The front door whips open, and Willow bounds in. Anne Marie trails her, and her eyes widen as we turn to face her.

"Oh, I didn't realize you had company," she says, but I don't miss the twinkle in her eye.

"Hi, honey," I say as I kiss Willow's head when she wraps her arms around me. I smile at Anne Marie. "Hi, have you eaten?"

"We did. Willow was just missing you, and the movie ended, so I walked her over."

"Thank you. I would have come and got her."

"Nonsense, it's a beautiful night. Hello, Nash, how are you?"

"Good and yourself?" he asks.

"Can't complain. Life is full and happy with my two girls home now," she says as she pulls Willow in for a small squeeze.

Nash smiles, and a look passes between Anne Marie and him that I can't decipher, but I can tell they have an unspoken conversation. Interesting.

"I'd better head out," she calls as she waves. We say our goodbyes, and I thank her for spending time with Willow. I know she'll have so many questions for me tomorrow, and I owe her a big update.

"Thanks again," I call and wave as she shuts the door.

"Hi, Nash. How are your horses?" Willow asks him since all her memories of him involve the horses at the ranch.

"They're doing pretty good. You'll have to come out and see them and get some riding lessons in." He leans back and casually tucks his arm behind me.

"Really?" she asks, looking at me and him.

"If it's okay with your mom." He shrugs.

"It's okay." I nod.

"Thanks!" she says as she jumps up, excited.

"Why don't you get your jammies on, honey," I say as Nash and I stand.

"I have to get going. Thanks for dinner." He leans over and kisses my cheek. I turn my head and catch his lips.

"Thanks for coming," I say as I follow him to the door.

"I'll text you times and dates to see what works, but I'd like to get Willow out on a horse."

I smile, excited for Willow. "She'll be thrilled."

"Alright." He leans into me and looks into my eyes.

"Can I talk to you for a minute?" Before he can respond, I open the door and yank him outside with me, scanning to make sure no one is walking by and in earshot.

"What if we're making a mistake, Nash? What if you realize that I'm not your type," I sputter, trying to make sense of the past twenty-four hours before I lose my nerve.

He crosses his arms and leans back, dragging his tongue across his lip. Biting his lip, he tilts his head in amusement. He challenges, "You know my type?"

"I'm not really anyone's type. Especially yours," I snap but shake my head as I look away. I don't know why he's doing this. He was supposed to be my dream guy. In my head. And now he doesn't even care about the consequences of this. For me. For him. If I lose the McCreedys, I have no one. We've been down this road before. Okay, maybe not this far down the road, but we were close. We did almost everything together—him, me, and Hayley. And then we weren't. It was gone, and it was scary, and I missed it badly. I can't do that again.

Does Nash get this? Probably not. Instead, he leans in and kisses me on the nose and says in my ear, "I've never had a type, Everly, ever. Just been chasin' shadows who weren't and could never be you. You're my type. It's only ever been you."

And with that, he pulls me to him, kisses me until I suck in a deep breath, then lets me go, leaving me standing on my stoop feeling even more confused.

I lean against my door and close my eyes. Nash kissed me. Again.

Teenage me would be freaking out right now. Twenty-eight-year-old me is freaking out right now.

CHAPTER 16

Nash

Did I just go there with her? Yes, I did. I'm thirty years old, and we're not kids anymore. I'm done pretending we don't have what we've got here between us. We always have. I wanted her long before the night she came to me and told me she was pregnant and moving away with Richie motherfucking Sullivan. The town douchebag. And that gutted me. I still love her. It was pathetic, but it was what it was. And I couldn't stop it. She's always been special and was too good for me back then.

It will take time to convince her, but I'll do it. I love her, and her kid is an amazing bonus. I want it all with her.

As I walk back to the bar, I think about how all of this has broken down over the past year. We've been slowly getting Everly back in her own time. She had to heal from the shit her ex put her through.

When Hayley called me last spring and said that we needed to go get them and bring them back to Cozy Creek for good, I didn't even think twice about it. I just got in my truck and hit the road. When we got to her house, she was so drained emotionally and physically. I don't think I've ever seen a more broken-down person. It was hard not to beat the crap out of that guy. She'd been crying, and her eyes and face were swollen and red. Richie was passed out on their couch, not even coherent. He didn't even come to as we packed up her stuff and loaded it up, but I was ready in case he did. I wanted him to wake up so I could pound the shit out of him. I wanted him to know how badly he screwed it up with the love of my life. He could have had everything. The life she and I were supposed to have together. She was willing to try to build a life with him, and he threw them away like they didn't even matter. The woman who I love with all my heart and her child. And fuck him for that. They're going to be mine now.

We hauled her stuff, mostly clothes and memorabilia and her daughter's stuff, back to the barn and got her set up at the ranch. She'd cried and leaned against the window of my truck the entire way back and said nothing. She was pretty much catatonic. She thanked me and carried her daughter into the farmhouse when we got there. She didn't even try to speak to me until last night in my office when I kissed the hell out of her.

I've watched her come back to life over the past six months. She got a job at the library and got her home back, which she's turned into a beautiful space for her and her daughter to heal and thrive in. I watched her enroll her daughter in school and make friends. The scared and timid kid came out of her shell, too. And her love for horses makes me so proud, and I want to help her with that. When Hayley texted me the picture of her homemade horseshoes, I went out to the barn and made four mini horseshoes for her stuffed horse. It took me hours, but seeing Willow happy was worth it. I want to buy her a horse of her own, but I'm biding my time. I want to give them everything because they deserve everything. I gave Everly her space and waited until she was ready. And she is, but she's got one hand up blocking and protecting. I can't say I blame her. I should have fought harder for her that night, but I felt the finality of it. She'd made her decision. Even though it hurt like hell, I had to let her go.

She's an incredible mother, and her daughter is one lucky girl to have a mother like Everly. I don't have a lot of memories of Everly's mother, but I do remember her being kind and a good mom. I remember her being sick at the end and going to her funeral. Then we got to see a lot of Everly. She became one of us in all the ways that mattered. And she matters to me a whole lot.

I see her in her kitchen and watch the way that they live happily here and the home that they've created. Fuck if I don't want that with them. I want to sip coffee at her kitchen table in the morning with coloring books sprawled out with crayons and colored pencils lined up. Tonight, I saw one page was sloppily colored and one colored in detail. She colors with her kid, and they are making memories here together. She's giving Willow what she didn't have here, and I know that's important to her. This place heals her in a lot of ways that she needs. Her kitchen is nice with a jar of homemade cookies out on the counter. She loves it there and takes good care of her kid and has made it a home that they want to come home to. I don't want to leave when I come here.

I loved the fall bucket list on the counter next to those cookies. They've decorated it in fall colors and with pumpkin stickers. A few things had been checked off with an orange crayon. Everly's always loved fall, and it's clear that her kid does, too. They had everything on there from pumpkin picking to baking an apple pie.

Everly and Hayley dragged Kincaid and me to a lot of Halloween parties, haunted houses, and our town's annual fall festival. Being the eldest, I was usually their mode of transportation, but I didn't mind. I also didn't mind when Everly got scared in the haunted house and would hold my hand or cling to me.

After Everly left, I hated everything that had to do with fall. If I could leave town and come back when the town transformed from fall into our tourist ski town full of snow, I would. Fall makes me remember Everly, and up until this year, I hated it. Now, all I can think about is helping them complete their fall bucket list and making sure every single one of the items on their list happens for them.

I can't mess this up with her. It's our time. She might not be there yet, but I am. And if I have to keep waiting for her, I will. That kiss told me everything I needed to know. She kissed me back as much as I kissed her, and having dinner with her in her kitchen felt so right.

I make it back to the bar and sigh when I look up at the dark windows above the bar. I don't even want to go up there. This has never felt like my home. I have a bed, a recliner, and a TV. And my office with basic office furniture. No plants, books, or personal touches anywhere like at her house. No red cast-iron enamel pot on top of my stove with some fall stew or soup simmering in it like she had. I sure as hell don't have fresh cookies on the counter in a cookie jar. It's not a home, just a place to sleep. And I've lived like this for years. This time, it's like life handed her to me on a silver platter, and I'm going to treasure everything about her and her daughter and treat them like they deserve. I'll try like hell to make her see I've changed.

I STEP OUT of the shower and see that the phone I use for property management has notifications. She's texting Reed instead of me. *Only it is me*, I groan as I read the text in anticipation.

Everly: Hey! Sorry, I haven't had time to text back. It's been a whirlwind over here. How are you doing?

Me: I'm good. How are things with your friend?

Everly: He told me he loves me.

Me: Oh, wow. How do you feel about that?

Everly: I've always loved him. But I just never thought he felt the same about me.

Me: How come?

Everly: Because he's . . . this ridiculously good-looking guy with a successful business who's got his life together. He's like the wholesome television show with an idyllic family and life. I'm just not sure I can measure up.

Me: Why do you think that? You seem like a good person and mother to me.

Everly: Well, thank you for that.

Me: Anytime.

What she's saying makes me sad. I want to grab her and kiss her and remind her that she's one of us and not a product of her prick father or how she grew up. Also, she called me ridiculously good looking, which makes me want to kiss her even more.

Everly: I don't know if I can put myself out there again. I was just starting to figure out who I am and what I want in life. Adding Nash to the mix . . . complicates everything.

Me: How does it complicate everything?

Everly: Well, if we don't work out, I lose his whole family, which is my family.

Me: Maybe it'll all work out. He seems like a great guy.

Everly: Do you know Nash?

Me: Sure, everyone knows Nash. He's a good guy.

I grit my teeth, trying not to make her cringe. I almost gave myself away.

Everly: He is a good guy. But I think I'm going to tell him that I need time to figure myself out first. I can't just jump into this like he can. I have a lot of obligations right now.

Me: Whatever you decide, it'll work out. You deserve to be happy. I'm rooting for you guys.

Everly: Thanks, Reed. I appreciate you listening. I hope you have a good night, and I'll text soon.

Me: You too.

She's probably going to be so pissed when she finds out this is me. I don't want to risk messing things up with her. Maybe I should just not talk to her anymore or answer any of her future texts.

When Everly left, I was not in a good place. I was working as a bartender at Bookers and getting into trouble. I was twenty-two and acting like an entitled shit. Her dirtbag ex got her for eight years, and we missed out on every single one of those years. But now she's back, and I have to show her how much I love her.

CHAPTER 17

Everly

"Send me the GPS, honey, so I can start my journey because I'm ready," Anne Marie calls as I walk in the main door to the library that's quiet and not bustling with patrons yet. She nudges a cup of coffee my way and sits behind the desk, ready for me to fill her in on all things Nash.

I bite my lip and grin as I slide into the seat next to her and pull my jacket and scarf off, setting it aside.

Picking up the mug, I hold it to my lips, breathe in, and close my eyes. "Mmm, coffee first." I just dropped Willow off at school, and neither of us wanted to get out of our warm and cozy beds today. Plus, I'm delaying telling her what's going on with Nash. I don't even know what to do about him. I'm still processing everything.

Anne Marie sits back and waits with her mug and says, "I haven't got all day, honey. People will be in here soon, and we won't have a minute to dish, so spill."

"Okay, okay, fine. He says he loves me."

"And?" she prompts excitedly.

"He likes Willow, too," I murmur as I pinch the bridge of my nose, still wrapping my head around this. I feel excited, and nervous, and a slew of other emotions entangled together.

"Ohh-wey. That boy is a good one, and he waited for you," she says, slapping the counter with a grin. "So hot!"

"I don't know that he waited for me," I protest as I look at her sideways.

"I have never seen him date anyone, Everly. He's like a monk living above that pub." She raises her eyebrows at me, sipping from her mug.

This surprises me, and I realize I had assumed so many things that weren't true about Nash. It makes me want to get to know him even more now.

The library door opens, and Hayley comes in carrying a box of donuts under her arm and a drink carrier of coffee cups.

"You didn't start without me, did you?" she calls as she sets the drinks and box down.

"Yeah, you got to hear this, honey. Your brother is *something*," Anne Marie says as she fans herself, her ruby-red lips pursed.

"Well, whatever you did, he seems to be in a good mood, and I'm thankful. He's not as moody and broody," she says as she slides coffee in front of us.

I drain the mug of the rest of the coffee that Anne Marie brought and reach for a donut. "Ooooh, this pumpkin?"

"Yeah, they're so good. There are apple cider donuts in there, too. Come on, tell me what's up," she pleads with excitement. As an afterthought, she reminds me, "Just don't tell me anything gross. He *is* my brother."

"Your brother loves Everly," Anne Marie says between bites.

Hayley waves her hand. "We all know that. What else happened?"

"*We* all did not know that. *I* didn't know that," I say as I purse my lips.

"Well, you do now. Then what happened?" She leans in, excited to hear more.

I cover my face. “I can’t believe we’re talking about this. But if you must know, nothing happened. Nash is a gentleman. We spent some time together. Ate dinner at my house and talked. Really talked for once. It was really nice,” I admit.

“Bummer. I thought the tea would be piping hot. But I’m so glad, honey. You need to leave Willow with me more often. That kid is a hoot. You need to go out and do young people things, and she needs to spend time with her Anne Marie,” she says, talking about herself in the third person, which makes me smile at her.

“I did have fun. And thank you for watching her. But I think Willow had more fun than you did,” I say as I take one of the fresh coffees Hayley brought and take a sip, closing my eyes at the sweet pumpkin flavor. Perfect.

“Impossible. I love having her. It made my day. Let’s do it again this weekend. You need to spend time with Nash,” Anne Marie says as she wipes crumbs onto a napkin.

“I was fine with my life,” I insist. “I have a good life. I love Willow. I never knew how badly I wanted to be a mom until I had her. I want to focus on her. I don’t need to go out, and I don’t need a man to feel complete. I can do this on my own. Nash and I just aren’t the same people.”

Hayley weighs in. “You can still have a life and be a good mom.”

“You and Nash are two souls meant to be, always have been,” Anne Marie points out.

“Are you two just going to offer solutions for everything I bring up?” I ask with a little shake of my head.

Before anyone can say anything else, the doors swing open, and Richard Sullivan Sr. and his son, Richie, stroll in. Instant dread washes over me. My stomach knots with tension and anxiety, my palms clammy and clenched tight. I set my donut down, no longer hungry.

Hayley looks over and says dryly, "Oh, look, a satchel of Richards just walked in."

Richie glares at her and narrows his eyes. "Don't you have a little sleazy bar to run . . ." Before he can finish, he breaks out in a fit of coughing.

Hayley inches away from him and wrinkles her nose in disgust. "Can you go die somewhere else?"

Richie glares at me as if it's my fault, and I should give him sympathy. "I'm sick."

"Not my problem," I say with disgust as I notice his hand is swollen and his knuckles scraped from hitting Nash. I shake my head, angry and upset that he's even here. I see Hayley looking at them too. This isn't going to go well.

Richard, who hasn't said anything, has been quietly looking around the library like he's calculating something. A feeling of uneasiness comes over me. They always have an ace to play. I'm just waiting for it.

"Can I help you?" Anne Marie asks but not in a friendly way. She doesn't like them, either, and she knows they are likely here to start trouble. There's no other reason for them to even come in here. They aren't usual patrons of the library and never have been.

"What do you want?" I shake my head, already tired of him being here in my space, at my job harassing me.

"Careful who you trust. Salt and sugar look the same, dear," she says with disdain at the Sullivans standing over us at the desk, trying their best to look intimidating.

"You need to come home. You've been messing around here long enough. And you need me. This job is not supporting you, and I've heard you've been struggling," Richie says like he's delivering news and talking to me like I'm stupid. As per usual.

I snort. "No, what you've heard is I'd rather struggle than be with you. We're divorced," I remind him. "And stop calling me your wife, for the love of God. I am not your wife!"

Anger fills me, and I'm just so tired of this.

"You have no business coming into her place of work and harassing her," Hayley points out to both with obvious disgust. "You need a restraining order, Everly."

"Hey, now. We came here just to have a friendly little chat. Can you give us a minute, old girl? My boy and I need a word with his wife," Richard says as he leans back, looking bored in his golf polo shirt and perfectly ironed golf pants. He looks absolutely ridiculous if he thinks he's going to win over Anne Marie with his charm. He probably needs to get to his tee time and doesn't want to be here for whatever nonsense Richie has dragged him into.

"Did he just call you . . . ?" Hayley asks as she looks between them and us with disdain.

Anne Marie looks innocently between Hayley and me, ignoring them. "Oh, I love it when people are rude. Because, oh my gosh, *my turn,*" she says as she turns and glares at them.

"What do you assholes want?" Hayley bites out, beating Anne Marie to it.

"I need to speak to my *wife,*" Richie parrots what his dad said, no doubt trying to show off in front of him.

"I'm not your wife, so please leave," I grit as I hold up my hand in a warning.

"You stay out of Bookers. You hear me?" he grinds out and points at me. "And away from McCreedy. I don't want that trash around you *or* my kid."

And there it is. He came here to manipulate, cause a scene, and throw a tantrum because of his behavior last weekend. And I'm so sick of this.

"Get out," I say sharply.

"This is your warning. If I see you there or around McCreedy, you won't like what happens. I'll make sure my daughter isn't being raised by the town whore and drunk just like her dad. And look how you turned out."

I stand from my chair. "How did I turn out? I have a master's degree in library science. I have a job and a home. I think I turned out fine."

"Out," Anne Marie demands. Standing, she's folded her arms over her chest and doesn't look much happier. I need them to go. They're embarrassing me in front of my friend and boss, and the patrons are starting to trickle in, seeing this unfold but pretending not to watch.

They don't get the hint, and Richie only seems to get more agitated. According to Anne Marie, the town has been buzzing with what happened with Nash and Richie at the pub. And Richie can't get past this one now. Nash made sure of it, and it seems like it's escalated Richie even more.

"What do you even bring to the table, Everly? You're a part-time library aide. How is it that you think you're qualified to take care of our daughter?" He hisses at me with a sneer as he threatens, "Maybe we should go back to court and change that."

I see red. I have worked so hard for the past six months to get my self-esteem back, and I won't tolerate this anymore. I've worked too hard on my peace to take his crap for even one more minute. It's time to send the memo.

I'm done.

I hold up my hand and stare him straight in the eye. "Richie, I *am* the fucking table. You just don't get that because you're not even a fucking chair. Get out!"

The room becomes silent. Mainly because I usually don't talk like this or stand up for myself. But when I'm done, I am done. I won't be disrespected like this. Ever again.

Richie and Richard look at each other, and Richard nods. And here comes their ace. I've been around this family long enough to know that they always have an ace to play. Always.

Richard looks at me and says, "We came to let you know that you're being downsized to a part-time library with part-time hours until the library is phased out. Your budget and your funding have been halted. And by the end of the year, we're closing the library and tearing it down to make room for a newer and more profitable business for the town."

"We're building a new hockey arena," Richie says with a smug grin. "It'll also be a big concert venue as well."

These words shred me, and I feel Anne Marie tense up next to me, but neither of us waver.

Richie looks smug, and Richard looks bored. Neither cares about this library and how much it means to our town. Both have something to gain by this.

I glare at both of them, saying nothing until they both finally turn and leave. I watch until they get into Richie's ridiculously large SUV, which is parked illegally in front of the library, and it drives off too quickly.

"Can he really do that?" Hayley whispers in horror as she stares at both of us.

Anne Marie looks worried, but she puts her hand over mine. "Over my dead body. I will be contacting everyone I can, and I will figure it out."

"This is the first I'm hearing about this," Hayley says. "And everyone talks about everything in the pub."

I close my eyes and blink back tears of anger and embarrassment.

I look over at Hayley and say, "We have to fix this. He can't do this."

"Of course not. We'll figure this out. The Sullivans don't have as much power as they think they do. They won't get away with this," Hayley adds.

"Now don't get too worked up until I've talked to a few people," Anne Marie says as she whirls her chair around to her computer and gets to work.

I sigh. "I'm going to call Richie's mom. She's not my favorite person in the world, but she is more reasonable than they are. Maybe she can talk to them and call them off. This is going too far."

Anne Marie looks over at us. "I'm going to keep the library open until I hear differently from someone from the town that isn't an asshat Sullivan." Then to herself, she mutters, "An ice hockey arena, what the hell? This library was donated to the town and can't just be torn down. It's a historical building."

I look at Hayley. "This is my fault. They wouldn't be coming for the library if I didn't work here."

"You'll be okay. The people in this town won't tolerate this when they find out the intentions of the Sullivans. I have no idea who is behind all this, but it won't hold up."

"And what happens if it does?" I ask, exhaling a deep breath.

She just looks at me and tilts her head. "You really think everyone will sit back and let this happen? The hockey arena is huge. That means all the local businesses around us are in jeopardy as well."

True. That brings me some peace of mind. People around here aren't going to stand for this. Hopefully.

"Nash is not going to like this either. And we are business owners in this town. We can get people to rally and back the library. Don't worry, this isn't going to bode well for the satchel of Richards," Hayley says as she puts an arm around my shoulders.

"Thanks," I say. "I'll figure out what's going on here and get with you about the baking schedule."

She stands. "Don't let them see you sweat. That's what they want. And Everly, one more thing. Richie never understood what you brought to the table until he saw you at another table."

I nod. This is what Richie does. Destroys everything for me. He doesn't stop until there's nothing left. And now that I've built a good life here for me and Willow, he's coming for that, too.

CHAPTER 18

Everly

When we hit a lull in the afternoon at the library, I sit down and work on a budget for my unstable future. Since Reed waived my rent for three months, which I'm extremely grateful for, we will be okay at least through the holidays. I've lived frugally, and since I no longer have any vehicle expenses, I can also take that out of the budget for now. Walking might get tricky, but we'll make it work.

Anne Marie doesn't return after lunch and is meeting with the town officials. She said she'll update me tonight on what she finds out. I'm pretty sure Richard can't do this and was blowing smoke, but we'll see. Richie is a chip off the old block, and he's learned his manipulative behaviors from his dad. I've seen it many times, so I wouldn't put it past him.

I organize our fall-themed book display and smile sadly. I need this job. It makes me happy and has been good for me. I've worked so hard on myself, our happiness, and our new life here. And I won't go out without a fight. How can they wipe out a whole library for a stupid hockey rink? We already have an expanding tourist town, and we want to keep it smaller and more intimate. This is not what the locals will want.

It's getting darker now, and it starts to rain. I need to pick Willow up from after-school care and get her home. I lock up and pull my umbrella out of my bag just as Nash pulls up. I recognize his truck now from when we were all out at the ranch.

He comes over and holds the umbrella for me. "Hey," he says in a smooth, deep voice.

"Hey," I say, relieved to see him. Without thinking, I wrap my arms around him and lay my head on his chest. His arms come around, and he pulls me in close. He smells so good.

"You okay? Hayley told me what happened." He has a different expression on his face that I can't read.

I shake my head. "No, but I'm going to be. I always am. I'll figure this out."

He nods. "I came to pick you up. Mom and Dad want us to come to the ranch tonight for dinner if you don't already have plans."

Relief surges through me. "That sounds amazing. For once, I wasn't looking forward to going home and having time to think about this anymore. I need good food and family right now."

"We've got you covered, beautiful. Let's go," he says as he holds the umbrella and leads me to the truck. He holds the door for me and goes around to get in on his side.

"You don't work tonight?" I ask, curious as he slides in next to me.

"Nope, I did farrier work today," he says as he cranks up the heat. I take in his profile as he drives, and damn, he looks so good. He's got a day or two of scruff on his jaw. It makes him look rough yet strong at the same time.

"How was that?" I ask, curious. I don't know this side of him, and I feel like there is so much I don't know about him now.

"It was good. I took care of Ed and Mabel's horses. They're always good for me," he says as he turns into the school parking lot and parks.

"Hold on," he calls as he gets out of the truck and comes around to get me.

Oh, man. He is just . . . *so good.* A girl could get used to this. Then I think to myself not to get used to it. Usually, it won't last with Nash. But it feels so good to be with him like this. I don't want it to end.

He holds the umbrella and walks with me into the school. Other parents picking up their kids give us curious glances, and a few eyebrows raise. This will make for great town gossip, I'm sure.

Willow lights up when she sees us standing at the door and comes running from a game she was playing with some other kids. Her teacher smiles and waves as I sign her out.

"Nash, you came!" she says as she slides a hand in his and walks beside him, chatting his ear off, which makes me smile. He can barely answer her questions before she barrels on to the next one. He looks over at me, and his mouth turns up a little as he helps us get in the truck. Then he starts it up and turns the heat on as he waits for us to get buckled.

"Your mom and I thought it would be fun to head to the ranch for supper. How does that sound?"

"Yes!" she squeals. "Can we ride a horse?"

He chuckles. "Not today, darlin'. This rain isn't letting up. But we'll have to do chores, and maybe we can brush them. You can get to know each of them a little after supper if that's okay with your mom."

I nod at her, and she looks a little disappointed but agrees, "Okay."

"I do have something for you, though. Look inside that bag back there." Nash nods to the back seat.

I watch her open the brown paper bag and pull out four mini

horseshoes. "New shoes for my horse! Thanks, Nash!" she exclaims, holding them up.

He looks over at me, and I smile and mouth, "Thank you." He says nothing but nods again and puts the truck in drive. Little things like this are big things to Willow. She clutched them in her hands all the way out to the ranch.

On the drive, Nash reaches over and takes my hand and holds it. I look at him, and he gives me a small smile, but his eyes never leave the road.

We get to the ranch, and when we open the door, the aroma of garlic, basil, and oregano envelops me in a state of paradise. I close my eyes and breathe it in. My eyes scan through the mudroom, and I see Anna in the kitchen at the stove stirring a pot, wearing her bright red apron.

"Nash? Is that you?" she calls as she reaches for a hand towel and wipes her hands, turning around.

"Does she know we're coming?" I ask, suddenly nervous.

He grins and shakes his head. "I wanted to surprise her. She makes enough to feed an army anyway. She'll be thrilled," he says to her and then calls out, "I brought company."

Her face lights up when she sees us, and it fills with emotion as she looks at the three of us standing in the kitchen together. She covers her mouth, then reaches out for Willow, who runs into her arms and wraps her in a hug.

"This is the best surprise of the day!" she calls as she hugs Willow. "How are you, my sweetheart?"

"Good. Whatcha making?" Willow asks.

I'm trying to be casual, but I'm nervous about being here with her son and wonder what she'll think. She seems really happy and can't stop looking at us and smiling.

"Well, right here, we have sauce simmering. And over there, I made homemade spaghetti noodles. And in the oven, I have some cheesy garlic bread. Want to help with the salad?" she asks as she holds out a little red apron for Willow that matches hers.

Willow eagerly agrees and stands next to Anna as Nash pulls up a stool for her to stand on to reach the counter.

Anna looks over at me. "Where's my hug, sweetie pie?"

I wrap my arms around her and hug her. She always gives the best hugs. She smells like home. She lingers for a moment longer, and when I was younger, I once asked her why she did that. I noticed she didn't do that with the other kids. She once told me that she does the extra time of the hug for my mom, who would want her to hug me extra for her. When she told me that, I cried myself to sleep that night, missing my mom so badly but grateful for Anna and her love for me. I cried because I thought it was unfair that my mom died and then my dad chose not to be around me when my mom would have loved to be with me. She wouldn't have left me if she'd had a choice. And I also cried because I love Anna so much. She always treated me like one of her own kids and made me feel special by doing things like that. Growing up around Anna was great because she keeps my mom's memory alive and talks to me about her. My dad didn't do that. In fact, he barely talked about my mother at all, and only if he had to, so Anna played a big part in keeping my mother close to my heart.

The ranch house has always felt like coming home. Worn dark wood floors covered in multicolored braided rugs. Worn but cozy couches have soft and warm quilts draped over the backs. Bookcases in nearly every room are overstuffed with board games and books. Board games are also under the coffee table in the sunroom, their boxes faded by the sun. The McCreedys have the kind of house where you can curl up with a book and take a nap, completely relaxed. It's a dream home for a kid like me who grew up in a quiet and lonely home.

Mack comes in, hanging up his hat and removing his boots. He looks surprised when he sees all of us, but he doesn't say anything. He just kisses my cheek and says, "Where's my best girl?" to Willow, who hugs him and sits next to him, telling him all about her day. Mack listens and asks questions, patient with her as a pop-pop would be.

"How's the new baby donkey?" Anna asks.

"You have a donkey?" Willow's eyes widen with excitement.

"We do. His name is Waffles," Mack says. "Hayley named him."

"I love it! I want to see him!" Willow says with the biggest smile.

"After dinner," Nash promises.

"Hey, son, when you get a chance, can you help me with the latch on the barn door? Do you have your toolbox handy in your truck?" Mack asks Nash.

"No, I misplaced it," he says as he follows him out.

I watch them go. Nash is a younger version of Mack, who is still a good-looking man.

After dinner, Anna and I wash dishes while Mack and Nash take Willow out to do chores and see the horses, and she takes this window of time to ask me, "So what's going on with you and Nash?"

I shrug, trying to play it cool. "He just invited us to dinner with you guys."

She grins and shakes her head like she doesn't believe me. "Okay."

"Okay," I repeat, and then we both laugh, knowing I'm full of crap.

"You'll tell me when you're ready." She lays a hand on my cheek, and I lean into it, loving her soothing touch. "I'm so glad you girls came out. I've missed you both dearly."

"We'll come more," I say softly. "Next time, I'll have you all over for supper if you're up for it. I love cooking."

"Just like your mom. And we would love that." She beams.

Just like your mom. She missed out on a lifetime with me, which makes me so sad. Every time I'm with Anna, I feel like she gives me a piece of my mom that I didn't have before.

When we got home, Willow was exhausted from her day, and by the time I got her settled, I walked out into the living room to see Nash sprawled on the couch, watching me with a hand under his chin and a softness to his gaze. A smirk forms on his face when I walk in the room.

"I just had to get her settled."

"Looked like she had a good time tonight," he says as he makes room for me on the couch next to him. I sit beside him but keep a little distance between us, which he notices and closes in.

"She did have fun. Thank you for tonight."

He puts his arm around me, pulling me close and tipping his forehead to mine. "Did you have fun?"

"I did, and we needed it. It's been a hard week."

"Yeah, he has to give up eventually. Why is he here so much anyway? Doesn't he have a dealership to run?"

"You would think. I don't know why he's here. I feel like he's never going to give up," I admit, feeling defeated.

"You're doing your best. Leaving a bad marriage from that shithead isn't easy."

"It's not. I hate it."

"We're doing this. I told you how I felt. You and me? We're going to explore this. And Willow?" He points his thumb down the hall. "She comes first."

"Thanks. Why are you such a nice guy?" I tease.

"Beautiful, I'm whiskey, and you're tea. We are opposite in so many ways, but we go together. I'm not a nice guy, but I'm a good guy. You need to know the difference. I'll always love, protect, and be here for both of you, no matter what." He strokes my cheek, and I lean my head on his shoulder.

"Thanks," I say, not sure what to say because there's so much to unpack in that sentence, and it literally made me swoon.

"You know you can thank me by cooking me dinner this week sometime," he says slyly.

"Oh, yeah?" I tease. "That could be arranged."

"Yeah," he murmurs as he tips my nose with his finger.

"You can come to dinner anytime, Nash. You know that, right?" I smile at him.

"I do now," he says quietly, looking into my eyes. My stomach dips in nervousness at the way he looks at me.

I bite my lip, and his eyes linger on my lips. His eyes darken a little as he leans in and kisses me softly on the lips. "Gotta go, beautiful."

"Okay," I say as my lips feel electric where he kissed me.

"Tomorrow will be better. Lock up behind me?" he asks as I get up to walk him to the front door.

"Yeah."

Nash looks out the window. "Dad just dropped off Bobby. I'm giving him a ride back to the ranch. You can use it as long as you like. Nobody's been using it out at the ranch anyway. Stay safe."

I start to protest, and he drops a set of keys on the side table and smiles as he tips his chin to me and shuts the door and leaves.

I lean my back up against the door and sink to the floor.

Nash.

God, I love this man.

CHAPTER 19

Nash

Sweat pours down my back as I pound the red-hot metal and shape it into a shoe. Farrier work is grueling and hard, but I love it. It's where my mind can wander, and instead of using it to drown out thoughts of Everly . . . she's all I want to think about now. I wonder what she's doing and where her mind's at on everything with us. I make an extra shoe, and it's hot and tiring, but my body needs it. Something about being outside with the horses clears my mind and makes me dream of what life will be like on my own property someday. This property has been in my family for four generations now on my mother's side. My father's family is from Ireland, and he's a first-generation American. Ireland has always been a special place for us. We'd spent a part of many summers there as kids visiting our grandmother. We'd stay with her and help her at her bakery, and she'd come here to visit us. She hasn't been well enough to make the trip over here for a few years, which worries us all. It's hard to be so far away from her. The back part of the land on my parents' ranch has forty acres, where I'll have my own ranch someday. I have a tiny home out there right now that I placed near where my house will be built. I like to go out there every now and then and dream. But it was hard to dream about a place where I couldn't see myself living until now. I can see Everly and Willow there with me, and it feels like it could really happen. I can see us having a big, beautiful home, lots of animals, and a horse for Willow to ride. My brother and sister have the same number of acres on either side of mine, so we'll be neighbors someday with our own families. None of us have settled down. Kincaid is off working the rodeo circuit and isn't home very often, and Hayley seems . . . lost. She's been different, and maybe it's because we've been so busy with the pub. Although she does seem somewhat happier now that Everly is back in Cozy Creek.

I look out over the mountains and dream of having a wife and a family that I can take care of here. I've only ever wanted to live here in Cozy Creek. Even in high school and after, when I was still doing dumb shit, I wanted to get it right. I just didn't know how. And now I feel like I'm getting it right. And I'm going to tread very carefully with Everly. I can't mess it up. They are everything to me.

"Penny for your thoughts, bro." I turn and see Hayley walking toward me with a bag of food and a few waters in her hand.

"That better be Gigi's subs." I grin as I wipe sweat from my forehead. I stand and set my hot iron down with the horseshoes completed next to it on a cooling place.

"It is, but it'll cost you." She cleans off the inside of my truck tailgate and sets the food down, then hops up on it. I wipe my hands off and head over, then hop up beside her.

"What's the price?" I grab a bag of chips, open it, and pop one in my mouth.

"Tell me what's going on with you and Everly?"

I look over at her and roll my eyes. "You didn't have to bribe me with food to talk about Everly."

"Yeah, right, you're not exactly Mr. Sharing when it comes to anything," she says as she unwraps the paper on her sandwich.

"What did you get me?" I ask as she hands me a sandwich.

"Barbecue brisket."

I sigh and close my eyes, realizing how hungry I am. "Thanks, I'm starving."

She looks at me and tilts her head expectantly.

"I love her," I admit. "I always have."

"And . . ." she pushes.

"I'm shooting my shot with her."

She looks at me cautiously. "For real this time?"

"This time?"

"You know what I mean. I think both of you were devastated when she left. You weren't yourself for a long time after that. It changed you," she says as she takes a bite of her sandwich and chews.

"We were young. And it's different now. I can't explain how, but it feels like this is our time. It's right; it was always supposed to be. She was the right girl, wrong time," I say, relaxing my shoulders as I let this out. We sit side by side, our feet dangling from the tailgate.

She zips her jacket up and shivers. "It's cold out here. I don't know how you're sitting there in a T-shirt and sweating." She wrinkles her nose.

"I've been working with the hot iron making horseshoes. Want to try it?" I ask her, raising my eyebrows.

"Eww, no thanks. I bake in a hot kitchen with hot ovens going. I don't want to work out here with more heat."

I laugh and take another bite.

"For what it's worth, I'm rooting for you both. I think you two have always been meant to be. And both of you seemed so lost without each other for the past several years. And we have Willow now, so that's a bonus."

"She's a pretty great kid," I admit as I reach for more chips.

"Mom and Dad are happy for you guys, too."

"I don't want to mess this up," I admit as I look out at the mountains, a mist of clouds settling over the peaks.

"I don't think you will. Just be patient with her. She's still going through it with Richie. He's not letting up, and her being with you isn't making it any easier for her."

"I hate that guy," I mutter.

"Join the club. I can't believe the crap he's pulling with the library." She holds up her pickle to me, and I take it and eat it. She never eats her pickles, yet always gets them and gives them to me.

"Thanks."

I'm disgusted and full of rage about what Richie is doing to Everly and Anne Marie. Coming for the town library? That's a new low, even for him. I want to take that prick and his father down a peg or two and teach them a lesson on what happens to bullies.

"Have you heard from Kincaid lately?" she asks as she takes her phone out of her pocket and checks it.

"I texted with him over the weekend. He's good, having a blast on the rodeo circuit. He said he'll be back in a few weeks. Mom and Dad will be happy to hear that."

"That's good. It'll be good to have everyone home together. Dad's going to Ireland in a few weeks to check on Grandma. She's not doing so good," she says, and I don't miss the worry that crosses her face. "It has to have been hard on him all these years being so far from his family."

"We're his family, too," I remind her. "He loves the ranch."

"Do you ever think about leaving Cozy Creek?" she asks as she stares out at the mountains.

I shake my head. "No, I never want to leave. Why? You feel like you want to leave?" I ask.

"Sometimes I do feel like I want to get out of here, honestly. I have this urge to travel and see the world. I want to meet people. I want to meet my person. I want what Mom and Dad have. And I feel like I won't find that here in Cozy Creek." She balls up her sandwich wrapper and stuffs it in the bag.

I look at her and finally see it. She's unhappy and has been for a while. I don't know how I missed it. She has the wandering bug like my dad, which brought him to the States, where he met my mom and became a rancher. He left everything he knew behind, stayed with her, and built a life. My mom and dad have always had a strong marriage and relationship and modeled that for us kids. They are meant to be. Sure, things weren't always perfect, but they love each other and are happy.

"You should go, Hayles."

She looks up at me. "What about the pub?"

"What about it?" I shrug. "We'll manage, and we can hire more help. We'll be fine. It'll be here when you come back."

"I'll think about it," she says as she hands me a brownie.

"You make these?" I ask as I unwrap it and take a bite.

"Nope, Everly did." She grins.

"Even better," I say as she nudges me with her shoulder.

"I'm happy for you guys," she says as she sways as we look out over the mountains.

"Thanks, Hayles. Go do what makes you happy. It'll all be okay here." I pull her to me and kiss the top of her head.

I just remember what I wanted to ask her. "Hey, have you seen my toolbox? The big green metal one? I can't find it, and I think I left it somewhere."

"Nope." She shrugs. "Maybe you left it at a client's barn or something."

"Keep an eye out for it, will you? It was Grandpa's old one, and I misplaced it."

CHAPTER 20

Nash

On my way back to town, I stopped at a pumpkin stand on the side of the road and picked up three good-sized pumpkins and put them in the back of my truck. I want to make everything on their bucket list happen. I wave at the owner as my mind drifts back to when Everly and I were thirteen and fifteen. Everly had the biggest crush on me back then, but she tried to hide it. I chose to redirect her as much as possible. Because she was Hayley's best friend, I never wanted to make it awkward for any of us. We had a good thing going, and I couldn't handle not having her in our life. Hayley, Kincaid, Everly, and I were inseparable. We would go big and get into every holiday, and fall was no exception. We carved pumpkins, went to the fall festival in town, and snuck beer behind the beer tent. We all decided that beer tasted and smelled like pee and opted for apple cider instead from the antique apple cider press. We tried to play it cool, but we just weren't. We would prank and scare each other at the corn maze and ride the floats in the fall parade and throw candy to the kids. The fall carnival was a favorite too. I don't have many memories without Everly in them. When her dad was home from long-haul trucking, he would be at the pub every chance he got, so she'd end up with us most of the time anyway. I never did like her dad. Most people didn't, and he wasn't missed around here when he moved. But Everly has always been loved by just about everyone. A lot of people were happy when she moved back.

I remember Everly telling me when we were about twelve and fourteen that I'd be her boyfriend someday when we were swinging on the big tire out back behind the barn. It was hot, and we were all in bathing suits. Kincaid and I had made a makeshift swimming pool out of the water holes for the cattle. We would swing and try to land in the water. We were eating our Popsicles as fast as we could because they were melting.

I had told her no way and that I'd be single forever. She just looked at me, smiled, and said, "We'll see." Then she jumped into the cold water, shrieking. I can still see her smile that day as she was so carefree and happy.

She believed in us back then. It's not that I didn't. It's that I just always knew she was special to me. And I didn't want to mess it up. Because when you have something that special, you hold on to it with everything you've got and make sure you don't ruin it. I never wanted to ruin things with Everly. I wanted to keep her safe and protected. When she left, I felt helpless, and watching her live as a shell of a person with Richie destroyed me. Now, I'm not leaving her unprotected. If Richie wants to come for her and make things hard, he's up against me and this town. Because this town won't let him do that to her—she's one of us, and we look out for our own. I've been talking to as many people as I can about Richie and what he's been doing, and people aren't down with that. He's got a battle in front of him, and I'm building my army. I wouldn't just protect Everly and Willow, I'd go to battle for them. These past few months of having her back have been good for her and good for the town. She does good work at the library and brings the town together, and people love and respect her. That's why it's hard to hear her talk about herself in the texts about how she doesn't think she belongs here and isn't good enough. I wish she could see what everyone else sees when they see her.

Stopping by her house on the way to the pub, I unload the pumpkins and position them on her front porch steps so they will see them when they come home. I had also grabbed a basket of random assorted gourds and squash that I left by her front door, too. They looked neat, and I thought she'd like them.

When I get back to the apartment, I shower and lean my head against the cool tile as I think of Everly. I hurry to get ready and check in with Marcus, who informed me that we're having a slow night and that I should come back later to help close. *Fine by me,* I think as I nab my keys and head back to Everly's.

I find myself on her porch examining one of the railings when the door opens, and I stand and say, "Porch looks good."

She beams, "Thanks, it's new. Landlord just fixed it. He did a great job."

I try to keep a straight face as I listen to her tell me about her landlord. I'm going to have to figure out how to come clean with her about this. I can't keep doing this to her.

She crosses the porch to me, her hands coming up to cup my face as she kisses me softly.

Warmth spreads through me as she wraps her arms around my neck and buries herself in my flannel. "Mmm, you smell good."

I pull her inside as I see a few of her neighbors out, and our show is not lost on them. Not that I care, but I don't want to share what we have with anyone just yet.

"Nash!" Willow calls as she looks up from where she's coloring at the table. The smell of good food hits me as I slide off my boots and pull up a chair next to Willow.

"How are you doing, kiddo?"

"Thank you for the pumpkins. Mom said we can carve them this weekend," she says excitedly as she scoots her coloring book closer to me and hands me a crayon to join in.

"I thought you'd like that. I saw your fall bucket list and noticed you hadn't yet crossed off carving pumpkins." I lift the crayon to shade in a pumpkin on the page.

"I claim the fat round one. That one's my favorite."

I look over, and Everly is watching us. Her face is happy and relaxed, her arms are crossed, and she has a small smile on her face as she's lost in thought.

"What's for dinner? It smells so good in here," I say as I meet her eyes, trying to look anywhere but her beautiful curves that make me want to reach out and hold her by the waist.

"Beef and noodles with homemade biscuits," she says as she reaches for a wooden spoon and stirs the big red pot on her stove.

"Does my offer to come to dinner anytime still stand?" I tease as I watch her bend to put biscuits in the oven. I try to hold back a groan and fail. She turns to look back at me, catching the heat in my eyes and the devilish smirk on my face. Her cheeks flush with delight.

She grins and turns to set the timer, her smile wide as she repeats, "Of course it does. Anytime."

I notice she has her kitchen decorated for fall and a wreath above her stove. Soft lights are on throughout the house, and a candle that smells like cider burns in the middle of the table.

"How was your day, Nash? What did you do?" Willow asks, her big bright blue eyes that match her momma's on mine. She looks a lot like Everly did at her age. It's surreal seeing a mini version of Everly.

"Well, I made some new horseshoes for a few of my clients. Then I had lunch with Hayley. And then I worked on a few horses. Then I picked up some pumpkins and ended up over here."

"Who are your clients?" she asks, interested and waiting for me to continue as if I just offered the most fascinating information.

"Well, I checked in on Soupy, Sparky, and Batman today. Those were my clients," I say as I reach for the green pencil to color the pumpkin stem.

"Soupy!" She giggles.

"Yes, Soupy. He's a red horse with wild hair. I saw him last week, but I brought him a fresh shoe today. He keeps breaking his on his fence. He likes to try to jump the fence, but then he messes up his shoes. He's a naughty boy." I try to sound serious.

Willow giggles and colors, her hand knocking into mine. "You're doing a good job there, buddy," she tells me.

I chuckle and look over at her. "Thanks, you are too. How was your day?"

"Well, I got up, and Mom made pumpkin muffins. We ate them on the way to school. We got to ride in a new truck. Then I had music today. But I don't like it. Then we played dodgeball after school, and this guy hit me three times with the ball. You only have to do it once, but he kept doing it. It hurt."

I stop coloring and say, "What's this guy's name?"

"Jayce."

"What else do you know about this guy?" I ask as I look at Everly.

"He's eight," she mouths, trying to hold back a grin. "Don't kill him."

"You know, when your mom and I were kids, there was a boy who bullied your mom," I murmur as I reach for another color.

"What happened to him?" she breathes, her eyes widening in anticipation.

"I ended him."

"Nash McCreedy, don't tell her that!" Everly says with mock horror.

"Alright, alright. I didn't end him. But I . . . had a talk with him, and he stopped bullying your mom," I say as my eyes meet hers over Willow.

It's unsaid who we're talking about. But Everly gets it. Her mouth turns up slightly, and she pretends to be busy setting out bowls.

"I'm glad. I don't want anyone to hurt Mom," Willow says seriously as she puts her hand on my arm.

"Me either. You know how to get back at Jayce?" I say to her as I hand her the orange.

"What?" she says as her tongue pokes out slightly as she concentrates on coloring.

"Pretend he doesn't exist. People who are mean only do it because they want a reaction from you."

"I can do that." She decides.

"When you stop giving a clown attention, they stop performing," I murmur.

This gets a giggle out of Willow.

"Yep. No attention for him."

"That's good advice," Everly says, looking relieved that I didn't teach her how to build a shiv or knock this Jayce kid out.

But the truth is, I hate hearing that anyone messes with them. We ate dinner together and had good conversation, and I could tell Everly was happy. She kept looking at us, and after dinner, I suggested we take a walk, and they agreed. It was a cool night, but it was not raining, so we put on our jackets and headed out.

I reach for Everly's hand and hold it as we walk. Willow skips ahead of us, collecting various fall leaves and acorns. Her "treasures," as she calls them.

"You're good with her," Everly says as our hands swing, and I pull her closer to me.

"It's not hard. She's a good kid. I like her." I shrug. I haven't been around a ton of kids, but I like them.

"It means a lot. She doesn't really have her dad, so it's nice that you're nice to her," Everly says. She turns to check for coming cars as we cross the street toward the town center where the park is.

"Have you heard from Richie since the library?" I ask.

"Nope."

"Good," I say as we watch Willow running to play.

"He has never been there for either of us. I want to choose someone who will be there for us next time."

"There won't be a next time," I told her.

Her eyes meet mine, confused.

"No more next time. This is it," I say as I bring her hand to my mouth and kiss her knuckles.

Her eyes soften, and she leans her head on my shoulder.

"Are you going to let me in?" I press, and she knows what I mean. She's holding back.

She takes a deep breath, and a small smile spreads on her lips. "My patience is basically like a gift card. Not sure how much is left on it, but we can try it."

I laugh. "Okay, I'll spend it wisely."

"Do you remember what you told me that night?" she asks softly.

"What?"

"You said that he wasn't going to turn around one day and suddenly realize what he has with me. You told me that if he doesn't want to be with me, I shouldn't waste my time hoping for him to come around. I didn't listen, and he never did come around. You were right," she says quietly.

"I hate that I was. But I'm glad we're where we are at right now," I say as Willow hands me leaves that she's been having me carry for her "collection."

We head back as the streetlamps blaze and porch lights light up. All three of us hold hands as we get back to Everly's. I get them settled in and have to check on the pub. I don't want to leave them, but I loved our time together. I realize that all these jobs I've been working will not work now that I have them in my life. I don't want to work all the time anymore. I want to be with them and make memories. Maybe Hayley and I are both going to have a job realization here soon on what we really want to be doing with our lives. The pub was good for us for a season, but maybe it will be a new season for both of us.

"Thank you for coming and for the pumpkins," Everly says softly as she kisses me on the porch.

"Thank you for dinner. Let's carve them this weekend."

"Willow will love that."

She looks like she wants to say more, but I kiss her and say, "Text you later." I boop her nose with my finger and shut the door softly as she steps inside. I wait for the lock to turn and head back to the pub.

CHAPTER 21

Everly

Richard Sullivan wasn't bluffing. The library funding was really pulled, and the library and several nearby buildings are in the process of being shut down. The ice arena project, which is a massive and expensive project, is really in motion. The town plans to bulldoze our beautiful old iconic library to make room for an enormous hockey arena, which the town promises will bring many income opportunities for Cozy Creek. Not only is the library at risk but so are other important landmark buildings that mean a lot to Cozy Creek. I end the call with Anne Marie, who is fit to be tied and beside herself upset about this. She's been in meetings all week trying to figure out what's going on and how we can stop it. I hate it, and deep down, I feel like this is my fault. If I hadn't had a target on my back, then maybe they wouldn't be coming after the library.

I tidy up my house I'm nervous cleaning and take the apple pie out of the oven I baked to take to the McCreedys'. It smells so good. I breathe it in and take a deep breath. I love cooking, baking, and taking care of the people I love. It feels good to be able to do things with the McCreedys again.

I called Mary, the town manager's assistant, who is also good friends with Anna. She said she couldn't talk while working but would call and update me later. At least I might have an ally there who can tell us what's going on so we can fight this.

I'm still helping Anne Marie at the library even though we aren't sure about the future of it, and baking with Hayley to supplement the lost income. The town suddenly can't lose its resources because of this, and Anne Marie needs my help. But we've been telling everyone we can what is happening, hoping others will be outraged and fight for the library with us. No one seems to be happy about this, and a lot of people are offering good ideas.

Working at the library is my dream job. I have loved books ever since I was a little girl, and the library here in Cozy Creek has always been my sanctuary and special place. It's a landmark for so many people here. They can't just shut it down and bulldoze it. Richie is making this personal. He's coming for something I've worked hard for. It's not just a fight against an unknown corporation coming to build a business. This is a battle to be free from Richie and his manipulative abuse.

I won't allow Richie to steal any more of my life. I will not stand around and let him take away *my* dreams as they shut the library down and raze it to the ground. But according to Mary, who finally called me back, that's exactly what will happen. On January first, the doors will officially close, and it has already been defunded. There has to be something more we can do; I can't accept defeat just yet. Not when so many people rely on our services.

But one thing they don't know is that I've still got a lot of fight left in me. The Sullivans don't have as much power as they think they do. Richie's mother was no help when I reached out to her. She said she thought the ice arena would be great for tourism and bringing income into the town and local businesses. She laughed at me and said I just needed to go home to Richie. "Stop this nonsense," she'd told me in a condescending fake voice. After we had hung up, I realized that she'd never even asked about her granddaughter. Not that I'm surprised. When we moved back, she asked if Willow had started school yet. She's in third grade. She's clueless and hasn't bothered to get to know Willow.

Note to self: his mother is out. This is a power play from the Sullivans to shut down the one place that I love and cancel my job. Anything to further manipulate me into going back to their son so he doesn't look bad.

Taking this job was my way to prove to the town that I'm reliable, and I'm not the town loser who grew up poor and on my own for the most part and married the town jerk because I got pregnant. I refuse to be knocked down. I'm back. And I'm not letting anyone take the library from us without a fight. Anger fills me as I look at the clock. No time to do anything right now. I promised Anna and Mack we'd come out to the ranch. Nash is going to work with Willow on riding a horse. I am nervous for her but happy she's getting to do what she loves; I quickly fix my makeup and hair. I glance down at my sage green sweater, jeans, and boots. I wonder if it's enough and realize if I wore anything else I'd look like I'm trying too hard.

Be cool. Don't be weird.

I head out to my porch and give it a quick sweep and shake the rug of the fallen leaves. I'm bent over arranging the pumpkins and mums when I hear behind me, "Hey, beautiful."

I look over, and he's wearing jeans that fit just right. His messy dark hair is tamed, and his beard is neatly trimmed. He walks up my sidewalk and looks like a dang snack. Scratch that, a whole meal. A feast. I bite my lip and stare up at him.

I give him a playful look, and he offers me a hand as I stand. His is rough but fits mine perfectly. He doesn't let go as I stand and pulls me into him against his wall of muscle chest. He lets go of my hand, wraps his arms around me, and pulls me in for a kiss. He feels firm and good. Safe.

"How was your day . . ."

Nash's lips touch mine, and I stop talking. My tongue touches his delicious lips, and he tastes minty and like Nash.

His hand goes to my hair, and he wraps a lock around his finger.

We finally pull away, realizing we're on my front steps for the town to see, and I smile at him. "Hello to you, too."

"Hello," he murmurs.

"I made pie," I say lamely, nerves starting to shoot through me.

He grins down at me. "I like pie."

"What kind of pie?" I tease, realizing he doesn't even know what kind I made.

"Your pie," he says. But something in his smirk tells me he's not really talking about pie.

My stomach dips in nervousness and excitement. I take him inside by the hand and call out, "Willow! Nash is here."

I hear footsteps down the hall as she crashes into him and hugs him. "I'm ready to go ride horses with you."

He places a hand on her head and says, "Me, too, kiddo."

This simple gesture warms my heart, and it swells seeing him interact with her.

"I'll get the pie in the carrier, and we can head out." I go to the kitchen, stopping at the stove to realize he's behind me and close.

"Can I help with anything?" he offers as he surveys the kitchen. "Hey, what happened to your faucet?"

"Oh, it broke today. I haven't had a chance to contact the property management guy. It's on my list," I say as I wave to the handle of the broken faucet.

He walks over and picks it up and looks at it, then sets it back down and looks at me.

"Really, it's fine. It still works; it's just snapped off at the top." I seal the lid on the pie carrier and say, "Are you ready?"

He takes it from me and places a hand on my lower back as he follows me to the entryway, where Willow is sliding on her boots.

He pulls the door closed behind us and reaches his hand in his pocket then freezes and says, "Beautiful, your keys."

"Did you forget this is my house?" I tease with a laugh as I hand him my keys.

His mouth turns up as he locks the door. "Yep."

The ride to the ranch is beautiful, the mountains showing off in a blaze of autumn glory. "We should go on more rides this time of year," I murmur as I take in the view.

"We can do that," Nash agrees.

"Remember how we used to go for drives in your truck as soon as you got your license? You took Hayley and I everywhere and took me home and picked me up countless times. You loved driving."

He looks over at me and back to the road. "My parents didn't mind, either. They liked that they could send me to town and run all their errands."

"Do you miss living out here at the ranch?" I ask him as I watch his profile, his face relaxed.

"I stay above the pub because it makes sense. But it's not home. I have a home."

"What? Where?" I ask, confused.

"Out on the back of the ranch land. Next to Hayley's house."

"How did I not know this? Since when?" I look at him in surprise.

He shrugs. "Since we were little, we knew. I don't have a real house built on it yet. I have a tiny home out there and sometimes stay out there. I'll build a house someday when I have a family." He glances over at me, then his eyes look in the mirror at Willow, who is glued to the window, probably looking for horses.

"Can we see it sometime?" Willow asks. "Do you have your own horse?"

He chuckles. "I don't have my own horse, but someday I plan to get a bunch of animals out there."

I stare at him in fascination. He catches me staring and says, "What?"

"Nash McCreedy, you surprise me."

"How's that?" he asks as his hand slides over and threads his fingers through mine. He stops at a stop sign and looks both ways, a muscle in his cheek twitching as his mouth turns up.

"You have come a long way from the teenage boy who hated ranch work and dreamed of getting out of Cozy Creek."

He shrugs. "I'm ready to settle down. I had my years to figure out what I want."

"And what do you want?" I find myself asking.

"A family to come home to and build a life with. A house full of kids with big family dinners. A barn full of animals."

My heart clenches because I want that, too. How is this feeling like it's too good to be true right now.

"What about you? What do you want?"

"I didn't have as many years to figure out what I want. But I figured out what I don't want."

Looking at me, he tips his head a little and squeezes my hand. "You can take your time figuring out what you do want."

I squeeze his hand back, and he holds it steady as we pull into the ranch. We barely get stopped before Willow is unbuckled and bounding off toward the barn, where Mack raises a hand and waves, clad in blue jeans and a flannel, dark brown weathered cowboy hat on his head.

"Be careful," I call as Willow races away, not paying attention to me.

"Hey, son, Everly. Can I talk to you both?" he calls as he stuffs his hands in his pocket. A look of concern passes over Nash's face as he takes my hand, and we walk to Mack.

"What's wrong, Dad?"

Mack's face crumples. "It's your grandmother, son. She's not doing well. Your mom and I are going to go over, but we need your help here at the ranch."

I suck in my breath, and Nash says, "Of course. I'm sorry, Dad."

I think of his sweet grandmother, whom I haven't seen since high school. She'd come over several times to visit when we were younger, but I heard she hasn't been well. She reminds me of the real-life Mrs. Doubtfire. A spitfire-spirited Irish woman who is a fantastic baker. She makes things you can only dream about tasting. She's just that freaking good. She also has the best stories. She reminds me of an older version of Hayley. They have a lot of similarities.

I pull Mack into a hug and say softly, "How can I help, Mack?"

"We need all hands on deck if Anna is going to go with me. Can you help, too? We have a lot to do before the weather turns. I've made a list for Nash, and Kincaid is going to cut his last stop on the circuit short and come home, too."

Holy cow. If Kincaid is coming back early, this has gotten serious.

"Of course," I agree immediately, relieved they want me to help. I'll do anything for them as they have always done so much for me.

Mack looks relieved, and his eyes drift to Willow sitting on the floor of the barn surrounded by baby barn kittens. She's smiling and petting them, lost in her own little world.

"I'm going to check on Anna," I say to them as I head to the house just in time to see Hayley pulling up in her SUV.

She gets out and joins me to walk up to the house. “Did Dad tell you about Grandma?”

Worry etches her face, and her voice is subdued as I put my arm around her, pulling her in for a hug. “I’m sorry, Hayles.”

She nods but blows out a puff of air. “I knew she wasn’t doing well. Apparently, she’s taken a turn for the worse. It just sucks.”

I nod, biting my lip, hating this for her. She has always been so close to her grandma, and they both share a love of baking. Her grandmother owns a bakery in her small town and has run it with her best friend for the last fifty years. This is heartbreaking for all of them as she is the pillar of their family.

“I was planning on taking a trip over, but now I have to stay here to help out while Mom and Dad are gone,” she says, looking upset.

“I’m here,” I say, “If you need to go, I’ll fill in at the pub, bake, whatever you need. I can even come out here and stay if that’s what’s needed.”

Hayley bites her lip as if she’s considering this.

We open the door and head toward a frazzled Anna, who is making frozen pizzas and looks up at us apologetically. I didn’t even know she had frozen pizzas. I’ve only ever seen her cook things homemade. She must be so stressed and overwhelmed.

I immediately get plates and start setting the table. “Anything else I can do to help?”

Anna pulls me into a hug and kisses my cheek. “No, sweets, but thanks. I’m just getting us packed and ready to head out. I assume Mack talked to you?”

I nod. “Nash is going over everything with him now. I’ll help with anything that you need. I have a lot of time because I’m not working at the library right now.”

“I need help cooking and feeding the ranch hands and just

keeping things going so Mack isn't stressed and can focus on his mom." She waves her hand around the kitchen and lets out a deep sigh.

"Of course, I can do that," I reassure her.

"Thank you, honey." Her lips turns down as she pulls out another pizza and cuts it.

I mix up a salad and throw in some veggies she'd already cut up on a cutting board. Tidying the kitchen as I go along to help.

"It'll be okay, Mom," Hayley says as she sets out salad dressing, looking worried.

She lets out a deep sigh. "I know. It just sucks. I thought we had more time with her."

I swallow a lump in my throat. I know the feeling.

CHAPTER 22

Everly

After dinner, which was quick and easy, everyone drifted off to take care of things. Anna was finishing packing, Mack went out to do chores, and Nash took Willow out to ride for a bit before we head back home.

Dinner was what everyone needed, just being together. Nash and Willow got into a thumb wrestling match, which Nash obviously let her win, and she took that as a great triumph, thinking she won against him. Seeing Nash and Willow bond makes me smile, and my heart is lighter and fuller of love than I ever thought possible. Our lives may be a shit show right now, but at least we have each other.

Hayley looks lost in thought. "Let's take a walk," I suggest as I join her in front of the kitchen window that overlooks the barn and pasture.

She nods, and we walk down the sprawling drive leading to the ranch's stone-gated entrance.

"I should have gone over to see her sooner."

"You can't 'should' on yourself and tell yourself what you should have done. You did your best. You've been busy with the pub and your baking business," I remind her as we take in the sun going down over the mountains. I wrap my jacket closer around me as the chill of the sunset sets in.

"Did you ask your dad about going with them?" I ask. "I told you I'm more than happy to bake for you and help with whatever you need."

"I offered, but Dad says he needs me here." She frowns. "All hands on deck."

I nod.

"What about you? How are you doing with Nash and the library? I'm worried about you, too."

"I'm fine. It just is what it is. I think it's another ploy to manipulate me and make me jobless. He thinks he can make me want to move back in with him after doing this."

"No way. You can't go back to the stinky shrimp house," she says with a smile. A smile I know she needs right now because life feels heavy for us both.

"I bet it smells so bad in there. Maybe we shouldn't have done it because now he's back in Cozy Creek more because he doesn't want to stay in his smelly house," I say as I shake my head with a laugh.

"Worth it. He better back off and go back home, or else I'll have to come up with something else," she warns with a smirk.

I shake my head and chuckle.

"It'll be okay. The library is the heart of our town. People are getting wind of this, and they have your back. This won't go down without a fight."

I nod. "I hope so. Things were just starting to go right around here," I say as I look over to where Nash sits on a horse, Willow in front of him, showing her the reins and talking to her, his cowboy hat on his head bent. He gets off the horse, holding her steady and walking with her as she looks over and waves with her little black helmet on her head. I smile, warmth filling my chest. "Nash thinks of everything."

"He's good with her," Hayley says as she watches them do circles in the horse pen.

"Yeah, he is." I wrap my arms around me and smile as I watch them.

"You're going to be alright, Ev. You and Nash will figure this all out."

"A lot is at stake here. If we don't work, what happens to us? We really have no family, then." I swallow a lump in my throat as I tell her this.

"I don't think you have to worry about that," she says as I watch Nash watch me, his face locked on mine with a look of pure love.

"I hope so."

"Hope is not a strategy, Ev. Get him if you want him."

I lean against the fence and watch them. I turn to Hayley and say, "I may not have started out with a family like this, but I'm going to make one."

"You've already got one," she says as she leans her head on my shoulder.

WE GET HOME, and I get Willow settled when I hear a knock at the door. I open it to see Nash with a bag and some tools in his hand.

"What are you doing here?" I hold the door open.

"I came to fix your faucet."

"My landlord can do that. You don't have to . . ." I say before Nash cuts in, and I see his smile dim a little at the mention of my landlord.

"I want to," he says as he gets to work. When he opens the cabinets, he takes out a few cleaners I had stashed down there and sets them to the side. He slides under the sink, and I see his shirt ride up, exposing tanned and muscle-lined abs and my core twitches. Damn.

He works under the sink and then stands and leans and takes off the faucet, tossing it into a bucket.

"I didn't know you were such a handy guy," I tease.

"I am very handy," he says as his eyes slide to mine. "I've learned a thing or two at the pub."

"I see that," I say as I sit at the kitchen counter and resist fanning myself. All of a sudden, Nash is the most fascinating thing to watch.

"Heard anything else from your ex or the library?" he grunts as he tightens the new faucet with a wrench.

I shake my head. "I'm just waiting for the next bomb to drop. First my car, then my job. What's next, my house?"

He looks over and says darkly, "Never going to happen on the last one."

I shrug. "I don't know. Richie seems to always know how to destroy me. I've learned to just wait for the other shoe to drop."

I trace the leaves on the tablecloth and hear Nash tucking tools back into the grocery sack he brought.

"That's your toolbox?" I tease, tilting my head.

"I've actually misplaced mine," he says as he wipes down the faucet where he caulked it.

"Thank you for doing this. You saved me from having to call my landlord. I'm sure he'll appreciate not having to come out and do this." My gaze flickers over Nash, watching for a reaction. "Can I pay you?"

He just looks at me and wrinkles his nose, sending me a look of disdain.

"Can I repay you in another way?" I ask as I bite my lip at my confidence. I haven't been able to stop thinking about Nash. The possibility of touching him, nibbling him, licking him . . . everywhere. And I may have meant dinner, but my own dirty mind took a detour right alongside Nash's imagination, and I like it.

He freezes, then turns to me. "What were you thinking?"

I slid off my stool and close the distance to him, pulling him to me. "I was thinking dinner, but I see where your mind went. Hold on a minute," I say as I step into my back laundry room and reveal the green toolbox.

"Did you forget something when you built my back stairs?" I ask dryly as I push it over to him with my foot as his eyes widen, and he freezes in the kitchen.

"Huh. Got nothing to say, Reed?" I cross my arms and tilt my head, waiting for him to explain.

"How long have you known?" he asks as he bites his lip and watches me closely. Damn. Why does he have to be so good looking?

"Since I found that you'd left your grandpa's old toolbox under my back stairs when you repaired them."

"Are you mad?" he asks cautiously.

"No, but you have some explaining to do."

At first, I laughed when I realized it was Nash. Of course it was Nash. It made sense how we clicked and hit it off so quickly. I decided to let him sweat it out about his toolbox for a little while. It serves him right for lying. Then, the more I thought about it, the more I realized how much he loves us. He just wanted to help us in his own way. How could I be mad at him for that?

He looks relieved. "I'm sorry. I just really missed you. I wanted to talk to you, but when you messaged me, I didn't want you to know I bought the house."

"So you do own this property?" My eyes widen, and I open my mouth, then close it, not sure what to say. He's confirmed all the things I've been wondering.

He nods. "I do."

I laugh and shake my head. "I should have known."

He crosses the kitchen and pulls me in his arms. "I promise I didn't mean to lie. I just wanted to make sure you guys were okay and you would have a safe place to live."

Okay, my heart is melting. I don't like being lied to but what could I say to that? He took care of us in his own way. He loved me even when he thought he shouldn't love me. Even when he thought I didn't love him back.

"Anything else you need to come clean about?" I ask as I look up at him.

"Nope. Wait, yes," he says as he looks at me, then bites his lip.

"Well? Let's have it." I cross my arms, waiting for another bomb to drop.

"I own about half a dozen investment properties around town," he admits.

I tilt my head and look at him in awe. "Nash, that's incredible. Look at you. I'm proud of you," I say as I realize there's so much about Nash that I didn't know.

"Yeah?" he says as he stands straighter, his eyes having so much emotion passing over them. I can tell he needed to hear those words, and based on how he is standing straighter like a flower, he was watered. Based on the wide smile on his face and the profound relief in his eyes as he gazes at me, he needed that.

I kiss him softly. "I wish you could stay. I don't want you to go."

"I can stay for a little while," he says as he sets his stuff by the back door and goes to wash his hands in the sink he just fixed.

"Will you hold me until I fall asleep?" I yawn and cover my mouth.

Nash follows me to my room, and I get ready while he lies on my bed, playing on his phone. He slides it onto the table as I curl into him, and he wraps his arms around me. This isn't the first time we've shared a bed. Hayley, Kincaid, Nash, and I camped all our childhood and curled up in a dog pile to keep warm often while camping. We slept in the old tree house in blankets and sleeping bags countless times, too.

But this time, it's different. I don't want him to go. I want him here. I want him in more ways than just holding me, but I need him tonight. I can't explain it, but I just feel so heavy in my soul today. And the way he's holding me tucked under his chin with his arms wrapped around me, I suspect he needs me, too.

I wake up to my alarm clock going off in a soft tone next to me. I feel the heat against my back and stiffen. Nash.

I glance at my closed door. Willow's still sleeping, but I've never had someone stay with me before.

Nash stretches and whispers in my ear, "I fell asleep. You just felt so good."

"It's okay. We needed it," I murmur as I push back into him, and he tightens his arms around me. I haven't slept well for months, and with him here, I slept so well.

"I am going to head out before she gets up." He sits up.

"Want to pretend that you just got here and eat pancakes?" I grin.

He laughs. "Sure. Then I do have things to take care of."

And just like that, we just became a family.

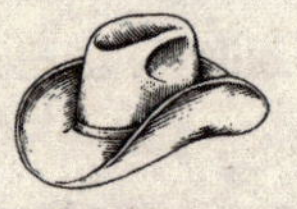

CHAPTER 23

Nash

After pumpkin pancakes and bacon, I head to my apartment for a quick shower. I have plans today but am not ready to share those plans with Everly yet. Waking up with Everly nestled in my arms and spending the morning with my two favorite girls, I felt like we're a real family. Something I can picture and long for every day starting and ending, from now on until forever.

I practically bounce with happiness as I head down to the kitchen and check in with Hayley, who is quiet and brooding as she bakes. She glares at me. "Why are you so chipper?"

Before I can say anything, her eyes widen, and she hisses, "Did you sleep with Everly? You did, didn't you?"

I cross my arms and lean on the doorway. "No, and don't be a dick."

"It's like we've switched places. I'm broody, and you're chipper. Not fair," she mumbles.

I pour myself a coffee and hold it up to her to see if she wants some. She nods, and I top off her Yeti mug with the bar logo on it.

"What's up with you? Other than Grandma. You haven't been yourself lately."

Hayley shakes her head as she stirs something in a bowl and doesn't look at me.

"What are you doing today?" she asks, changing the subject.

"Going over to city hall to talk with Sullivan. Want to come?" I say in a tone that is more clipped than I intended.

I'm going to bat today for the people who I love. I'm not afraid to dig up the dirt and get my hands dirty if it means keeping my family safe and happy. My thoughts drift to when I was younger, when it used to be my fists that did all the talking in fights, but now that I'm older and have much more at stake, I realize knowledge is power. And I'm ready for battle.

A look of surprise passes over her face, and she shakes her head. "Hell, no. I can't stand them. I can't be trusted around them. I can't even fix my face to be normal around them. Plus, I'm too pretty for jail."

I laugh at that. "Yeah, it would be a shame if you went to jail. No one would bake like you do, and we'd all starve," I say as I reach out and snatch one of her mini cinnamon rolls. She playfully swats my hand with a towel, but her smile doesn't reach her eyes, and she seems restless and caged.

"Everly would bake," she says, but it's still not lost on me that she isn't looking like her usual self. She's sullen and subdued, more reserved and sadder. Not the feisty spitfire Hayles that loves to pick at me.

"What gives, Hayles?" I ask gently, noticing her face etched with worry.

She takes out her frustration on her dough and says, "I am upset about Grandma, and I'm worried about Everly and the library."

"It's going to be okay. We won't let them get away with this," I promise. "I'm headed over to deal with that now."

"And you stay out of jail, too. Let me know what happens," she calls as I close the door and head out the back and down the alley to the sidewalk.

"No promises," I call back cheerfully.

I push the door into the glass building of city hall and stride past the receptionist, who jumps to her feet, exclaiming, "You can't go back there. You don't have an appointment."

Richard Sullivan sits at a long table with the town council members with his leg crossed and a smug look on his face that seems to disappear when I walk in. The conversation pauses, and the room feels tense.

"Leave immediately, or I will have you physically removed," Richard spats out, his face growing red. I can tell whatever he was in the middle of doing was not something he wanted to share with the class, and especially not me.

"Calm down, Richard," I say evenly as I stand in front of the room. "The only way I'm leaving is if you make me, and with all due respect, I don't think you have what it takes."

Crickets. Yeah, they didn't expect that.

"Now that I have your attention," I announce. "I think you all should think long and hard before you come after the library or any other buildings already happily occupied. I have dirt on each one of you, and I'm not afraid to ruin every single fucking person in this room," I say as I look at each one of their faces to make sure they know that I see them.

"Your decisions in here today affect the entire town, and you're not thinking clearly," I continue.

Richard starts to interrupt, and I hold up my hand. "With as much disrespect possible, shut the fuck up." I bite off the last few syllables as I glare at him, and he sits back down and sputters.

You could hear a pin drop in the room.

"Working at one of the most popular pubs in town here for the past twelve years, I know who is fucking who, who has a little gambling addiction, whose wife is fucking one of you." The last one got them all looking at each other with suspicious stares. Good, they can turn on each other.

"I will take down every single one of you, and I will enjoy doing it. So think long and hard before you vote to build something in a place that pushes your own agendas and not what's best for this town. You want your arena? Fine, build it somewhere else. I know where all your fucking skeletons are, and I'll lay them out one by fucking one, bone by fucking bone for everyone to see. All. Of. Them. I will simultaneously destroy you all."

I tilt my head to Richard as I notice his face is pale with disbelief and rage. "Anything to say?"

"You'll pay for this," he sputters about as his face flushes red.

"Ah, ah, ah, no, I won't. And you better reinstate the library budget today if you know what's good for you. And Sherry," I say the last part with a smug smile.

"Are you kidding me?" Barry asks since Sherry is his wife.

"You all have a great day now. I'll leave you to it. You have some things to straighten out."

No one in the room utters a sound, and jaws are dropped. I turn and head back out. The door shuts, and I pass the receptionist following me. When I get to the front door, she whispers loudly in awe, "That was *so* awesome."

I tip my hat to her and head out and down the block. I just made a ton of enemies, but I hope I got my message across. If they want to take down the library, they'll have to go through me first.

Everly: Thanks for staying with me last night. Do you have to work tonight?

Me: No problem, beautiful. Yeah, I'm working.

Everly: I'm going to come in and bake for Hayley tonight. Anne Marie is keeping Willow for a sleepover.

Me: Does that mean you get to have a sleepover too? 😈

Everly: Ummmm

Me: Or I can come hold you again, but it won't be until after I close the bar.

Everly: Close the bar early. Lol

Me: So I'll see you at the bar tonight?

Everly: Yes.

Me: See you tonight.

Music plays loudly, and we're surprisingly busy for a weekday night. I'm not complaining. Marcus and I have been going nonstop, and our server staff has been on their toes as well.

We have orders coming and going in the kitchen, and Everly is in the back of the kitchen where the ovens are going. The back door is propped open because it gets sweltering back there.

Everly wears a fitted T-shirt with an apron over it. Her hair is pulled up on top of her head in a knot, a few tendrils trying to escape. Her bright lipstick is on, she's focused and concentrating, and

I try to stay out of her way, but I can't help it. She's there. And I want to talk to her.

Our karaoke event starts at eight, and that's always a big draw for the crowd. Tonight, we have a bachelorette party, and their songs of choice are mostly Taylor Swift. Some of them are good, and the crowd is into it.

Everly comes and stands next to me behind the bar, touching me as she stands close. I wrap my arms around her and pull her in, kissing her cheek.

"I love this song." She sways slightly into me.

"What's it called?" I ask as I span my hands over her abdomen, keeping her close.

"'All Too Well,'" she says. "It's one of my favorites. It's what got me through when I lost you."

My heart sinks, and I lean in to murmur in her ear, "You didn't lose me, beautiful. I'm here."

She breathes a deep sigh and looks up at me as I lean down and kiss her.

"Get a room!" someone teases from across the bar.

"Later," I murmur in her ear.

Her eyes sparkle as she looks at me, then heads back to the kitchen. She's washing dishes now, so she must be close to finishing.

Having her here is what I need.

She approaches the door and motions to me, and I come over. "I'm going home to shower, and I'll be back. I'm covered in flour and sweaty from baking in the hot kitchen. Do you need anything before I go?"

"Got any soup at home?" I'm hungry, and her food has been so good.

"I do. I'll bring food when I return. Think you'll be able to get away and eat?"

I look at her and say, “I can definitely get away to eat.”

And I wasn’t talking about soup.

She freezes, but a grin appears on her face as she takes off her apron and throws it in the linens bag.

“See you soon,” I call as I work to get everything cleaned up and ready for close.

“What?” I say as I stock all the clean glasses and wipe down the bar, one of our regulars smiling smugly.

“You got it bad, man,” he says as he takes a pull from his beer.

I know I do. Everly is it for me. Always was, always will be. I will do anything to make sure I don’t mess this up with her.

CHAPTER 24

Nash

Everly comes into the bar and heads turn. Her long hair is down and wavy. Her makeup is subtle but sexy, and she has on tight jeans and a tight black top that hugs her curves like it was made for her. I hate it and love it at the same time. I mostly hate it because heads are turning and looking at her, and I want her all to myself.

Her black boots have a heel to them and make her seem taller. She saunters up to the bar, giving me a flirty smile, and slides onto a stool. She has a bag next to her and sets it down on top of the bar.

"Hey, bartender, give me your best drink," she says with a flirty voice to me that goes straight to my dick. Just watching her mouth makes me hard and want her.

I grin at her and make her a cocktail I think she'll like.

"What is it?" she asks as she sucks on the straw, and I have to take a deep breath. Her hands hold the drink, and her nails are dark plum purple. The way she holds the drink makes me think of her hands wrapped around my cock, and I try to get it together.

"Toasted pecan old fashioned," I say as I take a deep breath and watch her beautiful lips wrap around the straw.

"Are you okay?" she asks, tipping her head as she sips the drink.

"No." I shake my head, wiping down the bar.

"Can I help you with anything?" she asks innocently, which only makes me want her even more.

I look at the last few customers and wish they would leave now as I nervously run my fingers through my hair.

"Yeah," I murmur as I lean in and whisper in her ear.

She takes a big swallow but looks at me with desire in her blue eyes. "I'm staying with you tonight."

I tilt my head back and groan. "I want this pub to close now."

She looks at the clock behind me. "Fifteen more minutes. Play 'Closing Time' now, on *repeat*."

I laugh and pull out my phone to pull up the app that plays our music. I play "Closing Time" so people know it's time to get going. I've already called last call, and I'm ready to be with Everly.

Marcus and I get everything cleaned up and closed, and we lock the door when the last straggler leaves at five after.

"You got the rest?" Marcus calls, and I wave to him. "Thanks, man."

Everly has disappeared into the kitchen and is heating the food she brought. She brings out two bowls of soup and two plates with grilled sandwiches and sets them at the bar. I sit beside her, and we eat while discussing our days. I learned that she is a night owl like me and likes to stay up and sleep late. She tells me that doesn't always work out with Willow, but she prefers nights to days.

"Do you want kids?" she asks me.

"Yes," I say without hesitating. "I want a house full. I told you that the other day."

"Do you want to get married?" she continues as she finishes her soup, watching me.

"Weird way to propose, but yes," I say as I dip my sandwich into the broccoli cheese soup and take a bite.

Her eyes are wide. "I didn't mean . . ."

I know what she meant, but I turn to look at her and lean in. "Everly, I'd marry you right now if I could. *Right fucking now.* You're it for me. Let me make that very clear. You and Willow are mine. Just as I'm yours."

Her mouth is open, and she quickly closes it. Her eyes are locked on mine, and they're full of what I hope are happy tears.

"Do you feel the same way about me?" I ask her as I swallow, suddenly not sure of how she'll respond.

She nods. "Yeah, Nash. I do."

I lean in and kiss her gently, pulling her toward me on the stool. She's my soulmate. I know it, she knows it, and I appreciate the fact that we didn't spend time messing around about this. I don't want to waste another minute not having her as mine.

"I'm going to marry you and be a father to Willow. And I'm going to have as many babies with you as you want. We're going to build our dream house on the property and have horses, and everyone will be happy like we deserve."

She gulps and nods and leans her head against mine. "But I haven't seen the property. I don't know if I'll like it," she teases.

I grin as I run my fingers over her rib cage, tickling her. "Oh, you'll like it."

"I will?" She laughs.

I take her hand and lead her onto the floor of the pub and hold her close. "We can take our time making a thousand memories." I pull my phone out and push a few buttons to play a song for her. Her favorite song "All Too Well" comes on. "Then I'll play your favorite song so you can make a new memory of this one."

She quirks a brow and says, "Better be the ten-minute version."

I laugh and say against her mouth, "Oh, definitely. I'm taking my time with you." After listening for a bit, I lament, "This is a sad song."

"Yeah, but I like it," she murmurs.

I listen to the song as we dance, and I hold her. Something pulses between us that feels like forgiveness and starting new. We have a ways to go to heal, but I feel like things are so much better between us.

"I thought of Taylor Swift as just a pop artist. How am I relating to her songs?" I tease as I spin her around, my lips grazing her neck, and our hands intertwined.

"I'm sorry I hurt you," she whispers.

"I'm sorry I hurt you, too," I murmur into her ear. "I promise to make it up to you."

"No matter what happens, we will be there for each other," she declares as she looks up at me, her eyes full of promise for our future.

"I'm never letting you go again," I say as I lean down to kiss her. She kisses me back, her arms wrapping around my neck as our song comes to an end.

With a flash of my hand, I push our dishes off the bar in front of us, and I pick her up, her legs wrapping around my hips as I cup her bottom and set her on the bar. I kiss her deeply, hungrily, and that kiss spirals us into a needy desire.

Her hands are around me, cupping my face, pulling me in, her tongue touching mine, wanting me as much as I want her. I want all of her. Every piece. The piece that makes her an amazing mother, my best friend, and now my lover. At this moment, nothing else matters as long as she's mine and I'm hers.

She reaches up and pulls my shirt up over my head. Her hands caress my chest, her eyes on me, wanting more.

I press into her, showing her how I need her, want her. She gasps, kissing my neck, her hand sliding down and over my crotch, my breath catching.

"I can't have our first time be in the pub. On the bar," I say as I pull back, dropping my forehead to hers.

Her eyes widen, and she says, "I kind of like it. We're making a memory here. So every time you're working, you'll remember this is where it happened."

Her hands go to my pants, and she kisses my neck, tasting me as she works to unbuckle and push them down. She pulls me closer as she runs her hands down my sides and kisses me deeply. My hands do the same, and she kicks her boots off, her jeans sliding down to reveal the sexiest black lace panties.

My eyes come to hers in shock. "Is this what you've been wearing the whole time under your clothes?"

She laughs. "Yeah. I love sexy bras and underwear. It's kind of my thing."

I look up at the ceiling. "How did I miss out on this? I can't even handle this."

She steps back and pulls her sweater up over her head, exposing a lace bra that has her breasts toppling out of it, the black lace making me strain against my boxers.

"Oh my God," I breathe.

"Do you like?" she asks in a husky voice.

"I love it," I say as I pull her to me and say in her ear, "I'm going to fuck you so hard on this bar that you'll feel it for days and want more."

"I already want more, and I haven't even had you yet," she says with a smart mouth that I take my time kissing, my hands exploring her cheeky panties that I make disappear in one move, making her gasp.

"Don't rip them," she says.

"I'll buy you an entire room full of lingerie," I say as I kiss my way down her breasts, reaching back to unsnap her bra, getting her just the way I want her. Bare, exposed, and mine.

I clamp my mouth around her nipple, and I suck deep, causing her to moan and grasp my hair, clutching it as she tenses up. God, I could probably make her come just by sucking her tits.

I make my way down and find her wet and ready for me. God, she's so fucking wet. "You wet for me, beautiful?"

"Nash, if you don't fuck me so hard on this bar, I'm going to lose it," she whimpers.

I reach for my wallet and pull out a condom, quickly ripping it open.

"Can't have that now, can we?" I take off my boxers and pull her to face me, finding her pussy just as wet and ready for me as I cover her with my mouth, her moans getting louder.

"Nash . . ."

"Come hard, Everly, do it," I say as I work her hard, making her writhe and breathe deep, panting as she continues to pull my hair, and I fucking like it.

She tenses and lets out a small moan. "Oh my God."

She releases, and her body melts as I hold her. I make my way down her body, kissing her the whole way, stopping to take my time on her breasts as I feel her tense again.

"That's been a long time coming, sweetheart. I'm going to make sure you have this on the regular, like you deserve," I murmur.

"I need you . . ."

I turn her on the stool so she is bent and slide into her. She stills and moans in choppy pants.

"You okay, beautiful?" I ask as my eyes drift to hers, feeling deeply connected to her after all this time. It's so much better than I ever could have imagined. She fits me perfectly, gripping me tightly until my breath hitches and I see stars.

The scent of her hair—vanilla and coconut—pushes through my senses. The taste of her skin and the moans and pants from her mouth heighten the experience.

I can't wait to take my time with her, but right now, we're frantic. It's happening faster than I'd like, but we need each other urgently.

I want to be able to take my time memorizing and kissing every freckle and beauty mark. I want to map out the expanse of her graceful back, tracing her curves to remember every small detail about her.

She yelps and whimpers for me to go faster, and I lose my mind with pure sensation, giving all the power to her as her tight, wet heat hurls me over the edge. My jaw tenses and teeth grind as a low growl emanates from me, and I lose control.

"Are you okay?" I ask softly in her ear as we both come hard, and I feel boneless. And judging how I'm holding her up, she feels the same.

She wraps her arms around my neck. "If I'd known that's how it would be, I would never have left that night. I need your good, Nash. All the good things that make you. Your love, your fierce protectiveness, your heart. I need you."

"You didn't know, and you did what you thought you should," I say as I cup her jaw, making her look at me. "No more regrets, yeah? You have me."

"Yeah," she says softly.

"Now let's go upstairs to my apartment, take a shower, and I'll hold you until you fall asleep."

"Again?" she asks in a hopeful tone.

"Again and again," I tease as we pick up our clothes. She runs to the back stairs, squealing and laughing as I chase her and smack her ass playfully.

CHAPTER 25

Everly

Sun streams in the big windows, and I open my eyes, forgetting where I am for a moment. Then I remember that I'm at Nash's, and Willow is sleeping over at Anne Marie's since school is out for fall break. I checked my phone, and it's late. We slept in. There's a picture from Anne Marie of Willow and her having breakfast at the diner, and they're both smiling and sharing a stack of pumpkin pancakes. God, I love these two.

And unfortunately, six missed calls from Richie and several texts. I still laugh when I see the name that Hayley changed his contact to and saved in my phone.

Little Dick: Where are you?

Little Dick: Answer me.

Little Dick: I went by your house, and no one is there. Where's my daughter?

Little Dick: You are going to lose Willow.

I roll my eyes and slide my phone back onto the bedside table. It's too early for his bullshit. I need to seriously get a restraining order. This has to stop.

Nash sleeps next to me, his face toward me, and he looks so peaceful as he sleeps. His dark eyelashes are full on his cheeks, and his cheeks are scruffy and in need of a shave that he probably won't get to, and I will admit that I like it that way. It makes him feel rough and dark. I resist the urge to reach out and trace his jaw. Even though I want to, I don't want to wake him up.

I think about what he said last night that Willow and I are it for him. And he has no idea how much that meant to me to hear it. I can't remember a time when I didn't love Nash. He's always been the one I think about, default to, and dream about. And having him here with me and no longer being a dream but a reality is surreal.

His eyes open, and he looks at me, brings his arms over, and pulls me close. "Why are you staring at me like a creep when I sleep?" he murmurs as he kisses my forehead and pulls me closer.

"I wasn't," I deny but curl into him.

"I forgot to close the blinds last night," he complains as he buries his face into my neck. "Too bright."

I sit up and straddle him, and he grabs me and pulls me into him.

And I show him what a good morning it is.

"You want coffee?" Nash calls as he stands in his small kitchen and holds up a mug toward me.

"Yes, I need coffee. Like my soul *needs* coffee," I say as I take the mug and moan a little as I sip it. Heavenly.

"Did I just fall in love?" I say out loud.

"With me or the coffee?" he says as he snaps another pod in the coffee maker.

My eyebrows quirk as I look at him, taking in his muscles made by hard work and not the gym. Damn, Nash is so hot under his clothes.

"Is coffee all it takes?" He sounds amused as he brews himself a cup and watches me, his arms folded across his bare chest.

"You keep bringing me coffee like this, and you've got yourself a wifey for lifey," I tease back.

"Again, weird way to propose, but yes." He shrugs his shoulders playfully and brings his mug to his lips.

I laugh and then say more seriously, "I've missed you, Nash. You always made me laugh."

His warm whiskey eyes look at me and say, "Missed you too, Ev."

"So much has changed. We've changed," I say quietly.

"We have changed," he says as he lightens the serious mood. "Most people thought when I was in high school that I would wind up in jail."

"You still have time to live up to their expectations," I tease.

"After watching Richie pull his shit, it's not hard to imagine living up to," he agrees, but I can tell he's not serious.

"What's going on with the assault charges from the bar?" I ask him.

"He's trying to get them dropped," he says as he takes a sip of coffee and leans against the counter.

"He needs to be held accountable. He's a loose cannon." I frown.

"Funny, I'm the one we thought was the bad boy, and your ex is the one in trouble now." He sets his mug down and pulls me toward him, tucking a tendril of hair behind my ear.

"You're still a bad boy," I whisper, his dark goatee growing in and in need of a shave.

His head dips, and he kisses me, tasting like coffee and mint. The bad boy he tries to be isn't there. He's a good guy deep down, and we both know it. This town knows it. Nash has grown into a good man.

HAYLEY COMES INTO the pub kitchen in the back after taking Anna and Mack to the airport. "I brought coffee."

"Hey, how are you? Everything good with Mack and Anna?" I ask as I wipe my hands on my apron.

"Yep, this trip will be good for them. They haven't both gone together in over a decade. Usually, one of them takes turns going to see Baa," she says as she sets two coffees down and heads over to put on an apron and wash her hands at the sink.

"I worked out a schedule with two other people, and we have one schedule set up to make food and another for the ranch," I say as I pull bread out of the oven. "I shared it with you."

"That's why I'm glad you're helping. You're so organized. I don't know how Mom and Dad do all they do with the ranch. They need this break," she says, wiping her hands on a towel.

"You're here early today. What time did you get here?" she asks as she checks some of the bread and bags up the ones that have cooled off.

"Willow was with Anne Marie, so I figured I'd get a head start," I say, not looking at her.

Hayley stops and turns. "You stayed here last night, didn't you? Wait, gross, I don't want to know." She holds up her hand, laughing.

I finally meet her eyes and say guiltily, "I did."

She twists her mouth in a grin. "'Bout time."

"What's that supposed to mean?"

"You know what I mean. It's about damn time you and Nash got your shit together. I need you to become my official sister."

"Well, that seems fast, but I'd be honored to be your official sister-in-law. Maybe someday." I shrug, then add, "Do you think I'm crazy for just jumping in with him?"

"Well, first, you didn't just jump in. You have been in love with him since elementary school, and him with you."

"There was a pretty big break between there."

"So what? People grow up and go through things. It matters that you found your way back to each other," she says as she puts a load of bread on a tray to take out front.

I nod. "Yeah, I just don't want to mess things up. It's going well. Finally. But when Richie finds out I'm with Nash, he'll get even worse."

"Yeah, well, we're all sick of the satchel of Richards. Karma is going to get them," she points out.

I glance at my watch and look over. "I have to go get Willow."

"Thanks for catching up the baking. These loaves look amazing. Are you sure you don't want to be a baker, not a librarian?" she teases as she sips her coffee.

"Why can't I do both?" I say as I take off my apron and hang it up. "Can I take a loaf to Anne Marie?" I ask as I grab my coffee and purse.

Hayley waves. "Of course, anytime. Tell her I said hi."

"I will. Thanks, see you out at the ranch tonight. I'm staying out there with Willow. And Nash," I add with a smirk before I duck out and hear her reaction.

I make my way to my car, relieved that she's cool about Nash and me. It's still new yet not new in ways, but honestly, I don't know what to think. I'm still processing it all. It's not really a new relationship because we were close.

I don't remember a time in my life when the McCreedys weren't an important part of my life—except when I was with Richie. And it made sense afterward that anyone who keeps you from your family is a toxic person.

I stop by Anne Marie's and park in front of her small house with a bright pink front door.

She's sitting on a porch swing and sets her book down when I walk up the sidewalk. She smiles when she sees me. "Hi, sweets. Is that bread for me?"

"You know it. How's your day going?" I ask as I take in her face—no lipstick or makeup—and her eyes are suddenly more tired than I've ever noticed.

"I'm trying to stay busy. It's hard not being at the library, and everyone is upset. I am just waiting at this point to hear what the next move will be. I tried to keep it open anyway, but they shut that down, too," she says, sadness and frustration covering her face.

"We're going to fight this," I declare. "They won't get away with this."

"I know." She nods as she stands and holds the door. "Let's have some tea and toast."

Knowing she needs this time with me, I follow her in and pull out a cutting board. I slice the bread while she brews tea for us.

"How was Willow?" I ask as I grab the pumpkin butter from the fridge.

"Darling as ever. I love that girl. She reminds me so much of you at that age," she says, her face brightening at the mention of Willow.

Right here and now, watching her try to hide her sadness and her love for me, my daughter, and this town, I make a decision.

I'm going to fight so hard for this library. I will do whatever it takes to make sure that we get it back and this bullying from the Sullivans stops. Whatever it takes.

We sit and drink tea and catch up for a few minutes. But my brain spins with ideas. I'm going to be there for Anne Marie and the library the way she's been there for me.

CHAPTER 26

Everly

We pull up to the ranch, and I've barely got the truck in park before Willow scurries to unbuckle and bounds out of the truck, slamming the door without even looking back.

"Willow!" I shout but can't help but laugh, shaking my head. She's already disappeared into the barn, where she'll likely spend the rest of the evening. I'll have to drag her out to eat and to sleep.

A truck pulls up behind me and stops. A man gets out. He reaches into the bed of the truck and hefts up two large bags. He sets them on the side of the driveway and lifts a hand and waves as the truck backs out and leaves.

I stuff my hands in my pockets and wait as he turns to me. "Everly, what are you doing here?"

"Kincaid?" I say, surprised, as I take in the tall, handsome cowboy in front of me. He wears Wranglers, or more like the Wranglers are wearing him. Kincaid has always been the golden retriever version of Nash. Nash is more of a German shepherd, but both are very good looking. That McCreedy blood flows strong in these men.

I cross the distance and hug him as he pats me on the back with a wide grin. "I haven't seen you in a spell."

"It's been a while. I heard you were on the pro rodeo circuit showing bulls who the boss is," I tease. I haven't seen Kincaid since that night we moved back. But honestly, other than thanking everyone, that night isn't one that I remember a lot. I remember being so tired.

"Something like that," he says as his mouth quirks up on one side. "Where's Willow?"

"She's in the barn. Where she lives now," I joke. "That kid loves horses. This place is a dream for her," I say as we both head toward the big door of the barn.

"Momma, come see Waffles," Willow calls from one of the back stalls.

Willow stands in front of the baby donkey, stroking his head as she speaks to him softly.

Kincaid whistles through his teeth and says, "It's like looking back in time at you, Ev."

"You're not the first person to tell me that today," I say as I reach for the jar of apple cookies on the shelf and take a handful to give to Willow.

"Keep your hand flat like this." I show her.

She giggles as Waffles tickles her fingers with his mouth and nose.

"Want to help me with chores?" Kincaid asks as he leans against the stall, stroking Waffles and giving him a good scratch on his neck.

"Yes!" she says excitedly.

I smile. "Honey, listen to Kincaid and do what he says. I'm going to go start dinner."

I return to the truck, take out our overnight bags and my purse, and hurry up the front porch steps.

I stop and look back over the horizon at the sun starting to turn to the golden hour and the shadows it casts on the barn and porch. I sigh and breathe out. It feels like coming home when I come out here to the ranch.

I get to the kitchen, and the casseroles for dinner have been prepared. About a dozen hands work on the ranch, and they have their own dining area here at the main house with a door off to the side. They have a refrigerator stocked with snacks and various foods ready to eat. But there's always a hot breakfast and dinner for them. They have lunch boxes that they stock from the refrigerator for their lunches.

I read the note left by one of the other rancher wives sharing the work rotation. I have two dinners to prep and prepare for the next one for tomorrow, and there was a grocery delivery coming that I need to restock the refrigerators with. I check the breezeway and find the items stacked in boxes and grocery bags. I begin to haul everything in while the ovens preheat for the casserole. I set out plates and silverware and get everything stocked and set up. While it cooks, I prep the roast, potatoes, and carrots for tomorrow to keep the schedule flowing. It's been cool to see how many people show up for the McCreedys and help them when needed.

I look up and see Nash's truck pull up and park beside the farm truck I've borrowed. I smile and grab a towel to dry my hands. I see him start to head this way, and he stops to pick up Kincaid's bags that he'd left out there and bring them inside.

"Hey, Kincaid's here. Those are his." I point at the bags he set on the floor.

He looks relieved. "Good, I thought maybe a ranch hand threw in the towel. We can't afford to lose anyone, especially not now."

"I'll have you know my cooking hasn't scared anyone off yet," I say as I refill the butter container and slice the bread.

"Beautiful, the way you cook, the ranch hands would be doubling if other ranches got wind of your cooking," he says as he washes his hands.

"Aw, thank you. I try." I lean over and kiss his cheek.

"What do you need help with?" he asks, drying his hands on a towel.

"I'm all set in here if you want to go check on Willow and Kincaid. She's supposed to be helping with chores. He jumped right in, didn't even bring his bags in." I laugh, gesturing to the bags.

"Sounds like Kincaid. I know he's missed home. Glad to have him back."

"How long is he home for?" I ask as I pull hot casseroles from the oven and set them on the counter.

"Not sure, but I'll go get them for dinner," he says as he slides on his hat and steps in his boots.

I lean up and kiss him. He pulls me into him and pushes me up against the doorframe, my body melting into his.

The door to the side dining room opens, and a bunch of loud ranch hands come barreling in, interrupting us. One whistles and cheers us on as they see us break apart from kissing.

"I better get to them." I laugh as I straighten my hair and shirt.

"I'll go get our girl," he says as he ducks out.

Our girl.

That sends a warm zing through my body. And I can barely focus as I get everyone fed and clean the kitchen up as I go. It feels like home, and I don't want to leave. The only thing missing is Anna and Mack.

Nash heads back to close the pub, and Hayley comes in as I finish the loaves of banana bread for tomorrow morning. As an extra treat for the hungry staff, I threw in a few dozen pumpkin muffins, too.

I love being out at the ranch, baking and cooking, I realize as I finish cleaning the kitchen.

"Hey, hope you saved me something." Hayley looks exhausted as she kicks off her shoes and throws her hair up in a messy bun.

"Of course I did," I call as I turn off the oven, removing her plate. "How are you?"

"I'm fine. Just finishing up some inventory and our order at the pub."

"Where's the farm truck? I didn't realize you guys were here," she says as she heads to the oven.

Her eyes are tired with dark circles under them. I know she's close to her grandma, and hearing that she's not well is taking its toll on her. But I sense it's more than that. Something is going on with Hayles.

"I think Kincaid has it. He's back," I tell her as I slide her plate over and grab her a fork.

"He probably went to the pub, and I just missed him. Darn it," she says, taking the plate.

"Where's Willow?" Hayley asks as she sits at the counter and takes a bite.

"She's upstairs in the shower. I practically had to drag her in here since she insisted on saying good night to every single horse and donkey. Twice."

"That probably took a while." Hayley chuckles.

"She loves it here. Are you sure you won't miss this place when you leave?" I ask, gently bumping her shoulder with mine.

"Of course I will. I just want to travel. I can't explain it. I just have this urge to go explore and get out there."

"Then do it. We only get one life. Go find your hot Irishman," I say. "Hey, it's the opposite of your parents. Your dad came here and met your mom. You would go there to meet an Irishman. It's so romantic. I mean, this is like a Hallmark movie."

Hayley tries not to smile. "I just want to have fun. I think I'm giving up on finding love. I'm not even sure it exists anymore at this point."

"What exists?"

"Real love. What my parents have is something that usually only exists in books or movies." She quirks a brow.

"I don't believe that," I say because deep down, I've always been a romantic. I've always believed in love; I just didn't have it. Until Nash.

"Maybe you're the walking, talking Hallmark movie," she says as she looks over to see Nash come across my phone.

Nash: I'll be back late. But wanted to say good night to you.

My heart beats quicker just seeing his text.

I'm in so much trouble. I'm living in a freaking Hallmark movie. And I don't hate it. I love it. I want that for Hayley, too. Even if it's not perfect, love is messy sometimes too.

CHAPTER 27

Everly

Saturday morning is here, and we've been staying busy out at the ranch. I've realized there's always something to do out here. The work never stops. I've slept so well every night after working out here. I have a new appreciation for Anna and everything she does for the ranch. I've always known how hardworking she is, but now I am seeing this in a completely different light. And I love every bit of it. I miss the library, but working out here has been cathartic in so many ways. Slow starts to the morning while the sun rises wrapped in a blanket on the front porch with a steaming mug of coffee. Seeing joy on Willow's face and watching her with all the animals. Being out at the ranch is healing a part of my childhood wounds that I didn't realize I had.

And the best part is seeing Willow with Nash. Seeing them play and joke around and have the biggest smiles makes me indescribably happy.

Willow sleeps so well every night with all the fresh air and energy she burns off during the day. She goes to bed exhausted and wakes up barreling and ready to go. Taking care of the animals is a chore we don't have to argue about her doing. She can't get enough of them.

I clean up after breakfast and am relaxing on the porch with my book when Nash pulls up and parks. I've read the same page over and over for the past thirty minutes because I can't focus. My mind is all over the place right now.

He comes over to the porch with his grin, tanned skin, dirty T-shirt, and faded jeans that fit just right, stopping to talk to Willow on the way. She's entertaining herself by trying to get the feral barn cats to come to her. I tried to tell her most won't come to her, but she's bound and determined to make them all her friends. She's been able to get a few of them to eat out of her hand.

"Hey, handsome," I call as I stand, setting my book down.

"Hey, beautiful."

He crosses the yard, dips his head, and kisses me.

"Any plans today?" he asks. Leaning against the porch railing with his bicep stretched, he makes me feel hotter, and then I glance up at his face. He's watching me in amusement.

"Nope, just hanging out. It's been nice just being here."

He reaches for my hand, tracing my palm with his fingers. "Want to take a ride?"

"Where are we going?" I ask as I look over at Willow. She's now over by the fence waving at a horse who trots over to her. The horses adore her, and she's made friends with them as they follow her around the pasture like giant puppies. Their preferred currency of apple treats doesn't hurt either.

"You'll see," he says casually, but I can tell he's up to something.

"What should we wear?" I ask, trying to get some information out of him.

He's not falling for it. He glances down at me. "What you've got on is fine."

"Should I bring anything?" I continue, hoping he'll just give in and tell me. He knows I hate surprises.

He leans into me and boops me on the nose. "Pack a picnic for the three of us. We'll be gone for a while."

"Okay," I groan in frustration at his lack of sharing.

I CARRY A thermal bag with food and a cooler of water when I see Nash and Willow waiting in a UTV in the driveway. I place the food in the little storage space on the back and slide in next to Nash.

"Are we going to your property?" I ask him, excitement filling me.

He looks at me with his eyes hidden behind his aviators, under his cowboy hat.

"No."

"No? Where are we going?" I ask him, confused that we're in the UTV and not his truck. Surely, that means we're staying on the ranch.

"We're going to *our* property," he says as he starts to drive.

Willow pipes up. "Can we move there? I want to live out here."

I laugh it off, but I melted at his words. *Our* property.

It's only a short ride through a path I hadn't noticed before, but I recognized a few places from riding horses when we were younger. We finally pull up to a gate, and when Nash gets out to open it, Willow leans forward. "I like him, *so much*, Momma."

"I like him, too, baby," I say as I reach back and squeeze her hand.

We drive around, and Nash points out where he's set up a tiny home that is nothing more than the size of a garden shed. He drives around the entire property, and we end up back by the pond.

"What do you think?" he asks, looking at me and waiting for my reaction.

"It really hurts watching other people live my dream," I tease as I take in the gorgeous property. It would be a dream to live out here and see this view every day. And I'm not just talking about the mountains. I'm talking about him. I love him so much it physically hurts my heart sometimes. I take in all the fall-colored foliage reflecting off the pond.

"I can help you live out your dream," he says as his arm comes around me and pulls me closer, turning to kiss my head.

Willow's busy removing fishing poles from the back of the UTV in excitement. We set up on the dock. I set up our picnic blanket and spread out the food and drinks that I packed.

"Where will your house be from here?" I ask as I look around.

Nash points everything out to me, and I picture what it would be like to live out here with him every day. I shudder with goose bumps as I put my arm around his waist.

Our property.

Sometimes I wonder if we're moving too fast. Then I think about what Hayley said about us knowing each other for so long, and it feels like we're behind and not moving fast at all.

Time means nothing when it's real.

It's about damn time.

I wonder if that's what he thinks as I look over and see him calmly helping Willow with her fishing pole. She sits in her little chair beside mine, her hat that she borrowed from Nash pulled low, watching patiently for a fish. I think about how special it is that we get to do daily life like this, and it feels good. We don't have any drama or hard stuff out here. Life is easy and good. As it should be.

It's far more beautiful out here than any picture anyone could paint. The sky swirls with big, fat, fluffy white clouds, and the foliage is stunning, the property covered in mature trees mixed in color and evergreens.

He looks over at me and leans back, looking relaxed. His long legs stretch in front of him, his hat pulled low. He looks so damn good.

Almost as if he could read my mind, he grins slowly at me. I blush and look away. Caught.

"You know Hayley asked if she could have a little sleepover with you tonight, Willow," he says softly as she looks over at him.

"Really?" she asks. "Does she have a cool property, too?"

He nods and points. "Hers is over there. She already has a house on hers. Kincaid has a property over that way, but he doesn't have a house on his yet. It's just land for now," he says as he points in the opposite direction of Hayley's.

If Hayley has Willow, I can have some alone time with Nash. And I'm not going to turn that down. I love that Willow loves spending time with Anne Marie, Anna, Mack, and Hayley. She loves her new added family, getting spoiled and loved. Both of our hearts are so full and happy now back in Cozy Creek and my only regret is that we didn't move back sooner to experience this together.

"Will you be okay on your own, Mom?" she asks as her sweet face takes in mine, full of worry.

"Mom will be okay," he says as his sunglasses come to land on my face.

"I'll be just fine." I nod. "Are you sure you don't want to stay here with us?"

"She said next time we do a sleepover, we could do our nails," she says, looking hopeful.

LUCKILY, HAYLEY WAS just as excited about her time with Willow as we suggested and understood we were looking for alone time together. She rolled her eyes and chuckled, teasing us.

Nash's tiny home is surprisingly bigger than I expected and is really cool inside. He even has a bathroom, a shower, a full-sized bed, and a small closet. I took the tour, which took less than a minute due to its size.

"This is so cool. Why is it you don't live out here?" I ask as I trace the tiles on the tiny kitchenette.

He shrugs. "It's not big enough for someone to live here full time, and it's not as fun out here by myself. And I work so much that staying at the bar is more convenient. When I close, I can just go upstairs and crash there for the night. It's just easier."

"That's fair. But imagine getting up to see this view every day," I say as I look over the pond and mountain view.

"I do imagine this view every day," he says, but he's staring at me and not out the window.

He wraps his arms around me and pulls me into him as we take in the view together.

"Can you see us living here?" he murmurs into my neck.

I look up at him and tip my lips to his, and when I pull back a little, I say, "I could live anywhere if it feels like home. And you feel like home, Nash."

THAT NIGHT, WE sat by the firepit wrapped in blankets, staring at the stars and dreaming. We talked about everything from the past to the present. Things got emotional at times, but it felt good to get it all out, and it feels like we can both take on anything.

Listening to Nash talk about how he still feels unseen and not good enough in town broke my heart.

"You know you are an incredible man, right? Look at what you've built for yourself. You have three successful businesses, and you are going to build your dream home on your family's land. You are so handsome and so strong. You are a walking dream," I say, looking up at the stars.

Suddenly realizing he's quiet, I turn my head to look at him, and he's on his side watching me, emotion etched across his face.

"What's wrong?" I whisper, suddenly filled with worry that I said something wrong.

"I love you," he says quietly. "I always have and always will."

A lump forms in my throat as if he's said the most precious thing to me. Because he has.

"I love you so much. I'll spend every minute of the rest of my life loving you extra for all the time we lost."

He leans in and kisses me softly, his lips soft on mine, tender and loving. "We're gonna mess up, Ev. But the making up is what matters. We're forever, baby."

"Okay," I whisper.

He pulls me in closer, his hands rising to cup my face as he kisses me harder now, pressing me close, protectiveness radiating from his body.

He kisses me down my neck and across my jaw. His hands span across my ribs, and his knuckles graze my breasts, making my nipples pebble and harden for him. I arch my back in pleasure and moan into his mouth, making him groan slightly in return. I turn and straddle him on our bench, and he pulls the blanket around us tighter. I kiss him, my hands fisting in his hair, pulling him closer to me. Grinding on him, I feel him hard under me, ready for me.

He stands, picking me up. My legs wrap around his waist as I kiss his neck. He carries me to the back of his truck with the tailgate down. He pulls me to him after he lies down in the truck and kisses me softly, whispering that he loves me again into my ear as he takes his time kissing his way down my body as I slide down my leggings, pulling my shirt off me.

When I'm down to my panties and bra, he leans back and watches me in awe. "You are the most beautiful woman I've ever seen."

He leans down and kisses me again before I can speak, kissing me softly, showing me his love, and I have never felt more loved than I do at this moment with the way that he looks at me.

He slips a finger inside me and works me while he kisses me. My body feels like it's going to come apart, and I feel like he's just getting started. His mouth works me, kissing me like I've never been kissed before. God, I needed this. I needed him.

While I'm looking at him and up at the stars, my body shudders, and I come hard with whimpers mouthed into his. He kisses me softly, murmuring, "I love you."

"I need you, Nash," I say quickly, pulling his jeans down, him helping me urgently as he slides on a condom and fills me, stars in the sky, his body connecting with mine and my soul feeling complete with him. He makes slow, sweet love to me, alternating hard thrusts with a slow pace, and then kisses me while he fills me and completes me.

He builds up an urgent pace and whispers in my ear, "Mine."

He comes hard, his body tensing and tightening up around me, and my body clenches, feeling like stars shattered in the sky around me.

His hand wraps around mine, and he holds me close as we stare at the stars, holding each other.

Mine.

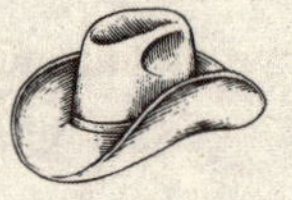

CHAPTER 28

Nash

Everly and I fell asleep in the back of my truck, staring at the stars after the best sex I've ever felt in my life. Being with Everly is just . . . everything, and it feels right. She's my everything, and I think I've always known it. But time hasn't always been on our side. And now that we have this second chance, we are going to make it. It's our time.

When it got too cold, I carried her into the tiny home and settled her under the covers. I cranked the heat and joined her, her body snuggling into mine.

I've always liked being out at the property. But when I stayed out here, I was restless and never relaxed. It was lonely and felt empty. A lot like my life did before Everly and Willow came back into it. Now it feels right being out here with them. It's like I can see clearly now what I'm supposed to be doing and who I'm supposed to be doing it with. Them.

The following morning, I woke up to the smell of coffee and bacon—two of my favorite things. I open my eyes and forget where I am for a moment. When I turn, she's got a blanket around her shoulders, standing at the stove in the kitchenette. Her hair is up in a messy bun on her head, a pair of sweats and her makeup-free face making her look beautiful.

I stare at her and think about what she said last night, telling me that I'm her everything and how proud of me she is. She'll never know how much that all means to me. But none of those achievements ever meant anything without having her. The years she wasn't here just melted into each other and felt like they were nothing. Just years that I didn't have her, and she had a kid and a life without me. Like what I was supposed to have and felt, in my bones, I had lost. That's enough to gut a man. But having her here in this place I bought and set up, hoping she'd someday somehow come back to me, really come true, it's surreal.

She turns and realizes I'm awake and smiles. "Hi."

"Hi," I say softly back.

"How did you sleep?" she asks softly.

"Good, and you?" I roll over, not waiting for a response. I stand, crossing to her and taking her into my arms, kissing her, and pulling her into a strong hug.

"I slept better than I have in years. This place is magical," she says as she waves her hand around the tiny home and toward the windows where the pond glitters from the morning sun.

"You should get used to it." I grin as I go to the coffee pot and pour a cup.

She makes two plates for us, and we make our way outside to the table and eat, watching the birds. She says softly, "Nash, look."

I glance over, and three deer stand on the far edge of the pond, drinking and eyeing us cautiously.

"It's like the three of us in deer form," she jokes as the two bigger deer and baby deer wander off to graze when they realize we won't bother them.

I chuckle, but I think about our future home here. I picture the huge front porch where we'll play with our kids and later grandkids. Horses, cattle, goats, barn cats, and dogs. A big kitchen where we'll have huge family dinners and a home full of laughter and fun. What I had growing up and what I want to have with my family.

It's what I've always wanted, but only with her. After feeling this with her and being out here, this is it. I can see it now. I want this, and nothing else matters. Life can try to take us down, but if we have this, it doesn't matter.

I POUR AN order of beers and slide them across to a few locals, then turn when the door opens, and Kincaid comes strolling in. I've noticed something has been off with him since he returned. We're all stressed about Mom and Dad and Baa. But they've kept us updated, and she's taken a turn for the better, which is a good sign. Mom and Dad have been taking care of her. But something is off.

He slides onto a stool, and I head over and say, "What'll it be, little brother?"

"A beer would be good, thanks." He runs a hand through his messy hair. Usually, Kincaid is the happy-go-lucky guy who is always having a good time and is the life of the party. And this guy before me looks stressed and put off by something.

I slide the beer over. "You alright, man?"

He exhales and tips the beer back and takes a long pull, setting the bottle down. "Yeah, I'm good. Just came to hang out. Needed to get out of the house."

I nod. "You just seem . . ."

"I'm good," he clips.

I put my hands up. "Alright."

"We can talk about you, though. Fill me in on what's been going on here and with Everly," he says, looking relieved to take the focus off himself.

It's been nice having him home, and I hope he stays for a while, but as restless as he's been acting, I'm not sure that will happen.

"It's been good," I say cautiously. "Hayles is thinking about taking off for a while to travel, so I might need some help around here if you are thinking about sticking around."

"I'm not baking, man," he says as he looks at me like I'm nuts.

I laugh. "I need bar help, not baking. Everly has been covering that. And we can always scale that back when she returns to the library. It was just a great side hustle for Hayles. She's always got to be baking something. It's like breathing to her or something."

"I saw the library is temporarily closed. What the hell's up with that?" he says, crinkling his eyebrows with concern.

"Richard and Richie Sullivan trying to screw Everly over and using the town projects and their wallets to do it," I say as I stack clean glasses down below the bar from the clean tray. "Town's fighting it."

"So what are we just not going to have a library? That's messed up." He shakes his head.

"I think they have plans to rebuild it somewhere else in the future, but they want that part of the town property for a tourist attraction. An arena."

"That's the stupidest idea ever. Our town doesn't need a huge arena in our downtown area."

"That's what I thought when I first heard about it," I agree.

He takes another pull of his beer. "So you and Everly finally got your heads out of your asses, huh?"

I playfully punch him in the shoulder. "Whatever."

"I'm happy for you both, man."

"Thanks."

A look of something passes over his face but I don't want to push him by trying to pry and I say, "What's next for you?"

"Getting tired of always being on the road. It's been fun for years, but now I'm just tired. So fucking tired. Like I don't belong anywhere." He shakes his head and stares off at several people playing pool in the corner.

"Tired of the buckle bunnies?" I tease.

He chokes on a swallow of his beer. "Yeah. I'm tired of buckle bunnies."

"Maybe you need to find a nice woman in Cozy Creek and settle down."

"That's the thing. I don't know if I want to settle down. I don't know what I want." He shrugs and peels the label off his bottle.

I see a lot of where I was in my brother now. I was lost like him and took on too much work to stay busy and not feel loneliness and hurt. I looked for a lot of distractions that helped me stay busy.

"You could travel like Hayley," I suggest as I pour myself a soda and take a sip.

"I wanted to come back home, but I don't know what to do here. I feel like an interloper who doesn't belong," he says as he looks up at me with frustration.

"I was serious. You can help run the bar with me," I offer.

"I don't know. But you don't want me baking," he says seriously.

I laugh. "I'm sorry, just trying to picture you baking. Like you'd be one of those Muppets in the back in a chef hat and hit the bell when orders were up."

"Did you just call me a Muppet, you dick?" he says with a scowl and a hint of a grin.

"Nah, I'm just messing with you. But we'd have fun," I say as I snap a bar mop and wipe down where the glasses sat and try to picture Kincaid here.

"We would," he agrees.

I look over as the door opens. Willow and Everly step in, and Everly scans the room and settles Willow in a booth by the window.

I cross over, kissing Everly on the cheek and squeezing Willow's shoulder.

"How are you guys? What are you doing here?" I ask as I try to hold back my stupid grin from just seeing them here.

"Well, Willow told me she's never gotten to come in here, and we thought we'd come and order sandwiches, some fries, and maybe a root beer." She smiles at Willow.

"Well, we can make that happen. How about I eat with you guys?" I offer.

"Yes," Willow says excitedly, scooting over in the booth. "Sit by me, Nash."

"Okay, let me go put in our orders first." I smile as I head back to the bar and ask Kincaid, "You want to eat with us?"

He glances over at Everly and Willow, and Everly waves and smiles at him. I see him smile and wave back. "Yeah, sure, man."

Kincaid is a lot more relaxed now, and I realize it must have been hard for him to come back after being gone a while. That was probably how Everly felt, too. I should have been there for her instead of giving her space. But I think she needed to find me on her own terms.

Kincaid looks back at me and says quietly as I put in the order at the computer, "She's a good one. Don't let her get away again."

"I won't," I promise as I turn to put the order in, realizing nothing is coming between them and me. No one. Ever again.

CHAPTER 29

Everly

"Thank you," I call as I wave to my cashier and head out to the truck. Two big bags of groceries are on my arm, and a coffee is clutched for dear life because, good Lord, I need it today. Life has been busy but good. Too good. I've started to worry sometimes that the other shoe will drop, but I refuse to live like that anymore. I want life to be good, and I'm choosing the good stuff. Willow and I deserve the good stuff. That's the mantra I keep telling myself, anyway. I smile as I feel the cool fall air on my face, and my boots squish the leaves beneath my feet.

I open my truck door and put the groceries in the back. I turn to get in the driver's seat, and Richie stands in my space. I jump, and my iced coffee pours down my front. He stands back and smirks.

"Found your shrimp," he says, practically spitting with anger.

"Why did you do that?" I shriek as coffee runs down my front, silently thankful that it was iced and not hot. I look up at Richie in horror, and he just laughs and smiles with satisfaction.

I shake my head as I reach for napkins in the glove compartment, coffee dripping down my front.

"You deserve it. You know what you did." He sneers and moves closer into my space.

I flinch and back up. "Get away from me, Richie." I nervously scan the parking lot. People are starting to watch and talk, and a few people come closer when they see him.

"No, you listen to me," he bites out and points a finger in my face.

I rear back from him and squirm to try to get away, and he moves in closer, pressing me between the seat and him like a vise. My stomach lurches from where his body touches mine. Fear clogs my throat, making my voice come out as a croak as I try to yell for help. My stomach cramps up with nerves. Richie is unpredictable and feels invincible, so there's no telling what he would do to hurt me, witnesses or not.

Fear pulses through me. "Help!" I finally find my voice to yell.

He continues pressing into me and doesn't back off as he demands, "You call McCreedy off. Tell him to stop coming to my dad's work and threatening my dad and me. This arena is happening, and you'd better stay out of it. You hear me? I will take you to court and take custody of Willow. I'll take everything from you. I will call in witnesses that will tell tales of you spending all your time in the pub just like your daddy and spreading your legs for every man in Cozy Creek. I will take her from you. You want that?" he grits out and adds, "Because I will do it."

I glare at him, tears piercing my eyes, and say nothing. I know he doesn't really want Willow, but I don't think he's bluffing. He will do this to me. He's already tried to sabotage me in every other way. I don't give him the reaction that he wants, so he continues.

"Why don't you ask your little fuck boy about his little property investment company and his investments in the new arena? You think his hands are clean in all of this, but they're not." He smiles as if he's proud of the ace card he just played. Just like he always does.

"Get away from me!" I scream at him. I see Kincaid come around the corner, and he gets between us.

Kincaid yells, "Get away from her!"

"You fucking him, too? Both brothers, huh? She wasn't *that* good, man," Richie sneers.

Kincaid raises a fist and rears back, and I watch as Richie looks triumphant like he's about to win, and I yell, "No! He's not worth it."

Kincaid stops. He gets in front of me, blocking me from Richie.

Richie turns to leave and calls back to me, "See you in court."

"What was that?" Kincaid asks as his arm is still in front of me. He pulls me in for a hug, and I realize I'm shaking and still covered in coffee.

"He was threatening to take Willow from me," I say, hot tears streaking my face in embarrassment and anger as I look at people watching me.

"Where's Nash?" Kincaid asks, searching my eyes, worried.

"He's doing farrier work today. It's okay, I'll be fine. I just need to get these groceries home and get cleaned up," I say as I look for my keys that had fallen on the ground.

"Okay, can I drive you?" he asks.

I shake my head. "I'll be fine, really, but thanks."

He watches me get in the truck and drive off and my hands shake as I pull up and park behind my house. I quickly put away my groceries and think about what Richie said. Surely, he's lying. Nash wouldn't lie to me about being involved in the library teardown. How could he? There's just no way. I fume as I wring my hands and then think, *I have to know.*

Part of me wants to believe that Nash would never do that and lie to me about it. But he did lie to me about being Reed and owning my rental house. I know he had good intentions, but he did lie. Would he lie about this, too? And another part is telling me that things have been going too well, and now they are falling apart, just like everything does in time. It's like I can't have anything good in my life. Everything will be taken away or destroyed, and I can't be happy.

I need to talk to Nash and figure this out. I can't keep going like everything is great when it isn't.

Me: Where are you?

Nash: Just got back to the pub and getting ready to take a shower. Want to join me? ☺

My stomach dips at this. I question how I could believe that he could have anything to do with the arena and the Sullivans. There's just no way.

I grab the keys and my purse and head to the pub. The only way to know is to confront him and get this over with.

"Where's Nash?" I ask as I come into the back of the pub and shut the door. I round the front of the pub, where only a few patrons are playing pool in the corner.

Nash looks over, his hair still damp, and his face freezes when he sees mine. "What's wrong?"

"What did you do to the Sullivans?" I ask as I fold my arms and wait for him to answer.

He looks confused. "What are you talking about?"

"Did you go into Richard's office and threaten him?"

His jaw hardens. "Yeah, I did."

"Why did you do that?" I ask, my voice shaking. "He's making things even worse for me. I didn't need you to go in and go commando on them."

"I did what I had to do," he says as he crosses his arms.

"What you had to?" I bite out. "You didn't have to do anything. You don't have to play the big bad wolf and try to save me from all my woes. I never asked you to do that!"

He glares, and his eyes narrow. "What's this about?"

"I don't need you to fight my battles for me," I continue.

"I . . ." he starts to say.

I hold up my hand. "And you lied to me."

"I didn't lie," he says, looking confused. "What did I lie about?"

"You know what? I was crazy to think we could make this work. I shouldn't have trusted you. You're just like them," I say, my voice breaking.

"Just like who?" he asks, now looking concerned and less angry.

"You're not who I thought you were, Nash," I bite out, angry and confused. "This was a mistake. You are not a nice guy."

I say these words, and once they've left my mouth, I know I can't take them back, and they're coming from a place of self-sabotage. I let Richie get inside my head, and I hate myself for this right now, but I can't take this back. I'm already feeling so far gone at this moment with anger, frustration, and helplessness. These emotions are rioting through me, and I need to get out of here. Step back from all of this and protect myself and Willow.

Now Nash looks pissed. Really pissed. "I never said I was a nice guy, sweetheart. But I have always been who I am, and that's okay because I'm a *good* guy. I'm fucking whiskey, not tea. And if I recall, you like your whiskey. And when you're ready to hear me out and really listen, maybe you will let me explain things to you and stop assuming shit you hear from your asshole ex-husband."

I stand back and swallow and shake my head and turn and storm out. He's freaking impossible. I look back through the doors and tremble as he leans on the counter, watching me intensely while looking like the sexy asshole that he is. Deep down, I want to think he wouldn't screw me over, too. Just like my dad and Richie. I won't let myself be hurt again like they hurt me. I can't take it. Not from him. I have to stop this before that happens.

I leave the truck and walk to the library, swiping angry tears along the way. The library isn't open, but I need to be there because it's my safe space. I slip my key in and am relieved that it's empty and quiet.

I find Anne Marie in the back going through paperwork, her glasses perched on her nose when I walk in. "Hey," she calls as she comes around her desk and pulls me in for a hug.

"What are you doing here?" I ask as I take a seat across from her desk.

She sits back down. "Just missed being here."

"I think everyone misses it," I say sadly.

"Let's talk about why you're crying, missy," she says as she scoots her chair across from me and waits for me to talk.

"Nash. He butted in and messed with the Sullivans about the library, and now Richie is threatening to take Willow from me. He said that Nash was involved in the arena project. I know you know he has a property management company," I say, and she doesn't look surprised.

Unlike me, she waits until I'm finished because she's a good listener. Probably comes with wisdom and being older.

She takes her glasses off, and they dangle on their chain, and she says, "I do know about his property management company, but I didn't know he had anything to do with the arena, and that surprises me. I can't see him being a part of anything like that. Our town means a lot to him, and he wouldn't do something that would hurt our town."

I wait for her to continue. See? I can practice listening.

"And since your boy toy went commando on the town board, things have been quieter. I think they're realizing that we're not going to just lie down and take it. We might win this, Everly. He might have done some good with that," she says softly as she looks at me, making me realize I overreacted.

"I don't want to believe either that he'd get involved in demolishing the library, but he did lie in the beginning about owning my dad's old property that we live in."

"You need to talk to him, honey. Give him a chance to explain. Why didn't you give him a chance to explain?" she asks as she searches my face for answers that I don't have to give.

"Because I didn't want him to hurt me like they did," I whisper.

It's stupid, I know. I self-sabotaged myself so that he couldn't hurt me, too. I close my eyes and realize what I've done. It was immature and stupid.

"Everly, he's not like your father or Richie. Nash isn't perfect, but he's a good man who loves you very much. Anyone can see that. Why can't you?"

"Because if he hurts me, I don't know if I can come back from it. He is . . . he's the love of my life. And I need him not to hurt me. I need someone to not hurt me," I say with a tremble.

Her hand comes over and covers mine. "Honey."

I look over at her, and she says, "Talk to him."

I nod and stand, and she gives me a big hug. The kind of hug my soul needs, and I let her hold me extra. "Love you, honey," she says.

"Love you, too," I tell her, exhaustion filling me with the emotions of the day.

"Call me when you get home and settled," she says as I head out.

I need to talk to Nash since I reacted and not well. I need to fix this, but now I'm wondering if I can. This fight reminded me of that night I turned him down and left.

I get myself together and pick up Willow.

If you wondered if this day could get any worse, well, it can. Willow was happy to see me, and we headed home. As soon as I got in the door, I started heating dinner. I flip through the mail and see an official letter and open it. I scan it quickly and mutter, "You've got to be fucking kidding me."

I have a letter saying that I missed jury duty and now I face a possible one thousand dollar fine and 90 days in jail, depending on the judge.

What the hell? What jury duty?

I look at the clock and realize I have a few minutes before city hall closes. I quickly called to ask, hoping this is a mistake.

Kathy Wilson answers, and I say, "Hey, Kathy, it's Everly." I explain everything to her, and she listens.

Then she says in a condescending tone, "We take jury duty very seriously here, Everly. That was very irresponsible of you. I hope you have arrangements for that sweet daughter of yours if you must serve jail time."

I hang up on her. She's a monster just like they are. Richard did this. I can tell. When will they leave me alone? What's next?

I want to call Richie and scream at him, but that's what he wants. And I don't want to give him any sort of reaction. I hate him so much. Even worse now.

I slump against the counter, defeat filling me. Come and arrest me, do your worst. I'm done. I can't take anything else today.

If you wondered if this day can't get any worse, well, it can . . .

"Mom! The bathroom is full of water!" Willow yells from down the hall.

My eyes widen, and I dart down the hall. "No . . ."

I rub the bridge of my nose. I don't want to call him, but I know I have to. I pick up my phone and go to text Nash but then scroll down and click on his property management number and text that number instead. Because I'm not ready to face Nash yet. I'm going to keep it professional and show him that I just need him to be the landlord, and that's it. I'm still getting pummeled by life, and I can't take him not forgiving me and accepting that I'm a train wreck.

Me: The bathroom is flooded, and I need help.

Reed: I'll be right there.

I LET HIM in and disappear into my room while he fixes the water heater leaking in the closet next to the bathroom. I hear him talking to Willow, and she asks if he's staying for dinner. She's excited and tells him that tonight's soup is her favorite, and he has to try it.

I don't hear his response, but they continue talking like nothing happened.

I busy myself in the kitchen, and he comes down the hall, his flannel rolled up at his forearms looking hot, and I look away.

He stands in the doorway and says, "It's all fixed."

I don't look him in the eye because I know I won't be able to keep it together, and today has just been so much. So much. I just want to go to bed and cancel today. I want him, and I want space. I don't even know what I need right now. I need to not be sent to jail by my daughter's asshole father.

He looks over at Willow and says, "I have to get back to the pub, but I'll see you another time, kiddo."

She looks disappointed and nods as she goes back to her room with her head down. I hear her door shut, and I look over and he's watching me.

"I'm dealing with a lot right now."

"What are you dealing with?" he asks.

"Things that aren't your problem, Nash. I can take care of myself."

"I know you can," he says firmly. "But why should you have to?"

I hold tight to these tears, not letting them loose. I keep them tight and tucked away just like I'm used to doing to protect myself.

"I have your back, Everly. Always have. You don't have to turn around to see if I'm ever still here. Because I've always been here and always will be."

I say nothing because I'm a coward and don't know what to say without crying.

"Jesus, Everly, even your kid gets it. When will you?" he says quietly. "I'm not them. I'm not going anywhere, and I'm not going to screw you over or hurt you."

"People like me don't get to have people like you in our lives. *I'm* the person who takes care of other people. I am a mom. I have to take care of my kid and protect her and me. I'm all she has now. I can't let her get hurt the way I'm used to getting hurt. It's not fair to her."

"That's complete bullshit, and you know it," he says, his voice cracking. "You know none of that is true. You're just pushing me away, and it's not fair."

I look away and blink back tears. "Yeah, well, life's not fair. Not for me. You should go."

When I finally look up, he's closing the back door. It clicks quietly, and he's gone.

I don't deserve him, and I can't risk what I had with him going to shit, so it's probably safer if I just end it now. *It'll protect me,* I think as I look at our now cold soup and wonder how did my life get to shit like this so fast. Richie destroys anything good in my life. I'm also mad that I took a chance with Nash and let myself hurt him again. I need to get my crap together.

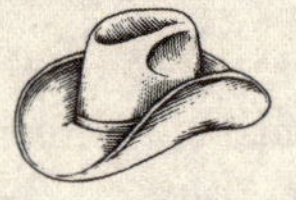

CHAPTER 30

Nash

I should have finished closing up an hour ago, but I can't stop replaying everything in my head. Why would she think that I could have anything to do with the library bullshit? The truth is that when the project came up, I had been approached by another property management company in an email asking if I would want to invest in the project. Initially, I said I was interested, but after reviewing the other investors, I said no thank you. I don't do business with the Sullivans. I never even knew the full project scope and what the investment entailed. I didn't even make it that far with any of that. How that fuckwad Richie found that out, I have no clue. Snakes have a way of getting in the crevices and wreaking havoc.

This hurts. She broke me years ago, and it feels like she's doing it again. And this time, it's worse because if I end up losing Everly, I lose Willow too. I love them both so much.

I cash out the register and shut it down, sliding our bank bag into the safe. I turn when I hear the front door to the pub shut heavily, cursing myself for not locking it.

"We're closed," I clip in a firm and irritated tone, hoping to deter anyone who was ballsy enough to walk right into an obviously closed pub at three o'clock.

And there she is. She's standing there in her long coat, pajama pants, a hoodie, and her hair pulled up in a messy knot on top of her head. Her face is hesitant and full of sadness and regret. She looks like a mess. A beautiful mess. My mess.

My heart softens. She's here.

We stare at each other longer than we should have, and I can't remember who started moving first, but we move toward each other. Before I can stop myself, my mouth is on hers. She presses hers firmly into mine, and my body relaxes into her.

I wrap my fist around her messy knot of hair and cling to her with relief washing over me.

Am I dreaming?

I must have said that out loud because she snorts with laughter and shakes her head at me.

She smells real, light, fresh, and delicious, and I kiss her again, hoping she feels how much I love her.

"I love you, and I'm sorry, Nash," she says as I pull back and search her eyes.

"It's okay, beautiful."

"No, I was wrong and immature to walk out like that. I should have let you explain. I trust you, and I love you so much, Nash. I just . . . I'm a mess. I don't even know," she says as her voice cracks a little and wavers.

My hands cup her jaw, and I say, "I would never have invested in that project. When I saw who some of the other investors were, I immediately pulled out. I never even saw where they had planned to put the arena."

She nods. "I'm so sorry for assuming something like that and listening to Richie. I'm an asshole."

I shake my head and say softly, "I missed you."

"I missed you, too. I don't like fighting with you. It's the worst."

"Where's Willow?" I ask her, relieved that she's here and we're fixing this.

"At home. Hayley stayed over, and she's asleep in the guest room," she says as her wet eyes reach mine, searching for reassurance.

I let out a deep breath of relief. "We're going to fight. And then the best part? We're going to make up. Want to make up with me?" I ask her before my mouth lands on hers, kissing her and pulling her tight into me, my hands on her waist.

She reaches for her coat. I say, "Hold on," as I jog over and lock the front door and come back to her. With one swoop, I pick her up and throw her over my shoulder while she squeals, and I take her up to my apartment and swing her onto my desk. It overlooks the bar on one side, and on the other is a full panel of windows with a view of the town and mountains.

"Where we started . . ." I murmur as I kiss her neck.

"We started long before this," she murmurs back.

"A few weeks ago, when you came up here, I felt like we finally had another chance, and I will do anything not to mess this up again," I tell her. "Anything for you, Everly."

I need her, and she needs me.

My hands pull her coat off; her hands unbutton my flannel and pull my T-shirt up and over my head.

I slide her hoodie up over her head, and she's not wearing a bra, thank fuck. Her nipples are hard and hot for me, and I lean down and take them one by one in my mouth as she arches her back and leans against the window, her palm holding her up. The lights are off, and the only light in the room is the moon shining on us. No one can see us up here, but we have a full view of the town.

"I love you so much, Everly. You're mine, and I'm yours," I murmur into her neck, kissing her feverishly with need.

Her hands slide down my hard cock over my jeans, and my breath hitches. I practically hiss I need her so bad as I strain against my zipper.

"I love you, too," she says as she pushes me back and then turns me around to sit on the desk. She moves between my legs and unbuckles my jeans, and I'm pulling them down as she's reaching in and wrapping her hand around me.

"We should make up more often." My breath hitches as she takes her time licking up the side of my cock.

She looks up at me and takes me in her mouth. Her hand moves up and down, and I grit my teeth. "Everly," I bite out as I hiss and lean back against the window, feeling like my body will explode.

I watch her, and she watches me. She moves her mouth on me, and I finally reach under her arms and pull her up and spin her around to face the window.

I slide her leggings and panties down and reach between her legs. She's already wet for me.

"Jesus, Everly," I say as I kiss her neck.

"I need you, Nash," she whimpers as her body trembles.

"See this town?" I say to her as I enter her. She looks out the window as I slide in and out of her. "No one in this fucking town will ever mess with what we have. We fucking own *our* story. And no one will take what we have."

I slam into her over and over, and she cries out my name, her palms on the window as I fill her and feel her body tense and collapse around me.

"No one, Everly. Say it."

She nods and turns her head, kissing me, and says, "No one."

"What we have, people write fucking stories about. The way I feel about you is unmatched to anyone else."

"I love you, whiskey," she says softly, making me smile.

"I love you, too," I say as I smack her on the ass and go clean up.

"I have to get back to the house. Hayley is sleeping over tonight," she admits.

"I'm coming with you." Hayley will kill me in the morning when she comes in and realizes I didn't finish cleaning up the bar. Tonight, I just want to hold my woman.

I drive us back to her house, and we quietly go in and get into bed, and she curls into me.

I don't fall asleep as quickly as she does, and I realize I've never felt my heart so full before. Whatever happens, whoever comes up against us, we will fight it. Because what we have is worth fighting for.

The following morning, I'm pouring my coffee when my sister comes out of the guest room, yawning. She doesn't even seem surprised in the least to see me in the kitchen.

I hand her a mug.

"Thanks." She accepts it and heads to the fridge for creamer.

"I didn't get the pub cleaned up from last night yet," I tell her quietly as we stand next to each other at the counter, nursing caffeine.

She shrugs. "I'll get to it after I get my bread going. I figured you were busy," she says, giving me a look.

I roll my eyes. "Mom and Dad are coming back in a few days."

She nods, looking sad. "I don't want to lose her. I hate that she's been sick."

"I know," I say as I set my cup down and put my arm around her. "It's going to be okay."

But the reality is that she's not doing well, and it probably won't be okay. But whatever comes our way, we're a family, and we'll get through it together.

Hayley heads to the pub to bake, and I bring Everly a coffee. Her dark blond hair is fanned over her pillow, and she is sleeping hard and solid.

I set the mug down on her bedside table, and she opens her eyes and smiles sweetly when she registers me. "Nash."

I crawl back into bed beside her and pull her in, kissing her head and holding her.

"I have to get up," she mumbles.

"No, you don't. Let me get Willow to school, and I'll come back, and we'll spend the morning together snuggle fucking."

She smiles sleepily. "Okay."

"Tonight is the fall festival, and I wanted to take you and Willow. I noticed it was on your fall bucket list," I say as I nod toward the direction of the kitchen table, where the brightly colored list waits patiently for Willow to cross off fun items on the list.

"Yeah, that would be really great." She yawns as she slides her hand into mine, and her eyes drift closed again.

"I also saw your jury duty letter," I say as I swipe a tendril of her hair back.

Her eyes open again, and she looks at me more awake, propping herself up on an elbow. "Yeah, that's Richie and his dad messing with me again."

"I figured. You know we're going to get that thrown out, and he can probably get fired for that," I say as I trace her shoulder with my fingers.

"I just want it to stop. I want them to leave me alone."

I nod. "Me, too. When is the last time Richie saw or spoke to Willow?"

She pauses, trying to remember. "It was sometime in the summer."

My eyes widen. "That's been months."

Unbelievable. I don't want to miss out on anything with that kid. And instead of spending time with her, he's trying to figure out how he can hurt and destroy her mother. And for what, because she left him? He needs to get over himself.

She nods. "He doesn't really want anything to do with her or her with him. The feeling is mutual. They've never really connected."

"I'll be here for her. Always," I promise as she lays her head on my chest.

Her face softens, and she leans up and kisses me softly. "I know. And we'll be here for you. Always."

CHAPTER 31

Everly

The smell of kettle corn and cider fills the air, and Willow practically skips between Nash and me as we hold her hands. I love seeing the excitement on her face as she takes in the fall festival. It takes me back to when I was a kid and felt the same way. I have a few memories of being here with my mom before she got too sick to take me. Then I remember Anna taking me with her kids, and while I missed my mom, the fall festival was one thing I looked forward to every year and missed when I had moved to another town with Richie.

The Cozy Creek fire brigade has its vintage red fire truck decorated for fall next to the town hall, with firefighters standing in front grilling hot dogs and handing out candy. We pass by vendor tables, sampling the legendary fresh fruit jam from the local Sutton farm and checking out tables by local artists. I see Lu Billings, a local artist, and look through her gorgeous art prints. Nash tells me to pick one, and we'll hang it out at the tiny home. We settle on a gorgeous mountain view watercolor, and she packages it up for us. We thank her and continue to shop. When we walk by a city hall booth, Kathy Wilson stands there talking to Richie's parents, and their eyes narrow when they see us walk by. Willow doesn't notice them, and they make no effort to say hello to her or acknowledge her. It dawns on me that she doesn't even recognize them. *Nice.* I exhale a deep breath and glance around nervously, wondering if Richie is here. I hope he isn't because I don't have the energy to deal with him or his trouble. We turn and keep walking, not looking their way or acknowledging them. The old me would try to smile, wave, and people please. I am not doing that to people who are intent on destroying me and everything that I love. If Richie wants Willow, which he doesn't, he can take me back to court. I'm done putting myself or my daughter in toxic environments to keep the peace. There is no peace when it comes to any of them.

No one.

I think about what Nash said as he fucked me up against the town windows. People can try to do whatever they want, but it's us against the world now. Not against each other. Whatever comes our way, I have him, and he has me. We are family now. We always were family, but now it's official and real. I squeeze his hand and look up at him as his eyes meet mine. He smiles, and the corners of his eyes crinkle.

God, I love this man.

The great pumpkin hunt has begun, and we laugh as we race and help Willow find a pumpkin to add to our growing collection that we still need to carve. So much laughter fills the air with the music, and the night is perfect weather for this. It's cool but not cold and feels and smells crisp. There won't be too many days like this before the snow comes and blankets our sleepy mountain town and turns it into a winter wonderland that attracts tourists, making it a busy time for the town.

After our pumpkins have been tucked in the back of Nash's truck, we play carnival games. Nash wins Willow a big stuffed ghost, which she jumps up and down with excitement over and insists on carrying with her despite its large size.

We sit and chat with Anne Marie and share treats while Nash goes to the cider stand for us.

"You look so happy, honey. I'm so glad you and Nash got your head out of your butts," she says as she plays with Willow's hair, who sits in front of her.

Willow laughs, and I cover my mouth. "Anne Marie," I warn quietly, but I can't help but smile. I love that she's in my corner, too. We're used to her just saying what comes to mind by now. And I will take anyone in my corner that I can. I've had too many shit sandwiches in my life not to know when I see someone good. I may not have had a supportive parent or spouse, but now I'm building the good around me, and Anne Marie is one of the most important people in my life.

Nash carries our cider over to us and hands a cup to each of us and slides in next to me, draping an arm around me like it's the most natural thing to do. My body still reacts to him, and a happy buzz fills me, having him nearby. He feels safe, secure, and makes me feel relaxed. Something I haven't felt for a long time.

We play tabletop games with Willow. We laugh and cheer each other on until Willow is lying on us, worn out from the day spent playing in the fresh air and hopped up on too many fall treats. After a dinner from the Tres Chica's food truck, Anne Marie pulls me aside and says, "Let me take Willow home and get her to bed. You two stay out a little longer and have fun. I know you look forward to this festival every year. Make the most of it." She winks.

"Can we read more of our book?" Willow asks with a yawn, looking at Anne Marie hopefully.

I chuckle. "I'm not sure she'll stay awake long enough for the book."

I look at Nash and back at Anne Marie wistfully. "It is one of my favorite events of the year. I wouldn't mind taking a sunset gondola ride with Nash," I admit. His gaze is on me, but he's unable to hear what we're saying. His mouth turns up, and he looks so good. His eyes on me make my stomach dip, and I smile back at him.

Nash and I hug them and wave as they make their way the few short blocks back to the house.

Nash takes my hand, and we head to the gondolas, where people take in the sunset and mountain views.

We get coffee while we wait, keeping our hands warm since the temperatures have dropped. I lean into Nash, and he wraps his arm around me, dipping his head to kiss my cheek.

"I love you," he says softly.

"I love you, too." I smile.

"What are you thinking?"

"I'm thinking that this has been one of the best days I've ever had, and I'm not ready for it to end yet," I admit.

"Well, it's a good thing it hasn't ended yet," he says as we're almost next in line to get on the gondola.

The ski village is busy with people mingling and taking rides, and the ski bar is busy and loud in the distance. A few people give us curious glances, noting our intertwined hands.

When we both slide onto the gondola and pull the bar down, Nash pulls me in and places his arm around my shoulders. "You ready?"

"For the gondola ride?" I laugh.

"No, for our next step. Our new life. We took a chance on what was right in front of us the whole time."

I nod. "In you, I've found my best friend, my lover, and my protector. I love you, Nash."

He leans in and kisses my lips softly, then pulls back, looking at me.

"Our love story is a mess. We have torn pages and missing chapters," I say as we look down at our town lights. The festival is still busy. People are dancing and filling our Cozy Creek downtown.

"It doesn't matter what the mess looked like. It matters that we keep writing our story and make an epic epilogue," he says.

"Then what?" I prompt.

"Then . . . we write the sequel." He leans in and says, "Spoiler alert: the next book is even better."

"Speaking my literary language." I smile.

He squeezes my hand, and we kiss again, only pulling apart when some of the people across from us on the gondola cackle and call out, "Get a room!"

We walk the town together, hand in hand, sending a message to everyone that we're together. Neither of us is bothered in the least. It feels good to finally get to be with him and not care what anyone thinks. This has been the best day.

"What are you thinking about?" he asks as he holds my hand, warming it with his.

I take a deep breath and exhale as I think about my father being unable to love me and then moving on with his new wife and step-daughters so easily.

Somehow, I always come back to the self-doubt that I'm hard to love, and if I wasn't, then why do all the people in my life not love me or keep me safe?

"Do you think I'm hard to love?" I ask quietly.

"Beautiful," he says as if the breath has collapsed his lungs.

I look over at him and wait for his response, wondering if we'll be able to make it or if this is just temporary.

His hand tightens in mine, and he spins me to look at him, wrapping his arms around my waist. "You are not hard to love."

"That's what Richie told me once. I was too guarded, too hard to love."

"No." He shakes his head.

"Why didn't my dad love me, then?" I ask, defeat filling me just saying it out loud.

"I don't know why Brian let you down in ways a father should never let down his child. And I don't know why Richie did that, too. The cards you've been dealt have been a shitty hand, Everly. Sometimes we need to reshuffle the deck. I haven't had very many relationships and never a love like ours. But I do know this—when the right person loves you, it's not hard. It's just love."

I nod and swallow. "Okay."

His face dips to mine, kissing me and making me almost forget that feeling of not feeling loved. Almost.

CHAPTER 32

Nash

"Did you see this, boss?" Marcus asks as he plops down some mail on my desk when I look up from my laptop.

It's been a few days since the festival, and I'm going through emails, paying bills for the business, and putting in an order.

"What is it?" I ask as I slide on my glasses and pick up a letter on the top of the stack.

Marcus crosses his arms and waits, looking pissed.

I scan the notice, and anger fills me. "What the hell?"

It's a certified notice saying that our liquor license is in question, and we have been identified as an establishment accused of serving minors.

"That's not true," Marcus bites out, looking defensive. He crosses his arms, shaking his head.

"I know," I agree. "I will give you one guess where this stems from. It's another attack from the Sullivans."

"Well, it's war because I won't risk my job. I didn't ask for any of this." Marcus shakes his head angrily.

"I'll handle this," I say as I run a hand down my face and over my jaw.

Marcus gets back to work, but I can tell he's worried. We've never had anything like this happen. My staff has always been extra diligent at checking IDs, and we've never served anyone underage. This is complete and utter Sullivan-manufactured bullshit.

I'm sick of this guy. He's coming for Everly, her job, the library, and now my pub. I've worked too damn hard to build a legacy for me and my future family for this guy to come in and mess it up. He had a chance to have a family, and he threw it away. I'll be damned if he messes up what I've worked hard to build here.

Richie thinks that the more he throws at us, the more inclined we are to give up and wave our white flag in surrender. But what he doesn't realize is that the more he tries to ruin and hurt my family, the more ammunition and determination that gives me. The more I'm ready to go to war for them.

I grab my keys and head out.

IT WASN'T HARD to find him. He was at the country club with his parents having lunch when I stormed through the club, heads turning as they watched me approach their table.

Recognition passes over his face when he sees me across the room coming toward him, and then his face darkens. "How did you get in here?" Richie practically spits out as I stop in front of their table.

"Coming for my pub? Really?" I look at their faces as they shift uncomfortably in their chairs, looking around to see who is watching them.

"I don't know what you're talking about," Richard clips as he tries to sit up straighter in his chair, shifting nervously.

"Oh, I think you do," I say casually.

"You need to leave," Brenda Sullivan hisses in a whisper, looking around embarrassed.

People are watching, and judging by the pursed lips and shaking heads, they are sick of the Sullivans too.

"No, I'm good. You see, I don't think you realize what you're doing. You're going to sink your ship and never come back from this," I say in an even tone, watching Richie and Richard exchange a look.

They know exactly what I'm talking about.

"Everly and I are together. We're a family. I will be around Willow, and I will show up for her and take care of both. I won't tolerate any disrespect toward either of them or anyone else in my family. You better wrap your head around this. Because this isn't going to end well for any of you. Do you understand?" I ask as I look at all their faces and take note that they're all refusing to make eye contact with me.

"You will lose everything," Richard mutters angrily. "I'll stop at nothing to destroy you."

"Consider this your final warning," I reply quietly, unable to contain a sadistic calm and eerie grin.

I turn and head out to my truck and realize that if the Sullivans are going to stand in my way, they're in for the fight of their life. I will stop at nothing to keep Everly and Willow safe.

I TAKE EVERLY and Anne Marie lunch at the library, which isn't technically supposed to be open, yet they're still there and strictly volunteering. But hopefully, that will all be fixed soon.

I think about everything they've put Everly through and see how strong Everly is. She had to start a whole new life by herself and make herself happy again because the two men in her life who were supposed to protect her failed her.

"Hi!" she calls as she comes from around the desk and reaches up to kiss me, taking a bag from my arms. "What's all this?"

"Lunch. Figured you might be hungry." I shrug as I set down a carrier of drinks and another bag.

“This was sweet,” Anne Marie says as she motions for us to have a seat at one of the big tables.

“I heard about what happened with your liquor license,” Everly says, looking concerned. “What does this mean for the pub?”

I shrug. “It’s been a mess. I think we’ll be okay for now, but it was just another way the Sullivans were trying to start trouble.”

Her face darkens, and I slide her drink over to her. “It’ll be fine. I think things will blow over soon.”

“What do you mean?” she asks. “It feels like we’re all under attack here.”

“I think you were right. The Sullivans are in over their head with this arena investment. Investors are backing out, and it turns out the Sullivans are broke and need money,” I say as I take a fry.

I’m going to figure out how to make sure they stay out of our way. I’m not sure how yet, but I will figure this out.

CHAPTER 33

Everly

None of this makes sense. I can tell something is off as I finish baking the last of the loaves here at the pub. Hayley's off making deliveries so I'm getting the baking done while I still don't have a job at the library. I don't have a good feeling about anything that Richie is doing. He hasn't said anything to me, but just Nash? It doesn't make sense.

I feel an arm come around me and pull me close. "Where's your head at, Ev?" Nash murmurs as he pushes a tendril of hair behind my ear.

"Concerned and confused," I admit. "What Richie offered makes no sense. There has to be something hidden here we haven't seen yet."

"Understandable," Nash says as he moves a tray of bread for me to take out more.

"What if someday she's just as sad as I am about losing my dad?" I ask as I fold and score some bread dough. "She might be sad that he isn't the dad he could have been and be so hurt. Something feels off, somehow, Nash."

"She might have questions later and some things to work out," he says. "But she'll have all of us to remind her how loved she is."

"I heard from my attorney today. She was able to get rid of the bogus jury thing. She said a lot of people are looking into Richard and his abuse of power here in town. A petition is also going through town calling for him to be fired. She's also investigating Richie and his finances," I say as relief fills me at the thought of this all ending.

"Yeah, apparently, a lot of people in town aren't happy. He's embarrassing himself for his man child, and people aren't taking too kindly to them bullying you and Willow and anyone else they can," Nash says as he takes a towel and wipes down the counters.

"Hold on, let me check this," I say as I look at my phone buzzing with a call on the shelf above the baking station.

"Hello . . ." I say as a roller coaster of emotions fills me with what I'm hearing. "What do you mean she was picked up early? By who?" The room spins, and I'm struggling to breathe as I hear the voice on the phone tell me something that makes my stomach drop.

"By her father. Someone filling in at the front desk let this happen, and when we realized, they were already gone. I'm so sorry. We called you right away," said a woman from Willow's school.

"No, I can't believe this," I say as I hang up and quickly look at Nash.

Bile rises in my throat. "Richie went to the school and picked up Willow after lunch and took her. He took her!" Panic engulfs me, my voice bordering on hysterical as I recount what happened. Hot tears stream fast and thick down my face as my hands shake so badly my phone almost slips from my hands.

My fingers fly over my phone as I text him.

Me: Where are you? Where's Willow? I'm calling the police.

Not waiting for a response, I hit the call button and call him twice, but both times it goes to voicemail.

Nash comes back from the front of the bar with one of the servers who looks just as worried and upset as he does. "Kristi will take over. Come on," he says as he pulls me behind him out the back and toward his truck.

"Why would he take her?" I cry.

"I don't know, beautiful. I'm so sorry, we're going to go get her," he says, his jaw hardened and anger radiating off him.

We drive toward the Sullivan's big ostentatious home on the edge of town and look for his SUV, thinking maybe he'd gone to his parents. I get out as he pulls to a stop and run to the front door, banging on it and ringing the doorbell.

It opens, and Brenda makes an annoyed face. "What do you want?"

"Where's Richie?" I ask as I dart inside her house under her arm that holds the door.

"Willow! Richie!"

"They're not here," she says as she rolls her eyes, looking confused and irritated.

"When's the last time you talked to him?" I demand.

She stares at me, looking like she's debating on answering.

"Tell me now," I grit out.

She steps back and says, "I haven't seen him since the club the other day when he got into it with his father. I don't know where he is. Even if he does have her, it's his child, too, you know."

I glare at her and turn and leave, getting in the truck. "She said she doesn't know." I put my face in my hands and reach for my phone and try calling him again.

"Mommy?" Willow's little voice answers in a panic.

"Willow, where are you?" I cry with relief.

"At our old house. But I want to come home. I don't want to be here . . ." she says and then the phone disconnects as she speaks.

I breathe heavily. "She's at his house."

Hayley and Kincaid show up and get in the truck with us, looking angry and frustrated on our behalf. Hayley and I get in the back, and I lean against the window, crying. Kincaid and Nash are in the front talking quietly.

"It's going to be okay. We're going to get her. I've already called the highway patrol. I also went by your house and got the parenting plan out of your binder," Hayley says.

Nash reaches across to the back seat and takes my hand in his, holding it tight, keeping me grounded. His touch gives me a little bit of strength to get through this, knowing that I have a truck full of people ready to fight alongside me.

"Thank you," I whisper, thankful that Hayley can think clearly to do that. All I can think of is what Richie is thinking, taking her out of school like that and out of town. He had no right.

"I'm just glad that you're so organized and told me where the binder is in case of emergencies. When we get there, we can show the highway patrol the plan if we have any problems," she says. "Don't worry, it'll be okay."

I check my phone, but there are no texts or responses from Richie.

"Why would he do this?" I ask, feeling full of defeat.

We get to Richie's, and Nash parks a few houses down. He and Kincaid go around the back of the house as Hayley and I go to the front, hoping we can get him to answer the door.

I ring the doorbell and wait but nothing. I knock loudly and ring it again. I see the curtain move to the side and still nothing at the door. His SUV sits in the driveway, and lights are on in the house.

I bang on the door and don't stop until it's yanked open. Richie, red eyed and a look of regret over his face, answers the door. "What?" he snaps.

Rage fills me. "Give me my daughter."

"I have nothing anymore! Nothing!" he says, looking full of defeat. "You took everything from me."

I'm staring at Richie, and Hayley is next to me. He goes into a tirade about his parents and losing Willow and is so emotional he doesn't turn around, and it's a good thing he doesn't because we see Nash come in behind him and guide Willow out the back kitchen door, unbeknownst to Richie. He continues and finally says, "I just wanted to say goodbye. And tell her why I had to do this."

It takes all of me to stand there and listen to him and make him not move so they can get out and back to the truck. I'm breathing so hard as adrenaline pumps through my body.

Hayley's on her phone next to me, and I assume she's talking to the police.

"Richie, listen to me. Do you want to be a parent?" I ask.

"No. Yes. I know I should," he finally says, pacing and running his hand through his hair.

"That's a lot of different answers. It's okay to say you don't. We can work something out," I finally say with a deep sigh, knowing Nash and Kincaid have her. No matter what he says to me right now, she's safe, and that's all I really cared about coming here.

He looks sad and relieved. "I wanted to be good for you guys. I just . . ." He runs his hand through his hair.

"She doesn't want to be here," he says, looking back into the house and then back at me, his brow crinkling.

"Give up your rights. She'll be fine," I promise.

He hangs his head, full of defeat. "Okay."

"And stop messing with my life, Richie. I don't deserve any of it, and you know it."

Before he can respond, Hayley grips my arm. I look at her, and she nods. We hear sirens in the distance.

"Richie?"

"What?" he asks as he looks down the street, knowing that the sirens are coming his way.

"Don't you ever fucking take my kid again," I say as menacingly scary as I can muster as we turn and run back to the truck.

At the driver's side of the truck, Nash kneels with Willow clinging to him tightly, her small body shaking with sobs. Nash's eyes are full of emotion, and he looks as angry as a bear. My heart shatters when I take in this innocent gesture. Nash comforting Willow who was terrified of her usually absent and distant father taking her from school and scaring her. I sob as I pull Willow into me and hold her tightly, Nash not moving and keeping us both wrapped up in him and protected.

"Mommy! I don't want to come here again," she whimpers, tears streaking her face.

"It's okay, I'm here," I sob with relief as I hold her tightly.

We wait for the police, and when they come, we make a report to put on file. He's not getting away with doing this to Willow.

Willow falls asleep on me on the way back to Cozy Creek, and I know one thing for sure: Richie will never take this kid again. I will do whatever it takes to keep her with me. I will be going down to the school tomorrow, and I will also be filing a restraining order.

I look over at Nash and Kincaid and Hayley who showed up for us, yet again. Because that's what family does. They show up. They love you in your worst times and your good times. And I love these people with all my heart.

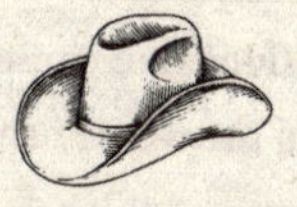

CHAPTER 34

Nash

We get home late, and when Willow is finally in bed, I stand with my hands stuffed in my pockets, leaning up against Everly's kitchen counter, my mind flooded with thoughts. Today, I was so afraid and worried, and I just wanted to keep them safe.

Everly finally comes out of her room, and she looks exhausted and her face red from crying.

I open my arms, and she lets me hold her. I rub her back and hold her while she lays her head on my chest.

"I can't lose her, Nash. I was so scared."

"Why do you think he took her?" I ask. She pulls back and goes to the stove. Taking her kettle, she turns to fill it with water.

"I think he's losing control, and financially, I think he's struggling. Something is going on with this new arena, and it's not good. He's grasping at straws because he didn't expect our pushback," she says as she turns on the stove and takes down two mugs.

"So he doesn't even really want her? He just wanted to scare you?" I state, and my blood feels like it's boiling. Seeing the fear in Willow's eyes when she was taken and then the relief when she saw Kincaid and me in the back door window. She immediately unlocked it and came with us. She knew what her dad had done was wrong.

"She doesn't leave our sight. We can go together and talk to the school," I say as anger fills me when I think about how the school should have never let her go with him.

Everly bites her lip, sadness still on her face. "We?"

"We," I declare. "I'm not letting anything happen to either of you. You're mine now, Ev," I say as I lay my palm to her face and then tuck a curl behind her ear. "Both of you."

"Okay," she says, leaning into my hand.

She pours us each a mug of tea, and we carry them into the living room. I get a fire going in the wood stove and stack extra wood next to the Buck stove for her after I leave.

I lean in to kiss her softly and leave my coat on.

"You have to go?" she asks as I come over and pull her into a kiss.

"Yeah, I have to go close the pub, but I'll be back," I say as I pull her blanket up around her and rub my thumb over her cheek.

"Thank you for all your help tonight. I love you. I don't know what I'd do without you, Nash."

"Love you too." I kiss her softly. She leans back and looks like she's going to fall asleep. It's been a long day for all of us, and we all need to decompress and get some sleep.

I do have to close the pub, but there are some things I want to work on and plan. I am really tired of the Sullivans wreaking havoc on this town and my family. It's going to stop.

My family.

Yes, Everly and Willow are my family. I am making them my priority. They always have been, but now they're mine and my problem.

I close the pub, get everything cleaned up and reset for tomorrow. I'm cashing out and heading up to my office when there's a pounding on my door in the back.

I look out the peephole to see Richie. I yank open the door and glare at him. He doesn't look like his usual asshole self. He looks . . . broken.

"What?" I practically hiss, my fists clenching.

"You got what you wanted. Congratulations," he says, his tone full of defeat.

"You got sixty seconds before I throw you in that fucking dumpster." I nod to the big green metal dumpster behind him.

"I want to sign away my rights. I . . . I can't be a dad," he says, looking away and not meeting my eyes.

"You're serious?"

He nods.

"I'll have the papers drawn up."

"You'll take care of them?" he asks, his voice hoarse and quieter now.

I tip my chin up, saying nothing to him.

He looks at me for a beat and nods and turns to leave. I watch as he gets into his SUV and pulls out.

Well, fuck me. That was not on my bingo card for the night. I figured I'd have to fight him on this, and I was prepared for that fight. This made my plans easier.

EVERLY AND HAYLEY are busy baking at the pub, and I have Willow. We went out to the ranch and made a horseshoe together. And she got to keep it, and we even painted it pink. We went and hung it in her room above her door for luck. She was so excited and said she couldn't wait to show her mom tonight.

Kincaid is picking up Mom and Dad at the airport. I'm happy to have them back because this ranch is a pain in the ass to run without them. But one thing I figured out while they were gone is that I love the ranch and prefer the work I do there with the horses to running the pub. I have some decisions to make, and they won't be easy.

For the past week, I've watched Kincaid thrive while bartending at the pub. He loves it and loves the people, and it's never run smoother. I look over at Hayley and Everly carrying on conversation and baking. I know Hayley isn't happy here either. The pub got us through, and we have made something great here, but it might not be what either of us has in the cards for our futures.

Hayley's making plans to go over to take care of our grandmother, so that leaves Kincaid and me. And I know now that I'd much rather work at the ranch than the pub. Sure, we've created a great place here, but I'm not sure this is where I'm supposed to be in the long run.

My grandmother practically made my parents leave. She loves her home and her bakery, and she told everyone she's not ready to die. She has been video calling daily and is adorable and stubborn. We all know she's not getting any younger, and her health has been failing her, but for now, she's doing okay. Her heart is having trouble keeping up with her mind, which is apparently still the age of twenty-five. My mom joked that she's not going to go out before she gets her rolls ready for each day. She'll die a hard worker. That's one thing about the McCreedys. We will work hard for life and chase what we're passionate about.

Paperwork has been caught up, and I need to get out of here and go do something. I look over at Willow, who looks as bored as me, if not more. She's watching a show and playing with a new Lego kit we bought at the general store.

"Hey, kid, want to get out of here and go get candy?" I ask as I lean my head toward her. She's propped up at the dining room table with crayons and coloring books spread out. We've watched more episodes of *Bluey* than I'll ever admit to anyone. And one of them almost made me cry. Almost. Willow and I decided that we'll be getting a blue heeler. I've already made a mental note to keep my eye open for one at the shelter.

"Yes!" she says as she shoots up from her chair, practically knocking it down.

"Alright, let's go tell your mom," I say as I nab my hat and keys.

I follow Willow down the back stairs to the pub kitchen and hear her telling her mom that we're going to the Cozy Creek Confectionery.

"Want us to bring you back anything?" I call as I wait by the back door.

Everly comes over and gives me a kiss on the cheek and hugs Willow. "No, but have fun," she says as she looks wistfully at us like she wants to come too. After what happened with Richie, she's on edge and doesn't want to let Willow out of her sight. We went to the school first thing, and they apologized profusely. Everly still kept Willow home and has been guarded since. Understandable. Things are just too tense right now with the Sullivans, and we don't trust to leave her.

We walk down the street and stop to pet Mr. Alexander's dog, a husky that howls and is very verbal.

Willow talks my ear off about puppies while we get closer to the confectionery. I don't mind because this kid is hilarious and makes me laugh. She now has me convinced that we need two dogs. You know, so it can have a best friend and all. I'd get this kid a dozen dogs if she wanted them.

I open the door as she ducks in ahead of me and hold it for a few other patrons entering the same time as we are.

I take my place in the back of the line and peruse the menu on the wall, opting for a banana nut protein shake. Gigi and Madi are at the counter. Madi smiles and waves at me, and I wave back. Willow's checking out all the candy and treats in the glass case full of everything you can imagine.

The door to the confectionery opens, and I glance over and do a double take when I see Everly's father, Brian. He looks older and has more gray in his hair and goatee than he did, and he's very tanned, with more wrinkles on his face. He's with a woman who looks slightly younger than him and has two teenage daughters lurking out front playing on their phones and laughing together. He looks happier than I have ever seen him, and he smiles and laughs with one of the kids. Something I never saw him do with Everly.

Confusion fills me when I think about how he has abandoned her, and now he's just casually back with his new family, almost rubbing it in Everly's face. I can't let that happen. She's had enough going on. I can't let him continue to break her heart like this.

Everly.

She never mentioned he was back in town, and it dawns on me that she probably has no idea. I look over, and Willow is tasting fudge samples from a colorful wooden toothpick with a leaf decoration on the end. She's not far from me, but she's sampling treats with Gigi, who spoils all of the Cozy Creek kids with extra treat samples.

Brian and his new family get in line behind me, and when I glance back at him, recognition hits him when he sees me, and he says, "McCreedy, good to see you."

It registers that he seems uncomfortable now that he's recognized me.

"Brian. I didn't know you were in town visiting," I say quietly.

He nods, shifts uncomfortably, and looks at his wife who is entering the store and his daughters who are still outside, trying not to make eye contact with me.

I stand staring, waiting to see what he does next. Honestly, I'm shocked to see him here right now. From what Everly has said, he's never even met Willow before, and they've only had contact over social media and sporadic phone calls.

"This is my wife, Jennifer," he offers, looking even more uncomfortable.

"Hi, I'm Jennifer," she says warmly, offering her hand and smiling.

"Hi, I'm Nash. A family friend," I offer.

She nods, and her eyes light up. "Oh, you're a local. We are just having such a blast here. We're staying at the Cozy Creek Lodge. Brian wanted to show the girls Cozy Creek, where he used to live."

I tilt my head and ask Brian, "Have you been in touch with Everly?"

I'm so pissed that he's just here and being so damn casual. How can he not think about them and have them be his priority when coming back here to town? Yes, her ex-husband was an absolute asshole, but Brian was the first man to break Everly's heart and abandon her when she really needed someone. I'm going to make damn sure no other man breaks her heart ever again. She's had a lifetime of it, and it's not happening anymore. Not on my watch.

I find it wildly ironic that they haven't even brought Everly up or said anything about her or Willow.

Brian's face falls, and he looks away and says sheepishly, "I'll give her a call."

Jennifer looks at him and asks, "I thought you said she was busy this week."

I tilt my head expectantly, and he at least has the decency to look embarrassed being caught in his lie. And I highly doubt that he will call her or the topic of her would even have come up had they not run into me.

He mumbles something to Jennifer, and the line moves forward.

"How have you been? Is that your kid?" he asks as he nods to

Willow who has her back to us, talking to another kid in line who she probably knows from school. No doubt he's noticed my eyes have been on her, and she's come over to hand me a few samples while I've been standing here talking to her grandfather who she has no idea is related to her. This is just so wild to me.

I freeze and look at him, wondering if he's serious right now. It's crazy enough that he's here on vacation and didn't even bother contacting his daughter. But now he doesn't even recognize his own granddaughter. He doesn't even know her. And she even looks like Everly.

I knew he had sporadic contact with Everly, but I didn't realize it was this bad.

Heat fills me when I think about how many people have let Everly down in her life.

I think about this for a minute before I respond, but I stare at Brian, and he looks even more uncomfortable.

I cross my arms and look at him and say quietly, "Brian, that's your granddaughter, Willow."

An anxious look crosses Brian's face, and Jennifer didn't hear me as she turned and waved at her kids to come in because their turn is coming up soon.

"How about that," he murmurs as he stares frozen at Willow. She turns and looks at me with her toothless grin and comes to stand next to me.

"Nash, can we get peanut butter cups for Mom? Those are her favorite," she asks, looking up at me. I know I'll have a hard time saying no to anything this kid asks me.

"Of course," I say as I hand her a twenty from my wallet.

I look over at Brian, wondering how he wants to play this, and he's gone. I look out onto the sidewalk, and he and his family are hurrying to an SUV across the street. Jennifer and the girls look confused.

Jesus. He ran out of here like the building was on fire. Coward.

Gigi has been watching this, and she looks angry and visibly upset. We pick out some treats to take back for everyone and share a brownie at the table with milk for Willow and a protein shake for me.

Willow talks my ear off about a game she's been playing, and I have no idea what she's talking about, but she promises to show me how to play it later.

It's crazy that he's here on vacation with his new family and didn't even bother calling his daughter and granddaughter to tell them he was coming.

I know one thing is for sure. Everly doesn't need this right now with everything she has going on with Richie.

WE GET BACK to the pub, and all the baking is done and packaged up and orders are being picked up. Everly and Hayley are both helping in the kitchen because the pub is pretty packed.

I put in two orders for Willow and me, and we eat in a booth in front of the big window so I can watch for Brian. I don't want him coming in to surprise her without giving her a heads-up. I don't think he will, but I can't be sure.

"Can I join you?" Everly asks, looking flushed and tired. She and Hayley have been working for a while now.

I move over, and she slides in next to me with a plate of fish and chips. "That looks good," I say, nodding to her food.

"It is good, and I am starving. What have you two been up to?" she asks.

"Nash and I are going to play *Minecraft* after this," Willow offers as she takes a bite.

"That will be fun. Thank you for hanging out with her," Everly says as she pops a fry in her mouth.

"Anytime. She's my favorite kid." I offer a smile.

Everly smiles and lays her head on my shoulder. "You're both my favorite."

Willow runs off to see Hayley, and they're having an animated conversation off to the side.

I take this time to say to Everly, "I ran into your dad today at the Cozy Creek Confectionery."

Her eyebrows wrinkle, and she looks confused. "Really? He's here?"

I nod and lean forward. "He didn't even recognize Willow. He asked if she was mine."

Everly's eyes close, and she takes a deep breath. I know that hurt her. And I hate this, but she needs to know.

She shakes her head like she's shaking off something. "It's fine. He probably just forgot to call. I'll call him later." But I'm not buying it. This hurt her.

I search her eyes and can tell she's undeniably bothered about this, and she has every right to be upset. I wish I could protect her from this, but I can't. But I can be with her through it and be there for her.

I nod and put my arm around her. "It's going to be okay. I love you."

"Love you more," she says softly.

CHAPTER 35

Everly

I bite my lip so hard, and I don't realize it until it hurts as I drive to the Cozy Creek Lodge and circle it in search of a parking spot. I was surprised to learn that my dad was in town from Nash. I was disappointed that he couldn't be bothered to call me himself and let me know that he was in town with his new family. Not mine, *his* new family.

And this hurts mostly because I don't understand any of this. Why haven't I ever been important enough to my dad? Why doesn't he want to be a father to me or a grandfather to Willow?

I'm tired of always feeling like something is wrong with me, so I'm going to find him and ask him. I have to do this. I'm tired of always wondering why. No matter how much it hurts, I'm going to find out tonight.

Nash is working his shift at the pub, and Willow is at home tired after a long day with Nash that she can't stop talking about. Hayley was angry and unsure about me going alone to confront him, but I convinced her that I needed to do this.

I get out and throw my purse across my chest and pull my jacket tighter, the brisk fall night finally feeling like we're closer to our first snow of the season.

I trudge up to the lodge and the front desk. I have no idea how I'm going to find him, but I'll find him. I didn't even bother trying to call him. Most of the time, my calls and texts go without a reply, so that's no use. I pull my gloves off and stuff them in my purse while waiting in line at the lobby desk.

As I wait, I take in the big stone fireplace with a fire going. Guests are around, luggage carts pass through the lobby, and soft music plays.

Dishware clinks and clatters in the restaurant, and I look over and see them. Having dinner like a family. My dad sits to the left, and across from him is his wife and the kids are on each side of him. He listens intently to something one of the kids says. I think one of them is Madison. Maybe I'm the asshole for not even knowing their names.

My dad's gaze happens to catch mine, probably since I'm frozen outside the entrance to the dining room staring at him. He registers my face and looks surprised. He says something and stands to cross to where I'm standing just watching him live his life like I don't exist. Baffled, I watch as he approaches me, and I feel nothing for him. Hurt, but nothing. No paternal bond, nothing. And I wonder if that's how Willow will feel someday toward her dad.

"Everly?" He breaks my thoughts as he stands a far distance from me. As if I'm a stranger and not his daughter. I don't know much about how normal families work, but I would guess that if a father hasn't seen his daughter in years, he would probably hug her. Not stand awkwardly ten feet away and hesitantly stare at me like Brian is doing right now.

"Brian," I say calmly as I stare at him, waiting to see his next move.

"What are you doing here?" He winces at me calling him by his first name. His words awkwardly come out, and he shifts his feet nervously.

"I heard you were here," I answer honestly, not sure what else to say. But then I bravely add, "Were you going to call me?"

He swallows and looks back at his family watching and then back at me.

"I'll take that as a no," I say as I fold my arms across my chest.

He looks over my shoulder and then quickly back at me. I turn and see Nash leaning against the doorway, his cowboy hat pulled low, arms crossed watching Brian.

He must have known I'd come here looking for him.

When he sees us watching him, he comes over and slides his hand into mine, standing tall next to me.

I smile at him quickly and shake my head, not surprised at all that he's here and has my back.

"I take it you two are together, now?" Brian asks, looking at Nash and back at me.

"I'm just looking after my girl," Nash says, lifting his chin. A pointed jut at Brian.

Brian at least has the decency to look ashamed. "I guess I deserve that."

"Can we talk for a minute? I have some things I'd like to get off my chest," I say quietly.

My dad nods, and we walk into the lodge library that is empty off the lobby. Nash shuts the door so we can have some privacy and stands in front of it, giving me space with my dad.

"I'm just going to come right out and say it. Why do I not matter to you, Dad?" I ask as I fold my arms across my chest, feeling cold.

Brian hangs his head. "It's not that, boo. I just . . . I failed. And then I didn't know how to make it up to you, and I didn't feel like I deserved to even try."

"You got married and didn't even invite me to the wedding," I accuse, hurt filling me.

"I thought in some ways if I just started over and made a clean break, then you could move on and be with the McCreedys. You were always happier with them. They gave you so much more than I could ever have given you," he says as he looks up and doesn't look at me.

"You left me a long time before you moved away with Jennifer and her kids. I have very few memories with you after Mom died. I tried to do anything I could to get your attention and spend time with you. But you chose the pub and trucking over me. You left me at the McCreedys'. You chose that for me," I say, feeling like the air just whooshes out of my lungs, finally feeling free as I get this off my chest.

"I know, and I'm so sorry, boo. I've been sober for seven years now. I'm trying to be better," he says.

"You're trying with everyone but me and your granddaughter. So you just don't want anything to do with us? If so, let's just get this done so we know officially where everyone stands," I say as I cross my arms.

"No, that's not it. I promise. I've reached for my phone to text and call you so many times, and I'm . . . I'm embarrassed, and I didn't know what to say," he admits, his red eyes reaching mine.

And for some reason at this moment, I see him. I really see him. He was a young dad doing his best to navigate grief for his wife and raise a little girl alone. And he messed up a lot. And that guilt ate at him. And when he finally dug himself out of his hole, he latched on to whatever he could, and it wasn't me. And while all this sucks, it is what it is.

"I don't know how to make it better," he says softly.

"What does Jennifer think about me and Willow?" I ask, afraid to hear his answer. I always thought maybe she was the one who didn't want us around.

"She wants to know you both and for the girls to know you, too. This is on me, kiddo. I did this, not her," he says as he shuffles his feet, awkward, looking nervous.

A soft knock on the door makes Nash turn and open it. I hear voices murmur, and Nash must have deemed them okay to enter because he holds the door open as Jennifer comes in and approaches us. "Hi," she says softly as she looks from Brian to me and slides her hand into Brian's, and his body relaxes.

Nash is still leaning against the door, and when he sees me look at him, he comes over and puts his arm around me. "You okay?" he asks as he searches my eyes.

"No, I'm not," I admit because I have no idea what to say right now.

Nash reaches for my hand and squeezes it gently, pulling me closer to him.

"I heard you're staying in our old place. We drove by, and it looks great," Brian says sheepishly, trying to awkwardly make conversation.

"I bought it for her," Nash says as he stares at Brian, and his face is determined to make my dad squirm. It works. He kind of deserves it. We aren't going to go too easy on him because he hasn't made any effort. He drove by the house but didn't think to stop or reach out to me.

"I should have just left it to you, and I'm sorry for that. I just didn't think you'd want it after you married Richie. What happened with him?" he asks, suddenly realizing that I'm with Nash and not Richie. Jesus.

"Richie was abusive and neglectful to his family. They are my family now," Nash adds, and I'm thankful for him being here because right now I'm going back and forth between crying and leaving. Confronting my dad is harder than I thought it would be, so I'm glad Nash came.

I watch his eyes as devastation and regret pass over his face, and his head bows in shame, a quiet sniff sounding in the library. He exhales a long breath, trying to catch hold of his emotions as he says quietly as if he's fighting for the air in his chest. "I didn't know, I'm sorry."

"You didn't try to know," I say, not letting him off the hook.

"I'm going to try to do better," he says, looking at Jennifer, who nods at him and me.

"I'm sorry," she says. "I should have pushed harder for you. I just thought this was between you and your dad. I knew things were difficult between you both, but had I known you were hurting like this, I would have stepped in."

"I would have loved to be a part of your family. Willow would have too," I say as I look at them.

"It's not too late," she says, looking at me, and I get the feeling that she's being genuine right now. She's a stranger to me, so I'm not going to hold my breath that what's being said is true, but she seems to have good intentions with what she's saying.

"Let me put your number in my phone, if you're okay with that," Jennifer says as she reaches into her bag and searches for her phone. She hits a few buttons and hands it to me.

I put my number in and look over at my dad. He nods and gives me a small smile.

"I'm proud of you, boo. And I'm so sorry that I let you down. I can't fix this right this minute, but I'm going to try," he says, his hands shaking as he reaches for me and then puts his hands back down.

I reach over and pull him into a hug. He chokes back a sob and pats my back, his body shaking as he sobs.

When he releases me and wipes his eyes, Jennifer leans in and pats my back. "I'm sorry, too, honey. You didn't deserve that. A lot has happened with your dad, but none of that is more important than you and your little girl."

We pull back from the hug, and I say, "I'm going to need some time. But maybe we can start by texting and calling."

My dad nods. "Whatever you want. That would be good."

I nod and turn to Nash, and he guides me out of the lodge and to his truck. He opens the passenger door and tucks me in, reaching over to buckle me. I suddenly feel exhausted. Like the heavy armor I've been wearing for years and that I've been so tired of carrying has been set down.

"Wait, the truck . . ." I say as I remember that I drove here.

"We'll get it tomorrow. Let's just go home, Ev," Nash says as he puts the truck in drive and takes me home.

Home.

That sounds so good right now. I'm so tired. Tonight was just a lot with confronting my dad, and I need to go home.

"Who is working at the pub?" I ask.

"Kincaid. My family needed me," he says as he puts his hand on my thigh and squeezes gently.

I'm not sure what the future holds with my dad and Jennifer, but I do feel more at peace about it. One thing I know for sure is that sometimes family isn't what you think it is. Sometimes it's the people who show up when you really need them, and it looks different from how you think it will look.

It feels messy and right.

Warm tears slide down my face as I look out over our town on the way home. They feel like tears of relief.

Nash doesn't say anything, but he pulls me closer to him.

When we pull up behind my house, I see in the windows that Mack and Anna are there, and Hayley comes out onto the porch when Nash turns his truck off.

"How did it go?" Hayley asks as she looks at me worriedly.

"It was okay, actually. I'm not sure what will happen with him, but I feel better going and seeing him. I'm glad you were there," I say to Nash as he stuffs his hands in his pockets and joins me on the porch.

"Want some cookies? Mom and Willow are baking." She nods toward the kitchen.

"Yeah." I smile as I step inside, and Willow has wet, combed hair like she's had her shower. She's wearing new pumpkin pajamas and has the biggest smile on her face.

"Mom! We're baking," she says excitedly as she comes over and puts her arms around my waist.

"It smells so good in here," I tell her.

I look up and realize that Anna and Mack are watching me and look worried.

"Hey, Willow tree, let's go read some more of your new graphic novel," Nash says.

"Okay! Be right back, Anna," she says as she races off to her room.

Anna pulls me into a big hug and holds me for one of her all-time longer-than-normal hugs that give a piece to my mom.

It makes me smile, and I close my eyes, breathing in her vanilla-and-cookie scent.

"We love you so much," Anna says as she releases me.

Mack promptly scoops in and tells me in his Irish accent, "We're so glad you're our girls."

"I love you both. Thank you for everything you've always done for me and now for Willow. I don't know what I did to deserve a family like you guys."

"You're a very special girl," Mack says. "We're all lucky to call you ours. Especially that boy of ours. He might be the luckiest."

I chuckle and smile at them. "You didn't have to come to town for us tonight."

"Of course we did," Anna says. "That's what family does."

Because sometimes family isn't who you started with; it's who you end up with.

CHAPTER 36

Nash

I look over from wiping down the bar and see Richie slide into the booth across from Hayley. He looks nervously around the pub, and he narrows his eyes when he clocks me watching him. I fold my arms and glare at him, and his shoulders stiffen.

Good. Asshole.

Hayley tilts her head and stares at him until he shifts uncomfortably and says, "Let's get this over with. Where's Everly?"

Hayley is all business as she opens a folder and slides papers over to him. "She won't be coming."

"How am I supposed to say goodbye?" He gives her an angry look.

"Sign it."

"Where's my money?" he demands as he leans back and folds his arms across his chest.

"What money?" Hayley asks innocently, not showing even the slightest reaction.

"You want the kid? I want money." He looks at Hayley like she's stupid.

Jesus, this guy has no clue who he's messing with. He thinks *I'm* the scary one. This should be good.

The pub isn't empty, but it's early, so we have just a few local regulars. But nothing could have prepared me for what came out of Hayley's mouth to Richie in an eerily cheerful and calm voice. It sounds like she's inviting him over for dinner.

Hayley leans in and says, "I have a shovel in my trunk. I will kill you and bury your smelly fishy body somewhere on this mountain, and no one will even miss you. I promise you that."

He glares at her. "Jesus, you're a psycho." But he looks legitimately afraid, and for that, Marcus and I are stiff with holding back laughter as we watch this unfold.

Hayley stares at him until he looks even more uncomfortable as he looks around the pub. Our regulars are sipping their beers awfully quietly while listening, also showing no signs of paying attention to what's happening behind them. But when Jimmy Huber meets my eyes, he knows and winks. Goddamn, that dude is scary, too. Someone said he used to be in the Mafia in New York before he moved here to retire. I'm not sure it's true, but I'm not sure it's not true either.

Richie shakes his head and snatches the papers, angrily initialing at all the colorful page flags. Then he flips to the last page and signs as his pen scratches furiously into the paper.

Before he could do anything else, the papers were seized and back in their folder as Hayley stands and turns back to him. "Now get out. You're trespassing."

He stares after her, and his eyes scan to me. I narrow my eyes as he stands and leaves the pub, mumbling something under his breath. That's it. It's done. Relief surges through me.

They're mine.

Just like that. Everly is free. We can move on with our lives and build a life together.

Hayley comes around the bar and drops the papers next to me with relief. "Can you believe that creep actually thought we'd give him money?"

I say nothing, but I can believe it. In fact, little does that bastard know, I was willing to pay if it came down to it.

Everly

Anna and Mack are ahead with Willow at the local corn maze, and watching her with them fills me with so much peace. I'm holding Nash's hand as we follow. Nash stops to get us each a steaming cup of cider as I gaze up at the dark sky lit with Edison lights strung throughout our cozy little downtown area.

Just when I think my nervous system will finally get a break to relax around the people who make me feel safe, Brenda and Richard appear and look at me like a rat crawling across the pavement.

"I hope you're happy. You ruined our family." Brenda glares. She looks bothered, not put together as she usually does. There's definitely been some upset to the Sullivan empire, and it's shaking on its axis. Good, they can feel what the rest of us feel when they mess with us.

Nash turns from the cider truck and walks over, casually handing me a cider and popcorn and looking at the Sullivans like they have lost their minds. His demeanor is strong and powerful, and he never wavers, which makes me feel protected.

"How do you figure?" I ask, confused and curious about their answer.

"You took our only grandchild away from us, and Richard lost his job. It's all because of you," Brenda says as she shakes her head, and her perfectly cut bob doesn't even move.

I almost laugh at what she's saying because it's completely wild to me that she could even believe this.

"Everly had nothing to do with that," Nash says as he eats a handful of popcorn and looks back and forth between Brenda and Richard.

I look up at Nash when he says this, and he gives me a look. A look where an entire conversation passes quietly between our eyes as we used to be able to do as kids. I swallow and wait to hear what they're talking about.

"You conned him into that!" Richard shouts.

I take a page out of Nash's playbook and sip my cider, remaining calm. I say nothing because it's not true, and everyone standing here knows it. What we have here are two supposed-to-be grown adults who have never taken accountability for their actions, and then they raised a little man-child to do the same.

"What, you have nothing to say? You're just going to find the next guy you can leach off," Richard practically spats at me.

I hand Nash my popcorn, and he calmly takes it, appearing very curious about what will happen next.

I hold my hand up. "Stop right there. Don't be rude to me because my rude will out rude yours, and I promise you that you won't like the outcome."

Brenda opens her mouth to speak, and I cut her off. "You can't do ugly things to people and expect a beautiful life. You will no longer be speaking to me or my family. Ever. Get away from me."

Both glare at me and grumble as they turn and head toward the parking lot.

Finally, I turn and say, "What are they talking about?"

"Yesterday, Richie came into the pub and signed over his parental rights to Willow. And I want to officially adopt Willow as soon as possible. I want you both to be McCreedys. I planned on surprising you tonight. But I didn't expect them to come up and ruin it," he says with a look in his eyes that makes me weak in the knees. Damn this man. He makes me feel so seen.

I stare up at him, happy tears filling my eyes. "He signed his rights away? He really did it?"

He nods. "Richie came to the pub that night after we went and got Willow. He knows he's in over his head and hasn't been the parent he needed to be or could be. I honestly give him credit for acknowledging that he can't do it, and he asked me if I'd take care of you both."

"Wow," I say. I didn't think it would go down that easy.

"Well, don't feel too soft for him. He was a dick about it and asked for money."

My eyes widen. "You gave him money?"

"No. Hayley was a badass and got him to sign without getting a single penny. I honestly think she scares him," he says, handing me back my popcorn.

"You did that for us?"

"Ev, I'd do anything for you both. It's your decision, but I want to be your husband and Willow's father. I wanted this all those years ago. I'm sorry it didn't happen, and we lost all those years," he says as he leans down and cups my cheek with his hand.

"We can start our new life together in Cozy Creek, all three of us, McCreedys," he says as I pull him in and kiss him. He wraps his arms around me and kisses me back.

"Any other surprises you have, McCreedy?" I ask, amazed at what he's telling me.

He looks at me and finally says, "One more."

"What's that?" What else could he possibly have up his sleeve?

"I got you a truck," he finally admits.

"A truck?" I reply, shocked. "You can't just buy someone a truck."

"I need *my family* in a safe truck. Plus, you'll need the hitch for the trailer."

"What trailer?" I ask hesitantly, not sure that I want to know more.

"The horse trailer," he says calmly like this should all make sense.

I shake my head and laugh, not following. "We don't have a horse, Nash."

"It's parked behind the pub," he says as he takes a swig of his cider, ignoring the part about the horse.

"Does it have a horse that comes with it?" I ask and laugh.

"It will eventually," he says, his eyes twinkling.

I sigh with relief.

"I hope it's okay if I love you forever," I say as I look at him and can't believe he's mine.

"I'm yours, no returns," he says as he slides his hand into mine.

CHAPTER 37

Everly

"The paperwork is filed," Hayley says as she slides across from me at Bookers.

Relief fills me, but I'm sad that it's come to this. I'm not sure how Willow will feel about this when she's old enough to understand it all. But sometimes parents just suck. Unfortunately, I know that firsthand.

While my dad has promised to change, I'm not holding my breath. Talk is cheap, but actions are what matters. Honestly, I think Jennifer was more excited about having contact with me than my father.

"How are you feeling about all of this?" Hayley asks.

"I feel like I'm ready to move on with my life and be done with the Sullivans for good."

"Did you know that their house is up for sale? They're in the process of moving closer to Richie. His dad resigned as the town manager. With the town reacting the way they did, he had no choice," Hayley says as she sips her iced tea.

"So the arena is fully off the table?" I ask, relieved.

"For now. It's not a terrible idea, but where they wanted to put it wouldn't work. They did it just to make trouble. And their idea of naming it The Richard Sullivan Arena was just asinine." Hayley rolls her eyes.

"Gross." I shudder.

"They're moving on. I think Richard is going to try to help Richie save his dealership. Apparently, he's struggling with it. Hopefully, they won't have reason to come back to Cozy Creek," she says, and I nod in agreement.

"Our Cozy Creek is safe. Thank you for getting Richie to sign those papers. When we talked about it, I never dreamed he would just do it without a big fight or some sort of hostage negotiation." I exhale as I sit back in my seat, relieved that it's finally over.

"The library is safe, and the entire block of downtown has been declared a historic protected place and safe from any developers. In addition, the library has a grant that fully secures your job until Anne Marie retires next year," Hayley says.

"It's over, and we're safe," I whisper, grateful for Hayley, Nash, and the rest of the McCreedys who stepped up for me and Willow.

My family.

"Hey there, fall hater," Hayley says as Nash comes in and sits next to me in his Carhartt overalls and a baseball cap pulled low.

"I'm not a fall hater," he grumbles.

"Right. You wouldn't let me put up a single fall decoration in here," Hayley says as she rolls her eyes.

"It's a pub. Not a damn Hobby Lobby. People don't come in here to see turkeys, pumpkins, and shit."

I stare at him in mock horror, being so negative about fall. "You hate fall?"

Nash puts his arm around me and leans in. "I don't hate fall. I just hated fall without you."

"Aw," Hayley drawls sweetly, then says sharply with a tease, "Get a room."

"Well, now, it's almost time to start planning for Thanksgiving and Christmas," I say excitedly.

"We should do a Friendsgiving here at the pub. For some of the locals who have nowhere to go," I say as ideas fill my head on what to make and how we can decorate.

Hayley and Nash exchange a look.

"What?" I ask.

"Some things will be changing around here," Nash says.

"What do you mean?" I ask as I notice Hayley isn't making eye contact with me.

"Kincaid will be taking over running the pub," Nash says as he watches Hayley, and she nods.

"What are you going to do?" I ask, confused.

"I'm going to travel," she says softly. "First, I'm going to Ireland to stay with Baa for a while. Then I'm going to travel the world."

Oh my God. "Hayley, that's amazing. I'm going to miss you so much, though."

"We can FaceTime, and I know we'll talk daily. I'll be back, but I need to do this. I just feel like I'm made to wander, you know?"

I nod and smile sadly. "I get it. You have always talked about wanting to travel. But we'll miss you."

"Who will bake when I return to the library?" I ask as I look at Nash.

"We're going to outsource it from the confectionery. It'll be okay. I'll still help Kincaid, but my focus will be more on farrier work and the ranch. Kincaid was supposed to help Dad on the ranch, but we're switching spots, so I'll help Dad."

"Which is what you wanted to do all along," Hayley muses as she looks at him and grins.

"I do prefer animals to people, alright?" He laughs, pulling his ball cap and curling it with his fist.

"Everything is working out," I say as I slide my hand into Nash's.

"Alright, let's plan Friendsgiving, but just know that Mom has a huge dinner planned at the ranch, and if we're not there, she's going to lose her mind," Hayley says.

"When are you leaving?" I ask Hayley, scared of her answer.

"After Christmas," she promises, and relief fills me that we have some time. "I'm going to help transition the pub and sell some things."

"What about your house out on the ranch?" I ask.

Hayley looks at Nash and raises her eyebrows.

He looks at me. "I was hoping you and Willow would live there with me while we build our own home."

My breath hitches. "Really?"

"Really." He nods. "It's right next to our property, so it makes sense that we stay close while we build. Plus, we can keep Willow's horse there."

Our property. He called it ours.

"Wait, Willow doesn't have a horse," I say as I wrinkle my eyebrows at him.

"She will for Christmas." He grins.

"You'd better get used to it. Willow has Nash wrapped around her little finger, and he can't tell that kid no for nothing," she says, cracking up. She playfully bumps her shoulder with his as she stands.

"I did notice that actually," I say as I look at Nash quizzically.

He raises his hands. "You're going to live on a ranch. You never know when you need a horse."

"Alright, we have something to talk about," I say as I stand and lean down to kiss Nash. "But first, I love you."

"I love you more," he murmurs.

"I know you did the grant," I whisper in his mouth, unable to finally keep from addressing what I know he did.

His eyes widen, and he looks surprised. "Anne Marie told you?"

"No. I just knew. That had Nash McCreedy written all over it. And I handle the library paperwork, which has your LLC on it as the donor."

"Just securing your place. It means a lot to you." His arms go around my waist, and he pulls me onto his lap.

"She's retiring after next year, you know," I point out.

He nods. "I know. But she'll still be around. We're not losing her."

I nod. "It won't be the same without her there every day."

"But this town will have you, so it will be okay. You matter here, Everly. This town is lucky to have you."

"Now that we got all of your surprises out of the way, I have a surprise for you," I say with a smirk.

"What's that?" he asks, sitting back, staring at me, and waiting with eyebrows raised.

"Two surprises actually."

I have been perusing all the local shelters and found one with two abandoned Australian cattle puppies. I picked them up, and they're back at my house and ready to surprise Nash and Willow. Those two are obsessed with *Bluey*, and I found them their very own Bingo and Bluey.

I pull out my phone and open it to the photos to show him. He reaches over and kisses my head. "Where are they?" he demands, excitement on his face.

"At home." I grin.

"Let's go," he insists, standing and pulling me with him.

EPILOGUE

Everly

I slide the pumpkin pies out of the oven and set them on the counter to cool. I put my Dutch apple pies in and inhale the smell of crust and baking goodness.

"Mom, can we go early so I can check on the horses?" Willow asks as she enters the kitchen, holding one of the puppies she refuses to put down and plays with constantly.

"Yes. As soon as the pies cool, we'll head out there," I say as I hear a knock on the door. I glance at the clock on my stove as I set the timer.

I head to the door and peek out and move back in surprise when I see my dad and his wife on the porch. We've texted a few times since I saw him last month. I texted more with Jennifer at first, and honestly, getting to know her has been fun. She's a very sweet woman, and we surprisingly have a lot in common.

I open the door, and before I can say anything, my dad says, "Surprise!" But the look on his face is hesitation and nervousness.

"What are you guys doing here?" I ask as I notice that the girls aren't with him.

"Mack and Anna invited us to Thanksgiving out at the ranch," my dad says as he nervously frets with his hands.

"Where are the girls?" I ask as I look around for them.

"The girls are at their dad's for the holidays this year." Jennifer smiles, looking hopeful. "We were hoping we could spend some time getting to know Willow and you. I can help you cook or with anything else that you need."

Wow. Okay, didn't see this coming, but okay. I look back and forth between them, and they both have a mixture of hesitation and excitement on their faces. But they're here, and they're trying. *Okay.*

"Come on in," I say as I hold the door open for them as they step in, and Willow looks at them shyly. She's playing tug-of-war on the floor with the puppies.

I'm not sure how to introduce them.

My dad looks emotional as he looks over at her and says, "Hi, Willow. I'm your grandpa Brian. Your mom's dad. This is my wife, Jennifer."

Willow looks surprised but says, "Hi. Want to see my puppies?"

My dad looks around our home, and his eyes fill with tears. The way his eyes land on different places in the house, I can tell he probably sees and feels my mother here and our family's memories. He lived here for almost twenty years; it would be impossible not to have memories that live with you here.

He nods. "I'd love that," he says, his voice hitching slightly.

"I'll show you around. Nash fixed it up before we moved in, but I did my best to make it feel cozy like a home," I say as I realize I'm rambling.

"My mom made pie, too!" Willow says, luckily breaking the emotional ice that had begun to thaw over in the living room.

"I love it," my dad whispers.

Jennifer looks at me, her eyes wet with tears, and she mouths, "Thank you."

I nod, emotion choking me as well.

Nash

Since the first moment I laid eyes on this kid, I've loved her. She holds my hand as we walk to the barn, looking up at me and talking my ear off. Sometimes I forget that she wasn't always mine.

Brian and Jennifer are here at the ranch, and at first, we worried it would be awkward, but it's actually been good for everyone to have them here. And Jennifer seems like a really nice person. She's already getting along great with my mom and Everly.

I'm relieved for her and glad that it's been going well. It could have gone the other way, and Everly would have been fine, too. She has us. But I know she loves her dad, so this has been good for her.

It turns out that Brian misses Cozy Creek, and Florida isn't where they want to be anymore. He asked me if I would consider selling him back his old house for a more than fair price. And now that Hayley is leaving and we're moving out to the ranch, that house will be vacant. I need to talk to Everly about it, but the money would be nice to put toward our home, which we're going to break ground on this spring. If all goes well, we'll be in our new house a year from now.

We're all curled up together on the couch, watching spooky movies and eating snacks. Everly gets up to make a cup of tea. When she's gone, Willow says, "Hey, Nash."

"Yeah, Willow tree." I'm lounging on the sectional couch next to her, our feet propped up.

"Do you think you could be my dad?"

Whoa. We haven't told her anything about Richie signing away his parental rights. She's so young and might not understand, and since she doesn't have much of a relationship with him, we figured we'd wait and talk to her about it when it felt right. She knows she doesn't see him and doesn't even ask about Richie, only to clarify that she never has to go to his house again.

"Do you want me to be your dad?" I ask, trying to keep it casual. I look up to see Everly in the doorway listening, and her face is full of emotion. I hold the blanket up and motion for her to join us.

"Yeah. I do. And Papa Mack and Nana Anna are like my grandparents, so I was wondering if you could just be my dad," she asks, looking at me hopefully.

"If you want to," she adds, looking down at her lap.

"Yeah, Willow. I'd love to be your dad," I say as I reach over and put my arm around her, pulling her into me and giving her a little squeeze.

She nods, looking relieved. "I promise I'll be a good kid."

"Willow, you're a *great* kid," I tell her, leaning down and kissing her head. "I'm so lucky that I get to be your dad."

"You okay?" I whisper to Everly.

She takes a deep breath. "I love our little family."

I do too.

Kincaid is running the bar full time now and loving it. It's like it's his calling, and he fits right in. I'm hanging back, letting him do his thing. He's the happiest I've seen in a long time.

After the holidays, we're moving out to the small house Hayley has built on her land. We'll take care of it for her while we're building our new home and she's traveling.

Everly loves being back at the library full time, and Willow is happy and thriving. Mrs. Caraway sold me Soupy, and my dad and I have been training him for Willow. She doesn't know it yet, but that's her Christmas present. I can't wait for us to show her next month. It's been hard keeping it a secret. And wouldn't you know it, now that Soupy is out at our ranch, he hasn't messed up a single horseshoe. I think he chose us, not the other way around. He's going to make a little girl so happy and have a good life with her.

I think about my Christmas gift for Everly, and I'm waiting for the perfect moment to give it to her. I've already asked my dad for my grandma's Claddagh ring, which he brought back from Ireland, so I can propose to Everly when the time is right. He said he couldn't think of a better person to wear his mother's ring. I'm ready for my family—Everly to be my wife, Willow our daughter, and our lifetime of memories ahead of us.

Life is good. Sometimes life is hard, but right now, it's good. And the hard times are worth it because we get the good in the end. I'm choosing to always believe that. And as I sit here on this couch with my arms around my girls, puppies asleep at our feet, I won't take a minute of it for granted.

Acknowledgments

To my family. I couldn't have done this without your support. Everything I do is for you.

READ ON FOR AN EXCLUSIVE BONUS SCENE!

Everly

"Hey, handsome. Where are we going?" I ask as I slide into the warm truck and look at Nash, who is staring at me.

"Home," he says with a grin. He leans over and cranks up the heat even more, then flips on the heated function to my seat. I shiver and give him a smile at the warmth that fills the cab of the truck.

I rub my arms, trying to get warm. "Thanks." I lean over and give him a kiss. His hand wraps around the back of my neck, pulling me in closer. He tastes good, and he feels good. I love this man.

He insisted on picking me up and telling me that we had plans, and he was very cryptic about it.

"I'm starving, Nash. Can we stop and get something to eat?" I ask as I pull off my gloves and set them in my lap, wiggling my fingers in front of the heater.

"I have a picnic basket packed and some snacks to tide you over." He nods to the back seat and reaches over and places it on the console.

"Yes," I say with relief. The library was so busy this morning. I worked straight through lunch, and now I'm famished.

I pull out a few granola bars and unwrap them, handing him one, which he smiles and takes.

"So where are we going?" I ask again, hoping it's someplace warm.

Winter is in full swing in Cozy Creek, and ski season has our small town as busy as ever.

"For a ride," he says as he slides onto the highway toward the ranch.

"In the truck?" I ask as I look at him and realize something is different. He's nervous.

He looks at me and smirks. "You'll find out."

"Okay, where's Willow?"

"She's at the ranch with Mrs. Caraway. They're baking apple horse treats together," he says.

We all love Mrs. Caraway. She's always been special to Nash, but she's just as special to us now. Nash bought a horse named Soupy and gave him to Willow for Christmas. We can't keep Willow out of the barn ever since. Those two have a bond like no other. Soupy used to be a naughty horse and was always getting into trouble for Mrs. Caraway. Since Nash brought him to the ranch and he has Willow by his side to take care of him each day, he's so much happier. Nash thinks he was bored. And with Soupy came Mrs. Caraway. She loves it out at the ranch and has become a part of our family.

"I bet they're having a great time," I say with a grin. "Are we riding horses?" I ask as I look out at the snow-covered fields when we pull up to the ranch.

"Yeah, just a short ride, beautiful. It'll be worth it, I promise," he says as he slides out of his seat, and I watch him walk around to open my door for me.

I get out, and he pulls the picnic basket out and takes it to the barn, where Mack stands with two horses saddled up and ready.

I give him a big hug. "Hey, Mack, how's it going?"

"Good. It's beautiful out, but a cold one." He nods out to the pasture.

"Your son seems to think it's perfect riding weather." I laugh as I run my hand over Stark and give him some pats before I throw my leg over his saddle.

"That he does, Everly. You two have fun." He winks as he saunters off, looking back at us as he walks away.

Nash throws his leg over his horse named Royal. "Ready?"

"Ready," I say, thankful that I wore my warmest coat with a sweater underneath and my hat and gloves.

We take off and head out the back pasture and toward the property we're building our house on. We've both been busy and haven't been out here for a while. We're staying in town, but getting ready to move out to Hayley's place to keep an eye on it while she's in Ireland.

We ride up, and I gasp and cover my mouth. "They broke ground!"

He grins and stares at me. "They did. Want to see where your library will be?"

"I have a library?" I say, holding my hand to my chest.

"With custom shelves for all your books. They're hoping to have it done before fall, as long as we don't run into any issues."

"Yes, I want to see," I say as we ride over, and he ties up the horses and walks me through where every room will be. It's only the foundation now, but it's amazing to think that an entire home will be here someday for our family.

Shivering, he pulls me close. "Let's head back. There's one more thing I have to show you."

We ride back together to the ranch, and I look over at him and can't believe he's really mine. After all this time and all that we've been through, it's all worked out. I love Nash more than anything.

He slows to a stop by the big tree in front of the barn. I stop next to him, and he points up at it. "Remember when you carved our initials in this tree?"

I cover my face. "Yes, you teased me about it relentlessly. I was twelve, Nash. I was so in love with you."

"I never teased you," he scoffs. But his face softens.

I smile at him and tilt my head.

"Okay, I teased you."

I laugh and shake my head.

"You believed in us before there was an us. I love you, Everly. I want you to know that with all my heart and everything in me, I'm going to put you and our family first for the rest of my life. My heart is yours, and you are mine," he says, not breaking eye contact with me, his voice breaking a bit with the emotion rolling over him.

I swallow back tears and nod. "I love you, too."

He slides off his horse and comes over and stares up at me, the horse turning his head to nudge his hand that holds a small box.

"Not for you, buddy," he murmurs, rubbing the horse's nose. "Everly, will you marry me?" he says as he opens the box to reveal his grandmother's emerald Claddagh ring. I know that ring well, because when she came to visit, Hayley and I would try it on when we baked with her and asked her questions. The special ring has been in her family for decades.

"Yes," I say. "Of course I will marry you. I love you so much, Nash."

I slide off the horse, and he takes my glove off and gently slides the ring onto my finger.

"This ring means so much to your family," I whisper. "It's so special. Are you sure I should have it?"

"A special ring for the most special woman," he says, pulling me into him and tipping his head down to mine. "I love you."

"Love you, too," I say as I kiss him. He pulls me in, wrapping his arms around me, and the cool metal on my finger reminds me that he's my forever.

He kisses me, and we hear cheering and look over to the entrance to the barn where Anna, Mack, Mrs. Caraway, and Willow are all clapping, and Willow is jumping up and down.

He whispers in my ear, "I had a mini version of the ring made into a necklace for Willow."

"Really?" I say, trying not to cry.

"Of course I did. I love our girl so much." He takes me by the hand and reaches for the reins with the other to walk us toward the barn.

Nash hands the horses to Mack, whose eyes shine, and he gives me a kiss on the cheek. "I'm so happy for you."

"Thanks," I say as I smile at him. Mack has always been so special to me.

Anna gives me a hug. "I'm so glad you said yes."

Mrs. Caraway huffs but smiles. "She'd be a fool to say no to that boy. He's the most wonderful boy in all Cozy Creek."

"Of course I said yes." I laugh as I reach for Willow and give her a big hug.

"Can I see the ring?" she asks.

"Actually, I have something for you, too, Willow. Since you asked me to be your dad, I think it's only fair that you get a special necklace," he says as he reaches into the pocket of his coat and produces a hunter green velvet box.

He opens it to show Willow, who looks like she doesn't know whether to cry or jump up and down. "Really? For me?"

"For you, sweetheart," he says as he takes it out and puts it on her neck.

I watch them and love this moment. I love their relationship and how close they've gotten. He's been so patient with her, shown up for her, and he already is a good dad in so many ways.

He looks up at me and gives me a look that makes me practically melt.

I love you, I mouth to him.

He nods and gives Willow a big hug, pulling me into it, too.

"So let's set a date!" Anna declares. "I have always wanted to plan a wedding. Can we have it here at the ranch?" she asks hopefully.

"There's nowhere else I'd rather have it," I agree, and look at Nash, who nods.

Mrs. Caraway says, "And you'll have a new home to move into soon, too."

"Yes, we will." I smile.

I look over at my family, and I'm so grateful. For all the times when we were lonely, and we waited for this moment, it was worth the wait. Because what we have is real. Sometimes family isn't what you're born into; it's the people you create a beautiful life with.

Stay tuned for Hayley's story next in *Bagpipes & Buns*. . . .

About the Author

ERIN BRANSCOM is a creator of happily ever afters, crafting spicy, Hallmark-like romances that make readers fall head over heels for charming small towns. When she's not writing heartwarming stories, Erin can be found anywhere where there are dogs, with a cup of coffee in hand, or lost in a good book. As a passionate Scorpio, she brings intensity and heart to everything she does. Writing small-town romances is her jam and her goal is to have you feel as if you truly visited the town and met the people when you're done reading.